# Shadow Language

---

## JP Bloch

---

PEGASUS BOOKS

Pegasus Books
3338 San Marino Ave
San Jose, CA 95127
www.pegasusbooks.net

Second Edition: July 2015

Published in North America by Pegasus Books. For information, please contact Pegasus Books c/o Christopher Moebs, 3338 San Marino Ave, San Jose, CA 95127.

Library of Congress Cataloguing-In-Publication Data
Jon P. Bloch
Shadow Language/Jon P. Bloch– 1st ed
p. cm.
Library of Congress Control Number: 2015935336
ISBN – 978-1-941859-24-7
1. FICTION / Mystery & Detective / General. 2. FICTION / Occult & Supernatural. 3. FAMILY & RELATIONSHIPS / Death, Grief, Bereavement. 4. FICTION / Noir. 5. FAMILY & RELATIONSHIPS / Dating. 6. PSYCHOLOGY / Suicide.

10  9  8  7  6  5  4  3  2

Comments about Shadow Language and requests for additional copies, book club rates and author speaking appearances may be addressed to Jon P. Bloch or Pegasus Books c/o Christopher Moebs, 3338 San Marino Ave, San Jose, CA, 95127, or you can send your comments and requests via e-mail to cdeluca@pegasusbooks.net.

Also available as an eBook from Internet retailers and from Pegasus Books

Printed in the United States of America

*For Tristan and his shadow*

"It was one of those March days when the sun shines hot and the wind blows cold: when it is summer in the light, and winter in the shade."

**Charles Dickens,**
*Great Expectations*

Police Chief Joe Hilario has a secret: he suffers from social anxiety disorder and chronic depression. He is happy only when he is alone. After losing his family, he quits his job and moves to an isolated cabin in the wilderness. His goal is to never see or talk to a living person again.

But Joe is obsessed with horrific visions of his dead wife and children. . . unless of course he is imagining things? Joe is never sure. He knows only that laughing voices keep urging him to die. Joe cannot bring himself to take his own life.

Myra, an FBI contact, tracks him down, and begs him to help her on a case that may be the answer Joe has been seeking. In a touristy seaside city, single men are being peacefully, painlessly murdered. Joe agrees to solve the case, determining in secret to become a victim himself.

Parents warn us not to go home with strangers, but Joe wants to go home with this stranger, and for the worst-case scenario to be played out. Joe meets an assortment of women suspected of the murders. Yet as the case becomes more and more emotionally charged, Joe unravels, and is ever less certain what is real. He solves the case, but the real nightmare is just getting started.

# SHADOW LANGUAGE

*I always dreamt about the Sun People.*

*They stood fifty feet tall, and hundreds of them frolicked on the beach, like a nightmare soft drink commercial. Their bright bikinis and bathing trunks assaulted my eyes, as if staring into the sun. They played with volleyballs the size of houses and never stopped laughing. Their opaque dark glasses and big white smiles somehow made them impossible to know.*

*Beach Boys music came out of nowhere, and everyone danced. Everyone, of course, except me. I moved out of the way to avoid getting stepped on, but it made no difference. They passed right through me, as if I didn't exist. I just stood there and watched, unable to speak.*

*I was not one of the Sun People.*

*When I woke in the morning, it took a moment to decide which world to believe in, especially in summer, when other kids played outside. I wanted to say to the sun, "No, I am not ape-shit happy all the time. Please leave me alone."*

*I got older and stopped having the dream. But not really.*

*The worst thunderstorm in years happened on the day I got married. Everyone joked about it, and a snippet of the wedding appeared on one of those ha-ha video TV shows. But privately, I understood what the thunder told me. I sensed my own shadow nodding in agreement about something dark and without falsehood.*

*"Thank you, friends," I whispered to my shadow and the thunder, when the moment came to kiss the bride.*

# 1

I remember being happy. I mean, really happy.

It happened in winter, my favorite time of year. I walked alone in a wild, overgrown park my ghost town of a city had long abandoned. In the gray weather, trash didn't look ugly, as it did on sunny days. Broken glass and the occasional discarded shoe blended in with weeds growing up through the cobblestones. I whistled an oldie, like I always do when I walk alone—or maybe I pretended to confront someone who scared me.

On impulse, I stepped across a knocked-down street lamp and climbed some rotting wooden steps to a boulder above the tree line. Standing near the edge, I saw the enormous gray sky turn black and powerful. And then it started to blizzard, as far as I could see. The whole world became a massive, drifting silence of black and white and brown. I couldn't imagine anything more incredible. The trees were bare, but I thought of them as resting, as if winter were vacation time for trees. Everything felt still, yet so full of power. Dumb as it sounds, I wanted to be one of those trees, just standing there—just being.

Sometimes, when I wanted to die in my sleep or wished that the world blew up, I remembered the happy feeling I had for those few seconds. And sometimes—even though the moment came and went while my life and the world went on and on—the memory convinced me that if I had one good moment, maybe there'd be at least one more.

Of course, if I explained to anyone why standing in the freezing snow in a derelict park made me happy, they wouldn't understand. But then, nobody had to understand because I learned long ago to tell people as little as possible. It's supposed to feel good to open up to your fellow humans, but I had no idea what felt good about it.

Sometimes even saying hello exhausted me. Years ago at some party, I stood there on the outskirts of a conversation, and this weird guy looked at me and he *looked* at me and then he tapped me on the shoulder and said, "Dude, social anxiety disorder?" He said it just like that, as if playing charades or something.

"Excuse me?" I said.

"Social anxiety disorder. SAD. Fear of. . . well, this." He gestured about the room of puppet-like drunks in suits and cocktail dresses. "I noticed your hand shaking. You're perspiring. You sound like you're out of breath. You look at your watch every few seconds, like you can't wait to leave. I bet you feel less lonely when you're alone, am I right? I recognize the symptoms. I have them myself, but now I take my meds like a good boy, so I'm as friendly as can be."

He raised his glass in a sarcastic toast.

It drove me crazy when people assumed they knew more about me than they did. I wanted to say that his meds—not to mention the drink in his hand, which probably didn't mix well with the meds—gave him the opposite problem. Now he came up to total strangers at parties and forgot to mind his own business. But, of course, I didn't say this. I didn't want things to go from bad to worse.

"I'm fine," I said with a smile.

"What do you do for a living? Does it add to your stress? I design video games, so I work alone. Or pretty much. Ever hear of the Alternate Universe Combat series? That's my baby. You know, I once thought people had parties to make fun of me. To point out how nobody liked me. But now I realize—"

"Look, buddy, I have to go. Best of luck."

As I walked away to leave, I heard him go on about how social anxiety disorder also included not accepting friendliness from others, and how ignoring a problem becomes the biggest problem of all. He sounded like one of those arrogant guys who got even more annoying when he tried to be touchy-feely. I thought the whole thing ridiculous.

I didn't have some psychobabble disorder. Most of the time I coped quite well, considering. I'd like to see other people try being me and see how they do.

Here's a scene from the horror movie of my life: I had to address a gaggle of reporters, though I wanted more than anything to lie in bed with a familiar book. I don't think anything makes me more at peace than lying under the covers and reading a book I already know.

Instead, however, I walked to the podium outside the imposing, Romanesque building. I let everyone film me and take my picture, as if I were an inanimate object. The bright sun gave me a headache, though people chattered like chipmunks about the gorgeous weather.

"Thank you for being here on this beautiful spring day," I said into the mic. "I only wish it were for a different occasion."

"Chief Hilario," said the first reporter, "the public wants to know if police are doing everything possible to catch the Blind Date Butcher."

Talk about a ridiculous question. In the first place, what did "everything" mean, not to mention with a total police budget of fifty cents? And anyway, what did he expect me to say? No, we're sitting around jerking off?

Glancing at the crowd, I saw behind the thick cluster of reporters maybe a dozen protestors carrying signs like *Cops Don't Care*, or *We Demand Our Right to Date*. Several people had sheets over their heads to look like ghosts. They held a banner that read: *Gone but Not Forgotten*.

"We're absolutely doing all we can," I replied to the reporter. "But we request that you cease to refer to this perpetrator by a catchy nickname. Whoever's doing this is a coward and doesn't deserve notoriety. Also, the families of the four victims surely do not appreciate seeing this worthless individual glorified in the media."

The profile signaled that this newest serial killer hated belittlement from authority figures. Or at least according to

Myra, the FBI know-it-all who invited herself to take over the case, and stepped over my metaphorical dead body.

"Chief," said the next reporter, "do you have any persons of interest in the Blind Date Butcher murders?"

I winced for the tiny wound to my soul; I never took it in stride when people ignored what I said, as if I didn't exist. You might say I picked the wrong line of work in becoming a cop given this character defect, let alone chief of police in a rundown cesspool of a city. And by far the youngest chief in the city's history, which made people disinclined to respect me. A popular choice when first appointed, I became scapegoat for everything wrong with the city.

"Again, please do not refer to the case that way," I replied. "But yes, there is a person of interest." In fact, we remained clueless as ever but I couldn't say that.

"Does it bother you to be called 'Chief Hilarious'?" asked a third reporter. A titter passed over the crowd, like hens in a henhouse.

"Completely immaterial and in bad taste, given the matter at hand. The important thing is for people to be careful. Do not, I repeat do not, agree to meet even for a cup of coffee with someone you do not know."

In truth, people called me "Joe Hilarious," "Mr. Hilarious," "Officer Hilarious," and now "Chief Hilarious" through the various stages my life. By the age of three, I rebelled against being called hilarious by never being hilarious. When people weren't telling me to be more open, they told me to lighten up.

"Do you think the Blind Date Butcher is a man or a woman?"

"Once again, we do not refer to the case by that name. We have reason to believe the perpetrator is a woman. That's all I'm going to say."

The killing method—axing young bachelors into little pieces and keeping their cocks and balls as trophies— suggested a man at work, since the crimes were so violent. As anyone who watches TV knows, most serial killers are men, and women murderers tend to poison or smother their victims. But three of the four young men mentioned going on a blind date with a woman, and ended up chaotic piles of bloodied guts and bone. The FBI smarty-pants decreed the killer a woman, one who suffered some horrible trauma, probably on a blind date.

Still, I pictured the killer as a man. Not only because of the violence, but because. . . because my cop instinct told me. I also thought it had nothing to do with blind dates. But as often happened, I had no evidence to back up my claim—or at least not yet—and I knew better than to come off sounding like some flaky TV psychic.

Also, I figured declaring the killer a woman increased the likelihood of pushing the unknown subject's psychological buttons. (Or as we experts called it, the unsub.) For not the first time in my life, I supported the dominant opinion when I believed it wrong. Though I had no idea why, it hurt my feelings when I pretended to know less than I did.

If the murders happened through an Internet dating service, tracking the killer could've been a piece of cake. But the unsub profiled as a clever online hunter who found personal web pages of guys in town, and then called them (never texting) from disposable phones to set up a meeting.

This suggested an eagerness to date on the part of all four victims. I had to admit that in their "before" photos— before being hacked to bits, that is—they looked pretty nerdy. As a woman detective said to a bunch of us pulling an all-nighter, "The great irony here is that none of these guys could've had big dicks," and in spite of ourselves we all laughed.

"Instead of trophies, she collects mini-trophies," offered a lieutenant.

"She stores them in Tic-Tac dispensers," added another detective.

"Charms for her charm bracelet," said someone else. Then, since there were three victims at the time, a bunch of people burst into a rousing chorus of "Three Blind Mice." I didn't join in, but when you're a cop, you laugh at such things at 4:00 a.m. to keep from going crazy.

Crime itself never bothered me. Hell, if crime didn't exist, cops wouldn't exist. I saw no reason to take offense when someone dealt drugs for big bucks instead of flipping burgers. And I comprehended that people lost their cool and shot their spouse.

Crime scenes never grossed me out; I gleaned a strange satisfaction from gory sights and smells that confirmed my hunch that life stank. The stupid crimes bugged me: children murdered in drive-by shootings or sex offenders and murderers who thought their problems more important than someone else's life.

I may not think much of life myself, but I don't go out of my way to make it everyone else's problem. I remember this one model of motherhood too busy fucking for crack to raise her daughter, so she had her own father raise the kid. Then, after getting busted for six or seven felonies, she said, "You have to understand, my father molested me."

I said to her, "So, let me get this straight. You gave your daughter away to the man who molested you?"

She grew quiet, until she said, "Gee, I never thought of it that way."

This kind of stupidity drove me up a wall. Over time, it broke my spirit. But I didn't like admitting it.

"I can answer one more question." From the podium, I looked at my wristwatch, as if piles of evidence demanded my attention that second. Public relations bullshit came with the territory. It didn't matter how much I cared but how much I appeared to care. If I let myself care, I'd lose my mind.

"Yes, Chief Hilario," said a reporter, emphasizing her usage of my correct surname. "I think the people of this city deserve to know why the crime rate has remained the same since you took office two years ago."

"Well, first let me say there's been a ten percent reduction in crime, and that shortages—"

"'Ten percent?' Do you call that good enough?"

I felt the anger build inside me. "With a thirty percent budget cut and thirty mandatory layoffs, actually yes, I would. I'm not here to trip over your nasty little word game. I'm not here to—"

I saw the FBI woman cut across her neck with her finger, meaning I shouldn't hang myself out to dry. Through an intense act of will, I regained control of myself. "These are hard times. I put in sixty to eighty hours a week, and I don't get paid for overtime. That's all I'll say."

Though I said I'd take no more questions, another reporter shouted out, "What would you say to the ghosts in the audience?" She pointed to the idiotic people with sheets over their heads.

"I've always believed it's the living we have to fear." It offended me when some people laughed, but I didn't say so. I wanted the press conference to be over.

"You didn't mention your family, Joe," said Myra, the FBI agent, as we walked back to my office. We entered the building through the swivel door, and the security guards waved us in. She pushed the "up" button for the elevator. Then she pushed it again, as if it would make the car arrive sooner.

"What do you mean, Myra?" Like a little kid, I enjoyed watching the lights above the elevator go from one floor to another. It let people in or out on the fifth floor, and next came the fourth . . .

"You should've said working so much meant you never saw your family. You could've wiped your eye or put a crack in your voice."

"Yeah. Okay."

"You know what I mean," she replied. "Joe, you're sweating. Wipe your brow."

I hated it when people told me what to do as they would a child. I never knew how to respond, besides doing as they said. I took out my handkerchief and mopped my brow.

"Are you feeling all right? Do you have a fever?"

"I'm fine, Myra."

The elevator doors opened; the people getting off looked either apologetic or resentful toward us for getting on. We stepped inside with a few other people, who exited on the third floor. I re-pressed the button for the sixth floor, even though it remained lit, to help the doors close sooner. For some reason it bothered me when a few people exited, but then more people entered, as if a game went on called "Empty the Elevator."

"You never talk about your family," Myra said. "I find that fascinating. You don't even have their pictures in your office, which speaking of PR is just plain dumb."

"Look, you stole my case. You won. Are you also my publicist?"

"Joe, we're working together. I didn't steal anything. Not everything is about winning, you know."

"Fine. Whatever you say. And as for my family, maybe if someone tried to kill your wife and kids, you'd be a wee bit inclined to keep them out of the public eye."

I could tell I made a small crack in her cheery countenance.

"I'm sorry. I had no idea."

"I'm a walking giant-sized folder of classified information."

We got off at the sixth floor, and I led her down the dirty hallway that the city cleaned maybe once a month. Myra's high heels clunked behind me on the grimy fake marble tiles. We entered the outer office, and through force of habit, I scooped up my mail from the receptionist's inbox.

I shuffled through the envelopes, several of which I recognized and handed back to the receptionist. Someone kept writing that the Blind Date Butcher belonged to an unground zombie cult, while another poor soul said his dead wife did it—stuff like that.

"The usual nut jobs. Send a form letter. Tell them to go to hell."

"Yes, Chief," said the receptionist, who now also doubled as office bookkeeper.

I held the door open to my inner sanctum, and Myra smiled as she entered. I'm not fussy about furniture, but my office would've depressed anyone. It consisted of a banged-up metal desk and file cabinet plus a couple of chairs with cracked plastic upholstery. The desk had a sticky substance on it that wouldn't come off, and one of the file cabinet drawers didn't open.

Overhead, the cracked fluorescent fixture made an annoying hum that, when I had a headache, made the headache worse. The one window, painted shut from years of soot, featured a cheap plastic window shade. Yet I permitted no clutter; I hated clutter. Sometimes I threw away letters or e-mails that would've come in handy later, but I am the opposite of a hoarder. I hate saving anything.

Various imitation bronze plaques and certificates in plain black frames covered the walls. Some were for my police work; I received commendations for solving some heinous crimes. Others came from local booster organizations and charities. When not at work, I could be found at luncheons with roomfuls of strangers, where I shook hands and threw the first pitch at local ball games and made the same speech over and over.

I gestured for Myra to sit in one of the cracked chairs, while I sat in the broken wooden swivel chair behind my desk. She liked to sit with her legs crossed, her hands encircling her upper knee, as if she were a guest on a talk show.

"So, Myra—anything new?"

"The case—nada. But on a personal note, Lisa made the honor roll again."

I registered puzzlement. "Lisa?"

Myra sighed. "Hello, anyone home? Lisa, my younger daughter? Ring any bells?"

"Sorry, but I told you, I'm not good at remembering these things. I remember your husband died fighting in Afghanistan." I leaned back and almost fell over since I forgot the chair had broken.

"I have three kids," Myra said. "Laura, Lonnie, and Lisa. One, two, three. I've only told you about them a dozen times. I miss them as we speak. I try not to let my guilt affect my judgment."

"No one's stopping you. You can leave this case any time you feel like it."

She gave me a sidelong glance, the way you might look at a kid telling a fib. "That's not the point. When you profile a case, in a way you also profile yourself. In the Bureau, that's one of the first things you learn. Serial cases change the people who work on them. Hopefully for the better. But not always."

"Gee, who knew the FBI could be so profound?"

"Call it what you want. You're stubborn as a mule, but you know what I mean."

"The only thing I feel guilty about is that another day is going by without cracking the case. Some fuckhead is out there butchering people. What else matters?"

"Why are you mad at me?"

"I'm not mad at you." Though the rising decibels of my voice suggested otherwise.

We both sat there. Neither of us spoke. At length, Myra said, "Can you remember the last time you slept?"

I thought about it. "No, I honestly can't."

"Please. Go home. Sleep. Even for a few hours."

"I'm not crazy. Stop treating me like I'm crazy. I hate that."

Myra laughed. "Who said anything about crazy? It's sleep deprivation. Let's pretend I'm in charge of the case like you said, and I'm giving you an order."

She could tell she hit a sore spot, so she added, "Or not. But Joe, you're only human. Everyone needs sleep."

"I guess I can't argue with that." I called home and heard the voice mail. I stated I'd be home soon. Then I grabbed my briefcase and followed Myra out of the office.

"You should find something to take your mind off all this," she said. "For me, it's Victoriana. First edition novels, clothes, penny dreadful stories, and of course the architecture and furniture. I practically faint at the sight of an antimacassar."

When I didn't express amusement, she continued. "Seriously. If you have a hobby, make time for it. If you don't, find one."

I reached, nay, surpassed my limit for her small talk. "I'll see you tomorrow."

"That will be fine." She touched my hand as we walked down the hall to the elevator. "Oh, and Joe?"

"Yes, Myra?" I couldn't believe how exhausted I felt.

"I know you didn't mean to raise your voice at me. I know that's not the real you."

I faked a smile. "Thanks."

Driving home to the suburbs, I realized it was a Saturday afternoon going on evening, so I expected everyone to be home. In practical terms, this translated into little chance of getting sleep. Ralph, our sheepdog, never failed to greet me with his big sloppy tongue, and I never had the heart to make him get down.

Caitlyn inevitably gave me a tepid kiss to the cheek before telling me the storm drains still hadn't been cleaned or that she apologized for her work papers being everywhere. My son, Joe Jr., now sixteen, would tell me he needed money for something, while my daughter, Stephanie, now fourteen, would tell me *she* needed money for something.

Criminals often said how if only they hadn't succumbed to a particular temptation, their lives would be on track. Increasingly I felt the same way about being a husband and father. No one twisted my arm to get married and have kids, but like most people, I never stopped to think what it meant. I plunged right in. I loved my wife and kids, but I sucked at letting them know.

Most of the time I teetered between burnout and super burnout. It took a lot of effort to throw those baseballs and make those speeches when you're thinking about murderers and rapists, but nobody understood. My kid's problems were so trivial that I had a damn hard time taking an interest in them. At their age, I subsisted in foster care. I survived, so why couldn't they?

As I drove across the bridge to my town, I wondered how long it would be before Caitlyn divorced me. When the kids got out of control, she said they wanted my attention. She tired of telling them I worked hard and demanded to know when things would change. I never had an answer. I didn't even know if I understood the question.

Would I put up a token fight for joint custody of the kids, or just let her take them? Maybe I'd only see them once every five years. Worst of all, I wondered if I'd get remarried.

I got a call from Myra marked urgent, but I didn't pick up. On the radio I heard another body had been found.

2

I should mention that two years earlier, some crackpot tried to kill my family. During our once-a-year barbeque in the backyard he decided to show up, pointing a Glock G41— a gun used for hunting. He screamed that cops were communists. Thinking fast, I grabbed the tongs and threw a hot coal at his trigger hand, which made him drop the gun. I tackled him to the ground and grabbed his G41, pointing it at his head until a couple of squad cars arrived.

I predicted a Kodak moment: the four of us plus the dog huddled together in All-American wholesomeness. Instead, Caitlyn slipped into this weird mood about how we had to clean up the "mess," though she kept the yard pristine. She flinched when I touched her.

"Can't you help me this once?" she demanded. "When is it going to stop—all these terrible people?"

Twelve-year-old Stephanie said, "Thanks a lot, Dad," and went on about how she hoped the neighbors hadn't seen anything because it "humiliated" her to have a cop for a father since cops were so uncool.

Ralph, the heroic watchdog, slept through the entire incident. When I saw Joe Jr. crying, it tipped me over the edge.

"I'm s-so scared, Dad," he said.

For the first and last time, I hit my son, smacking him hard across the face with the back of my hand. "Be a man," I shouted. "Damn it, I've never been so ashamed of you." This made him cry more. "How stupid are you?" I yelled at Stephanie. "You could've been shot to death. How's that for feeling humiliated?" She started blubbering, too.

Caitlyn put her arms around both our children and caressed them tenderly, as if they were still babies. "Can't you see they're traumatized? What's wrong with you? You're such a bully."

I stared at them, as if I never saw these people before in my life. "You've broken my heart." My voice became hoarse with rage. "All three of you. I'll never forgive you." I heard Caitlyn join in the crying as I stormed off to police headquarters to do mindless paperwork.

The next day, I apologized to everyone, bearing gifts of jewelry, perfume, and video games. Yet as we smiled and hugged, I knew that something ugly transpired. My effort to change things only made them worse. I felt a heaviness in my chest as we spent the next two years in a state of tension no one talked about. Caitlyn made it clear that we shared the same bed only to sleep. Once she caught me jerking off in the shower and called me a pig. She considered it cheating on her, though I didn't mean it that way.

The favorable publicity from the incident gave me a double promotion to chief of police. (Also, let's face it. No one else wanted such a hot potato job, given the city's economic decline.) The general understanding was, I wouldn't let my family be interviewed because I didn't want them traumatized.

But truth be told, I worried over what they might say to the press. The mayor's office told me that all of us could get therapy courtesy of the taxpayers. But I replied that I had no time for it, and that the most fucked up people I dealt with were therapists.

So much for the talking cure. Chief Hilario, town hero—and my wife and kids hated me for it.

Still, driving home on Myra's suggestion, I felt exhausted and I dared to hope I might get some rest in my own home. With a sense of relief, I pulled into the driveway. But I heard Ralph barking, so things did not bode well.

Opening the front door, I realized Ralph had to be out back. For all my pissing and moaning, I missed his usual soggy greeting. The house appeared to be empty. *Shit, it's my birthday*, I realized all at once. Though not in recent years, my wife and kids gave me a small surprise birthday party. Maybe this meant a desire to reconnect with me? Ralph barked and scratched at the back door. From the corner of my eye, I saw that the dining room had a banner that read: *Happy Birthday, Dad.* The timing couldn't have been worse for the healing we needed. But I knew I had to play along. Farewell, beloved sleep. I wondered why my family just didn't work. Somehow, we were always off our game.

I let the dog in. "C'mon, Ralph," I said in a loud voice. "Let's find Mom and the kids."

With the wisdom of a dog in the movies, Ralph barked some more and led me up the stairs. He stopped at the closed door to the master bedroom, so I opened it as Ralph kept barking. "Oh God, what a surprise," I called out with a big, forced grin.

I saw Caitlyn sprawled across the bed—or at least what remained of her. She'd been slaughtered to pieces with an ax, like the other murder victims.

Next to her were remnants of my son minus his genitals.

A few feet over lay the remains of my daughter. In addition to nine ax wounds, she'd been scalped. All three of them, hacked to pieces.

I went to each body and tried breathing it to life. But it did no good. Covered in blood and body matter, I remember thinking to myself: I've seen this many times before, is it wrong to feel differently now? Like I had to solve some abstract philosophical quandary.

Ralph wouldn't stop barking. It hurt my ears. I wanted to yell at him to shut up, but I kept it together and drew my weapon.

I heard the door to the master bath creak open. Startled, I turned to see a man. He held an ax, and blood dripped from his body like a slow-burning red candle. He panted like an animal. He wore a conservative, dark-blue business suit with a two-corner sky-blue handkerchief that matched his tie. For some reason, I hated that handkerchief so much I couldn't stop looking at it.

"Remember me?" He smiled with satisfaction. If he noticed my gun, he didn't seem to care.

I have no idea how long it took me to respond. "No."

"The party?" he yelled. "I told you about my social anxiety disorder. I opened up my life. I told you I made video games. And you told me to fuck off."

"I don't remember saying that," I replied, forcing my hands to keep steady.

He held up his free hand in oath. "I swear on my father's grave, may he rot in everlasting hell. Those were your exact words. 'Fuck off.' 'Fuck off, you fucker,' to be precise. Good God in heaven, all I want out of life is a friend."

"I already told you, that's not how I remember it. I wished you good luck."

"You know you told me to fuck off."

He came forward, swinging the ax, as if killing me fulfilled his wish to have a friend.

Then I shot him. I remained calm enough to shoot him in the leg, so that I didn't kill him, and he'd live to face justice and all the other crap I was supposed to believed in. Nobody could say I murdered him in the heat of the moment, or that I violated his precious civil rights.

But one shot didn't do the trick. His adrenaline kept him moving toward me.

I shot him in the other leg.

Finally, he fell to the floor, alive but immobile.

I took out my cell phone and called for help. I made sure I said nothing that a defense lawyer could use against the DA. Ambulance and backup needed, the usual song and dance.

Next, as if an automatic reflex, I pointed the gun at my right temple.

"No, don't!" screamed the crazy, shot man on the floor, writhing around in the bloody mess he made. "Killing yourself is a very bad thing. It's a mortal sin."

Ralph whimpered. I knelt down to assure him. He licked my face with his foul dog breath as I held him with everything I had. He felt like the one good thing in the world.

I set the gun down, though I don't remember doing it.

3

Waiting for a familiar face from the department felt like the longest stretch of time in my life. I don't know if it took five minutes or fifty.

The man who slaughtered my family screamed, "If you love that dog, why can't you like me just a little?"

Over and over he said it, like a rhythmic cheer at a football game, tapping his hand in time on the sticky red floor. When the cops arrived, he smiled with shyness. "I couldn't hurt the dog," he murmured. "I'm not that kind of person."

He looked at me, as if my moral superior. The ambulance workers lifted him onto a stretcher and carried him out. I don't remember much else about the day, other than giving Ralph a bath. Under normal circumstances, he hated baths, but this time he sat up in the bathtub, as if he'd been traumatized, too.

The press trumpeted with ecstasy that the Blind Date Butcher had been caught. But those of us in law enforcement experienced no surprise when the crazy guy who butchered my family turned out to be a copycat of sorts. The murderer killed another blind date right after we locked him up.

Eventually Myra from the FBI brought in the real perp, though she did it with evidence I collected. She asked if I wanted to share the glory with her and took my lack of response as a "No."

The Blind Date Butcher turned out to be a man, just as I suspected. The motivation had nothing to do with blind dating, which affirmed my hypotheses two out of two. He saved the severed penises and testicles in pickling fluid to mail to his ex-girlfriend as a wedding present for his finale. He found it easy to sound like a woman on the phone—he talked in a falsetto and told the guys at the other end that he had a cold.

Upon meeting, he grabbed them from behind and knocked them out with a hammer. (In a couple of instances, he knocked them out so well that they technically died from hammer blows.) He got their apartment keys from their pockets, snuck them in, chopped away, and harvested his trophies. His parents insisted there must be a mistake because years earlier he volunteered for Meals on Wheels. He received life without parole.

The guy who killed my family received the death penalty. Unlike the Blind Date Butcher victims, my family got axed to death while conscious. He killed Caitlyn first, to frighten the children more when their turn came. My kids got slaughtered together, a blow to the one and then to the other. If his description of events can be trusted, Stephanie and not Joe Jr. fought back.

When I thought more about this, I remembered that Joe Jr. never liked roughhousing as a little boy, so I stopped doing it. Stephanie, for her part, tried to boss us around. Caitlyn caved most of the time, but I didn't. For whatever it meant—and it meant very little—Stephanie died her father's daughter, despite our complicated relationship.

The killer reiterated his motive: to teach me to face up to my social anxiety disorder. He hated that I got away with being such a haughty person when he knew how unhappy I was. Some people speculated that he had a crush on me, if that's your idea of love. The theory went that he couldn't deal with his closeted feelings. I didn't know, and I didn't care. I knew plenty of gay people who managed not to become mass murderers.

On death row, he found Jesus, or some approximation thereof, his worship of Him interrupted only by his endless appeals. He wanted to write me to apologize, but a judge forbade it. His new lawyers plus the anti-capital punishment people deemed it cruel to deny him the opportunity to make amends and said I'd benefit from finding closure.

Myra landed a huge publishing deal, and titled the resulting book *The Blind Date Butcher: The Untold Story*, even though she made a big stink about not calling him that in the first place. She quit the FBI and took an early retirement to Jamaica. The book sold well and became a TV mini-series. I turned down several offers to have my life story ghostwritten as a book or sold to the movies.

I received a postcard from Myra in her tropical digs, saying that she thought of me often, she couldn't have solved the case without what she called my unique insights, she delighted in finding so many antiques, I should come for a visit, and that if I needed to talk to someone I should give her a call. She signed it with love. I thought about it for a moment and tore up the postcard.

Everyone screamed at me, "Psychiatrist, psychiatrist," but I didn't see why I should be treated like some nut case. I didn't go around butchering innocent people. I remember being told I had to "come to terms" with what happened. Well, why? Why the goddamn motherfuck why? It seemed to me that only a crazy person came to terms with something so horrible.

I took an early retirement instead. Given the circumstances, nobody protested the added expense of a generous lifelong pension. If I lived a simple life, I never had to work again.

Or see anyone again, or talk to anyone again.

Unless Ralph the sheepdog counted as someone.

But some of what I mentioned took years to happen. First, the issue of the bodies needed addressing—or that is to say, the evermore mangled pieces of bodies, once the crime lab finished with them. I opted for cremation with no funerals. The thought of those axed-up corpses continuing to exist made it hard to sleep or sit still, and I saw no point in staging some contrived farewell. Caitlyn's family objected to both decisions and intimated legal action to stop me. My lawyer threatened to out them as pill-popping drunks, and I never spoke to them again.

I had no family to contact, which, as I grew older, I saw as an advantage, considering all the adults I knew who hated their parents. The only child born to a junkie mother, I went from one crummy foster home to another until joining the army at eighteen. The woman who gave birth to me OD'd before my third birthday, and no one had any idea as to my father's identity.

People frequently commented on how well I did, considering how things started out. It took me a long time to understand why hearing this pissed me off. What if I hadn't overcome my upbringing? And anyway, who wants to live a life that's only about showing how you've overcome something? When alone, I pretended to confront people with these abrasive sentiments. I enjoyed imagining how I rendered everyone dumbstruck.

My initial thought was that I wouldn't pick up the cremated ashes, but then I decided I'd feel better if I did. At first, I wanted to throw the urns in a public trashcan. Since God or Fate or just plain bad luck had thrown my family into the garbage, I thought it only fitting that I do the same. But I forced myself to drive to a well-kept park the next town over, which we went to in better times.

Driving with the ashes in the car made me jittery; I might as well have been a drunk driver. But I made it to the tranquil picnic tables and swings, and scattered the ashes in a grove of trees. I saw a woman walking with a happy little girl, and I vomited blood.

At home, I threw away all reminders of the three of them: clothes, photos, perfectly good computers and smartphones, Caitlyn's inexpensive jewelry, all the bed sheets, everything. Soon I decided to empty out the entire house. Every item went straight to the city dump. I didn't want anything to go to charity. I didn't want anything to be seen or used again.

Then I decided to go all the way. Since I had the legal right to do so, I had the house demolished, with every last stick of it again going to a landfill. Everything needed to be nothing but garbage. Still not satisfied, I poured bleach and salt on the remnants of the lawn to kill it, cut down all the trees and shrubs, and had the swimming pool filled with dirt. Pulling strings at City Hall, I had the sidewalk in front of my property replaced. I coaxed my backyard neighbor into letting me put in a new fence. I lost a lot of capital when I sold the vacant piece of land, but I didn't care. When the life insurance claims went through, I took a sum of cash out of the bank and went to my favorite abandoned park, where I deposited a wad of twenties here and a wad of fifties there, like an Easter egg hunt.

I did all this with an ice-cold businesslike precision, as though life consisted of nothing more than one task after another. People might as well have been insects, to my point of view. I knew everyone expected me to cry, but I didn't. I only felt numbness, as if my heart were made of petrified wood. I decided I must be a very bad person.

The word "clean" became sacred to me. I needed to feel untainted. Yet I felt dirty after everything I did. I scrubbed myself in the shower until my skin turned raw and drew blood. It hurt in a satisfying way. Everyone told me not to blame myself. But I kept reliving talking to the man at the party, only being nicer to him. I fantasized picking some other line of work. Most of all, I wanted to take back the many times I came home in a cloud of anger, wishing my family to leave me alone.

A number of people offered to let me stay with them until I resettled, some willing to let me bring Ralph. But I refused them all. I bought a used pickup truck, and Ralph and I slept together in the back, along the side of a road. During the day, I walked the dog in the abandoned park. He loved all the smells, though for the sake of his paws I had to be mindful of broken glass.

There were old abandoned cars in the deep trails, and one of them functioned as a cave for a pack of wild dogs. They scared Ralph, so I stopped taking us there. Besides, summer arrived, and the park didn't look the same.

My property didn't take long to sell. Only a few months after the killings, I realized I had to make a decision about my life. I considered moving thousands of miles, or to another country, but it sounded like too much effort. Besides, only a few hours outside of the dirty city you could live in the wilderness, away from everyone—which is what I did.

I bought a spacious one-room cabin once used as a hunting lodge. It came with a sizeable acreage of woods. The cabin lacked insulation, but it had a fireplace. I installed an indoor bathroom, complete with an extra-large Jacuzzi. I wanted to stretch out and soak in hot water for hours and hours. The walls of varnished log remained bare because I threw away my plaques and certificates from work. I had no TV and no radio, though I kept my cell phone and laptop.

Having discarded all my business suits, I saved only minimal outdoor clothes for warm and cold weather. The sun bothered me, so on more temperate days, I walked naked into the thick of the shady woods. At first, this hurt the soles of my feet, but they grew thick calluses. When my clothes got too dirty for even me to wear, I soaked them in the Jacuzzi tub and then showered off the soap. I dried them indoors in front of the fireplace.

I used to go hunting, but since the slaughter I couldn't anymore. Instead, I bought a book on edible indigenous plants. I also ordered food and other supplies from a store in the nearest town, which delivered what I needed. I texted a message, and paid the bill online.

I hoped never to speak to another human being again.

I thought I could live without books, too. But within a few weeks I ordered new copies of my ten favorite books, the older ones having gone to the landfill with everything else. I made sure the new editions had different covers.

I spent hours online. I never communicated with anyone, but I started an e-collection of family photos. I couldn't get enough of happy families posing with their kids. I'd Google for images, and when I liked one I went to the website, to see what I could learn about the family. I bookmarked all the links and began adding pictures to a photo album on my desktop. Sometimes I used software to bring out a nicer hue in a photo, as if in some way taking care of the family.

Seasons came and went. I felt better when the weather cooled off. Following the vivid, peaceful autumn, came winter and the snow. Ralph and I chased each other and tumbled in the snowdrifts for hours, and ran indoors to curl up together around the fireplace. When I split the firewood, he guarded me, sitting up and barking. Now and then the ax served as a reminder, but as long as it snowed, I could make the feeling go away.

In fact, when I stared out the snowy window, I made believe the rest of the world really had gone away. I'm the only person left alive, I told myself. And I recognized this sensation as being as good as anything would get.

Naturally, Ralph loved living in the woods, and I swear he understood how we needed each other after what happened. Every night, he put his front paws on the bed to lick my face before going to sleep. One night late in the summer, he climbed all the way on top of me. He weighed a ton, but I let him lie there and lick me and lick me before he lay down on the floor.

That night, he died in his sleep. I cried for the first time since age ten. In fact, I bawled like a baby for several days. I knew it defied logic that I cried so much over my dog but remained unable to shed a single tear for my family. But over time, I realized I couldn't face where grieving for my family might take me. I feared my rage the way someone fears his own shadow.

I made Ralph a beautiful burial mound not far from the cabin. I permitted myself a few fleeting seconds of imagining my family joining me in planting flowers.

But when I finished mourning Ralph, it all caught up with me.

I became unneeded.

I might as well have been the tree falling in the woods with no one to hear it.

I tried telling myself that I felt something other than loneliness, but I never knew such loneliness could happen. I knew where it might lead me, yet the thought of going back to the everyday world seemed so impossible that it hurt even more.

Then something happened.

Or at least I thought it did.

For the first time in years, I dreamt about the Sun People. Same as always, their huge bodies danced and laughed and ignored me.

When I awoke, I knew something inside me morphed into something else. I can't explain it, I just knew.

4

It started one evening as I searched the Internet for new family photos. At first I assumed the faint sound came from outside. Maybe trees rustling in the wind. But after a few minutes, I knew it couldn't be. I sensed an unmistakable presence of whispering, too faint to make out, but there all the same. It sounded like people giggling in the next room—that kind of muffled effect. But my cabin had only one room.

I stood up and looked outside. I saw no one. To be on the safe side, I grabbed my rifle and shot into the sky. I thought maybe kids from town came to make fun of me. Well, hopefully the rifle shot scared them away.

Sure enough, the whispers disappeared.

But when I came back inside and closed the door, the voices started up again. I felt like a little kid in bed, hearing what the grown-ups said before he fell asleep.

After about an hour, my intrigue dissipated. The whispering became a nuisance, and I tied a bandana round my ears to muffle the sound. I wondered if I had a problem with my hearing. But I wondered much more if I had a problem with my brain.

Now is as good a time as any to say I never had an interest in hocus-pocus stuff and assumed that reports about hauntings or the supernatural were crap. (In other words, your generic lapsed Catholic.) But since I also deemed therapy to be crap—I thought it didn't work—I didn't leave myself much wiggle room. I fell asleep believing I went off the deep end, with no way back up.

When I woke the next day, I relished in the relief that the voices stopped. Yet, now and then—maybe, say, twice a week—they came back, and not always at night. One morning while walking in the woods I heard them, and another day I woke up to the sound. It came in spurts about an hour long. I could never identify the speakers, or what they said. This went on for maybe a month.

The best way I can describe what happened next is that I sensed someone standing near me in the cabin one night. My skin felt breathed upon, as if a shadow entered the room without its body. The air became somehow thick, almost like a roomful of cigarette smoke.

Then things got strange. I know it sounds crazy, but it's the truth.

A filmy vision formed, like some invisible sculptor forging a statue out of air, or someone slamming down hard on a dusty cushion. It reminded me of a hologram, only more fragile. I wanted to stick my hand through it, but something told me not to.

As the image completed itself, I saw a beautiful tableau of Caitlyn standing with her motherly arms around our kids, Joe Jr. and Stephanie. They looked like the happy photos I downloaded from the Internet—regular folks in their nicest clothes, smiling for the camera. A peaceful aura, like a cloud, enveloped them. Under the bizarre circumstances, I experienced little surprise when I realized they were the ones I heard whispering. But I still couldn't tell what they said.

I had no idea what to do besides marvel. Even if it meant I'd gone insane, it didn't matter. I wanted to keep looking at my family. I worried that if I said something, it would all go away. The vision seemed so delicate, and yet so real.

Then, as if it were the next logical step, the image changed.

It started with a hue of red overtaking the protective cloud. The red deteriorated into blood, and then into severed body parts. Caitlyn still stood there with her arms around the kids, but my sweet threesome became a massacred jigsaw puzzle. Body organs spilled out in crimson waterfalls. Loose eyeballs hung by a thread. Yet their mouths never stopped grinning.

After a minute or two, they vanished. Until the next time, that is, which came later the same day.

The visits from my butchered family didn't last long, but they dominated my life, like an encroaching incurable disease. One time they appeared with a banner. As it took shape, I saw the words: *Happy Birthday, Dad*. However, the word "Dad" appeared as cut up arms and fingers. Then, their axed faces called out to me in one voice: "Surprise!"

For the first time I understood what they said.

I tried to say something—I don't remember what—but they didn't acknowledge my words. They kept laughing and staring.

I never saw them the exact way they were murdered. Instead, I lived within a giant, bloodied kaleidoscope that made them appear hacked to pieces one way and then a different way. Armies of maggots harvested the decaying remains, only for a new, rearranged mess to appear. But no matter how hideous each member of my family became, they looked joyous, as if at my never-ending birthday party.

I've heard it said that people experience one of four emotions: fear, anger, sadness, or happiness. Yet what I felt upon seeing and hearing my family seemed more of an absence of emotion. I decided my entire life led to these never-ending reminders of sordid murder. I found my reason for being born. I stayed alive by technicality; the deadness in me took over.

I looked up websites about the paranormal. I figured I had nothing to lose. But I couldn't tell which sites to trust, assuming I could trust any of them. They all appeared to want my credit card number as much as anything else. On the other hand, when I looked up hallucinations and mental illness, any number of authoritative sources offered the free advice that I had experienced a psychotic break.

I spent days following one link to another. Finally I stumbled upon a long out-of-print book on sale for one cent plus handling fee—a small, thin paperback entitled *Supernatural or Psychotic?* The author, Annabelle Sleet, had a PhD, for whatever that meant. From the product description,

I learned the upshot of the book: some people saw weird things because they were crazy, but sane people saw weird things, too. The book looked promising; it considered both sides. As soon as it arrived, I started reading it.

The worn, brittle pages were brown along the edges so I turned them with care. I looked up Annabelle Sleet online and learned that she vanished after her book came out. Perhaps she passed on, but I chose to believe she ran away, same as me. The book didn't have a photo of her, and I couldn't find one online, either. Since she was the closest thing I had to a relationship with a human being, I wondered what she looked like and what type of person she was.

First, I took a lengthy quiz with complicated scoring procedures that determined if you tapped into the supernatural, or qualified as a good old-fashioned nut job. The quiz did not contain obvious questions like, "Do you believe in ghosts?" Instead, questions consisted of things like, "In the morning, do you read before you eat?" Or, "Do you listen to music to feel happy?"

I didn't receive a perfect score in either direction, but I got the message—11 percent for supernatural, 89 for psychotic.

Undaunted, I read the book. A previous reader underlined a paragraph and scribbled a large question mark beside it:

"In extreme cases, the dead may beckon to the living to join them, out of revenge, jealousy, or loneliness. Of course, such apparitions also are associated with schizophrenia and may serve as alibi for suicide, homicide, or other acts of violence."

Another highlighted passage read:

"It would appear that a heightened sensitivity is needed to experience these apparitions. The sensitivity often manifests in times of crisis or tragedy. It is possible for two people to be in the same room, and one person claims to have a supernatural encounter while the other does not. People lacking this special form of awareness may even have a dampening effect on the experience and cause the supernatural elements to cease, rather like parents unexpectedly walking into a teenager's party. The relationship of the living person to the dead one may also be a factor."

Some of the book made sense, but elsewhere it didn't. Surely I never experienced "heightened sensitivity." Even after these horrendous visions I didn't feel anything but numb. How sensitive is that?

Yet I held on to the slim volume and read it cover-to-cover five or six times, hoping that something would leap out at me, and everything fall into place. I didn't know what else to turn to. I started carrying it with me as a kind of good luck charm—the times I wore clothes, anyway.

An answer came to me, if you want to call it an answer. The blood-splattered vision of my family appeared again, only this time the unmistakable voice of Caitlyn said, "Come join us, Joe. Die, and set us free."

I heard the same sweet voice she used when she wanted piano lessons for the kids or to redo the master bath. Despite the awfulness of her butchered body, a strange calmness drew me in. Caitlyn looked more at peace than she ever did in life. Yet, as always, when I talked to her, she didn't seem to notice.

I wondered if it happened through the power of suggestion. Annabelle Sleet described this very phenomenon of the dead calling out to the living to join them. But it didn't seem like my imagination. Or at least I didn't think so.

"Daddy, come play with us," said an exuberant Stephanie, her scalped head oozing what appeared to be brain matter down one side of her face.

"Teach me to be a man," urged the neutered remnants of Joe Jr. "Let me make you proud."

Caitlyn added, "We will never be free until you join us."

"Be with us. Set us free," the three slaughtered bodies said in unison, over and over, twenty or more times a day.

Cleaning out my old house had not been enough; I needed to demolish it. Now I realized that living away from everything and everybody hadn't been enough, either. I had the right idea when I wanted to shoot myself through the head at the murder scene. Now nobody could stop me. I felt certain no one would miss me if I were dead.

I told myself it made perfect sense. My wife, son, and daughter got trapped in some terrible cosmic halfway house, and they needed my death to complete the incomplete. I'd lead them from a netherworld of horrors to a place of peace. We would all be free. We would all be together. I could think of no other way to atone for all the times I yelled at them or missed soccer games and did a terrible job as husband and father.

I'm doing it for my family, I told myself. I had to do it. And if it turned out to be a bunch of psycho nonsense—well, when someone is that crazy, he might as well be dead, anyway.

I reached for one of my handguns and aimed it at my head.

5

I couldn't pull the trigger.

I told myself it would only take a second. I told myself every negative thing I could think of. But I couldn't do it. I faced death many times as a cop and withstood two serious bullet injuries without complaint. I joked with doctors when they removed my stitches without painkillers. Everyone knew I had a high threshold for pain, like the way I never lost my lunch at a crime scene. Yet though I seldom enjoyed being alive—though I thought I had no right to be alive—I couldn't bring myself to take my own life. Some people cannot carry a tune or learn trigonometry or throw a football. And some people cannot commit suicide.

In between the surreal visits from my slaughtered family urging me to die, I spent two or three days doing little more than stare at the ceiling and listen to the stirring of leaves outside my window. At night the crickets and owls kept me awake. I told myself to relax in the Jacuzzi, but couldn't muster the energy to do it.

I kept my cell phone turned off, but on occasion I turned it on to text a store order. I noticed I had a voice mail and deleted it without listening. I spent a week lying outside with my clothes off, though the weather turned cooler. When I turned the phone on again, I found that the same number left several more voicemails, and a text message that read:

*back w fbi couldnt stay away call me new serial m case big consultant fee 4 u myra*

I deleted the text and the unheard voice mails—all from Myra— and put a block on her phone number. I returned to my vegetative state for a week. I lay in a fetal position on a pile of leaves outside, with my hunting rifle nearby. One day, as I savored the nip of the cool air on my naked skin, I heard someone say, "Oh my God, Joe, is that you?"

I woke, stood up, and pointed my gun. I emitted an animal-like growl.

Myra looked me up and down. "Well, I've seen better and I've seen worse."

I grabbed some leaves in a vain effort to cover myself up. I didn't do it out of modesty. I didn't want to feel in any way vulnerable in Myra's presence. I resented that she found me at all and spoiled my streak of however long it had been since I had direct contact with another flesh-and-blood human being, though I knew it had been over two years.

I noticed that her mere presence made any sensation of my family's nearness go away. The whispers, the breathing, the bloodied bodies—it all seemed far off, as if it never happened. I remembered what Annabelle Sleet said about people too grounded in the mundane for the otherworldly to care about. Still, I freaked out at seeing Myra. She knew me before. . . well, before.

"Get the fuck off my property," I said.

She nodded her head. "Nope, afraid not. What are you going to do, shoot me?"

I fumbled with the gun and my handful of leaves—which caused Myra to suppress a chuckle—and gave up. "Screw it." I held up my hands in peace. "Look, I know why you're here. You think it would be good for me to solve your stupid murder case, and everyone wins. I don't care. I'm never going back. I can't."

Myra frowned. "God, your hair turned gray. When's the last time you shaved or had a haircut?" She cleared her throat. "Or worn clothes?"

"Okay, okay." I hurried into the cabin, put on a faded pair of jeans, and strode back outside. "What I do is none of your business. Now, will you go?"

"My hunch is even more on the money than I realized. Lose the beard and trim the hair to make it look presentable. But no one will recognize you." She bit her lip in thought. "Yes, you'll be perfect. The victims—they all had that hippie thing happening. You won't need a wig."

"You never could listen, could you? You're not talking me into it. This isn't going to end with me getting back on the saddle. Go be a Girl Scout to someone else." I walked to my cabin door, entered, closed the door behind me, and locked it. I'm not sure what she did next. She couldn't understand how a respectable guy like me turned into such a wild animal. Well, so what? I locked the shutters on the windows and fell back asleep.

Night arrived by the time I woke. I went outside to get the rifle I left in the leaves and to my surprise saw Myra sitting in her car, parked about twenty feet away. The dome light lit up the inside as she typed away on her computer tablet. She waved at me and smiled. I shot her the finger.

I woke again to darkness. Only this time I opened my eyes to Myra, standing over me like a doctor studying a patient's prognosis. "You forgot to lock the door," she said.

"What the fuck?" I sat up.

"If you'd like, I'll have sex with you. I mean it. If that's what it would take to at least get you to listen."

I thought I must've heard wrong. Myra? Sex? I couldn't comprehend the two phenomena at the same time. Not that I'd been setting any world records in that area. I hadn't even touched myself since I lost my family. But Myra didn't need to know that.

"You'd whore yourself out to get me on a case?"

"Line of duty gives certain acts a different context. I had a case in New York City where I—" She stopped herself. "Let's not go there. I know I can't even imagine what you've been through, but—"

"But what? That's what people always say when they think it doesn't matter what someone's been through. 'I know I can't even imagine it.' You forgot to add that you have no right to be telling me what to do, which motion I for one would second."

Myra sighed. "Okay, fine. I care nothing about you. I just want to solve my case. Does that make you feel better?"

I thought about it. "In a way, yes. It's closer to honest."

Myra clasped my hand. "Joe, if you only knew how much I—how much so many people care about you. You wouldn't be here all alone. Cutting yourself off like this. It's the cruelest thing someone can do. And you've done it to everyone in your life."

I pulled my hand away. "Okay, let's see if I'm keeping track of everything. I'm mean, I'm selfish, I'm a wimp—that's what you think, isn't it?—and I'm forsaking my sacred oath of duty. Did I leave anything out?"

Myra slammed her fist into her hand. "Damn it. Give me five minutes, okay?"

I realized that Myra had, in her clumsy way, gotten straight to the heart of the matter. She claimed to want only five minutes of my time. That was the story of my life—always giving in so that people could have their lousy five minutes of my time. In the last couple of years, I stopped giving five minutes to anyone. I'd been cursed at birth with a lethal personality: It seemed impossible to be true to myself and somebody else at the same time. I knew Myra went out of her way to find me. Yet I decided an important principle had to be upheld. I needed to be rude to her.

"Have you ever grieved at all?" she said. "Or do you keep everything stuffed inside, where it festers like poison? I know that showing your feelings doesn't come easy to you. On second thought, I take that back—anger you've pretty much turned into a science. But I know about loss, even though you think I don't. My husband, remember? My children had to grow up without a father. You of all people should know—"

"Okay, fine. You have five minutes. Anything is better than a lecture on the meaning of life." I didn't bother telling her how I cried after Ralph died, and that it accomplished nothing. What little I learned about crying as an adult led me to deem it an overrated activity. I gave in to her desire to tell me about the case, but in the strange battle of wills before me, I wanted to hold on to at least some things.

Myra's visit proved precipitous in ways she couldn't have imagined. For as I let her describe the case she wanted me to solve, I found my deepest wish all but handed to me on a silver platter. If I couldn't kill myself, I could have the next best thing—getting someone else to do it for me. To be specific, Myra's unidentified serial killer.

An insane idea. I knew it even then. But somehow crazy and sane got all mixed up. I could only do what I could do. And as I kept telling myself, my family needed me. I felt like the world's bravest coward. My return to civilization would not be to make a fresh start or help other people or any of the other nonsense that made you feel better. My comeback would assure me that I'd never have to come back again.

"This case, Joe. . . It's like nothing you've ever seen before," Myra began.

"What's the modus operandi?"

"Did you really just say, 'What's the modus operandi?' God, you are rusty. But I'll give you the MO anyway."

In so many words, here's what happened:

In some other part of the country—a famous touristy city that touted itself as a year-round ocean paradise—someone snuffed out young professional men, and always in the men's homes. So much for paradise. The men's races and ethnicities varied, but they all had one small detail in common: they wore their hair on the long side.

The FBI thought the perp to be a woman because all seven victims died after participating in a speed-dating event—those pathetic things where you have a few minutes to meet with someone before switching tables and meeting with someone else. Also, the manner of demise fit the profile of a woman.

First, over dinner at the man's home, the killer knocked the man out with heavy doses of Rohypnol (better known as Roofies). She snuck the lulling powder into food, never drinks—maybe so it would not change color. Roofies lowered inhibitions, so as the men relaxed or stood on their heads or dozed like babies, she snuffed them out with a pillow. They died in a state of oblivion, none the wiser. No evidence indicated that any victim struggled. She dragged them to the nearest bed or sofa, and placed their hands across their chests and moved their dead lips into a smile, as if they were relaxing away the day in a hammock.

The seven male victims to date were all between the ages of thirty and forty and classic metrosexual types—you could tell they spent a lot of time working out and buying clothes and all that baloney. To no surprise, they had uppity white-collar careers, including stockbroker, cosmetic dentist, and marketing VP.

One, a defense attorney who developed a reputation as the kind cops hate—got the sleaziest crooks off with a slap on the wrist—and faced disbarment until death took him first. Another filed for bankruptcy when his human resources consulting firm went belly up. But they were all on the fast track. They could afford silly pursuits like speed dating. None had ever been married. That they each invited the killer over for dinner suggested an eagerness to make a good impression and settle down. However, another murdered lawyer had been arrested for domestic violence. No evidence suggested that any of the men knew each other, besides perhaps nodding hello at a speed date.

No DNA could be found at any of the crime scenes, which signaled someone skilled at bumping people off. Still, over the past month or so since the first murder occurred, the FBI narrowed the list of suspects down to three different women present at all the speed dating sessions the seven men attended. Phone records indicated each of the victims had spoken to or texted all three of these women. By process of elimination—and given the scant evidence—they seemed to be the only reasonable suspects. But all the public knew was that men were being murdered.

Since the evidence against any of the women proved circumstantial, the FBI dealt with legal maneuvering about violating the suspects' civil rights by tailing them round the clock, let alone getting search warrants for their homes.

Adding to the usual bureaucratic obstacle course, only a year earlier the Bureau found itself sued big time for causing an innocent suspect to kill himself. Not the kind of publicity you pay for. An edict came from on high within the Bureau that the suspects could not be tailed unless more substantial evidence appeared. Therefore, someone had to go undercover at the speed dates, meet each woman, and take it from there. My job would be to date the three women and profile them—or, of course, catch them in the act of drugging my food. If nothing else, I'd watch for them to say or do things that warranted full-time surveillance and search warrants.

The Roofies signaled a woman seeking revenge for being raped or molested, reclaiming her power over whoever took it from her. But I only thought about falling asleep with the soft world of the pillow over my face. I'd be like a baby in a crib, slumbering to a lullaby. That's what I needed and wanted. How could I refuse?

I'd find the killer all right, but unbeknownst to Myra, I'd make damn sure to be the next victim. My family would be free. The killer would be caught. It was an easy "two birds with one stone" scenario. And my life will have been. . . "worth something" may be too upbeat a way of putting it. But at least not lived for nothing.

Doubtless some fancy psychiatrist would disapprove of my sicko delusions, what with my life's goal being that a crazy person would kill me. But, as I'd been learning from my new favorite book, you could take anything—even why you liked scrambled eggs or a TV show—and explain it one way, and then some other way.

"Do it," I heard Caitlyn whisper. "Joe, I miss you so much."

## 6

As we buckled up to drive into civilization the following morning, Myra patted my knee and said, "I knew you'd do the right thing. My instincts are dead on, if you'll pardon the expression." When I didn't say anything, she added, "You have this hang-up about believing you're a good person. But you really are. And the finest detective I know. Personally, I think you wasted your talent as chief of police. You need to be where the action is. Not that people didn't have the utmost respect for you as chief. Everyone did. They told me so."

I looked back at her with the most sincere expression I could muster. "Thank you, Myra, that means a lot." But I thought to myself, *Soon I will never have to look at you again.*

My cabin rested behind an old, curvy single-lane road. If, over the next few hours, we saw a cow or even another car, it would be a highlight of the ride. I never spent this much one-on-one time with Myra, and did not brim over with anticipation.

"This is going to be fun," she said. "We have so much to talk about."

"Yeah, I guess."

Like people check their pockets a thousand times to make sure they haven't lost their plane tickets, I acquired a sense of security from patting my copy of *Supernatural or Psychotic?*, hidden in my inside jacket pocket. Or I did for about ten minutes into the trip. The book popped out of the narrow pocket and onto the car seat.

Myra, being a total buttinsky, grabbed it before I could. She looked at it and burst out laughing as she handed it back to me. "Oh God, I can't believe it. I forgot all about that book. I read it. . . I can't remember, I must have been in high school. Or maybe junior high. Isn't it hilarious? Why are you reading such nuttiness?"

"I think it's funny, too," I said, thinking fast. I felt guilty for hurting Annabelle Sleet's feelings.

"As I recall, there's some ridiculous quiz about whether you're crazy or seeing ghosts."

"Is there? I must've skipped over it." I could've just let the subject drop, but curiosity can be hard to resist. "Did you take the quiz? How did you score?"

Myra giggled, looking straight ahead. "Who knows? I can't remember."

"Do you believe in ghosts?"

"Of course not, why would you even ask? I'm an empiricist, like you."

When people acted one hundred percent sure of themselves, it made me uncomfortable. In a way, I treated everyone like a crime suspect.

"I heard the author disappeared."

"I'd disappear if I wrote such a silly book." She honked at a driver who cut in front of us.

I put the book in my paper bag, next to my toothbrush. For maybe three minutes neither of us spoke.

"What about the case?" I asked. "Shouldn't we be talking about it?"

"Relax. If you remember how, that is. It's a long ride to the airport. Let's enjoy a little R-and-R."

"I've heard hunting serial killers called many things, but never relaxing. I want to do this and get it over with. I want—" I caught myself in time. "I want to get back to my cabin as soon as possible."

Myra pulled the car over to the shoulder of the road and stared at me like she couldn't comprehend my inability to see beauty in all things. "One thing hasn't changed, Joe, and that's how much you have to offer the world. I know you don't believe it, but it's true. It's always been true, and it always will be." She leaned over and kissed my cheek.

"Thanks for the vote of confidence." I stared out the window, hoping she didn't notice when I wiped away her intrusive kiss.

"Oh, I'm sure you'd do the same for me. We're friends."

I wanted to say that no, we weren't, we were barely acquainted. But I figured that would make her more determined to snap me out of my funk.

I heard myself say, "Do you still collect Victorian stuff?" I didn't care one way or the other, but it seemed a neutral enough topic.

"Do I ever!" Her smile took up half her face. "I just found original copies of *The Fancier's Gazette* from 1874. And in mint condition. A magazine for animal breeders and exhibitions. So very charming."

I thought about saying, *Calm down, Myra, it's not like I asked you to fuck.*

"You haven't asked about my kids," she scolded. It didn't occur to her that maybe the subject of one's children raised issues for me.

"How are your kids? Alive, I assume?" My mounting irritation needed some release.

"Oh, I'm so sorry. I thought it might be good for you if. . . never mind what I thought. Forget I said anything. There's plenty of time to talk."

I didn't bother replying.

Myra said, "Okay, Mr. Ants-In-Your-Pants, if you want to know about the case that badly, I'll show you what I have."

It struck me as odd that this should be her attitude, after all she went through to get me this far. But Myra conceded nothing without a little dig.

She pulled the car over, opened her briefcase, took out her razor-thin computer tablet, logged in, and clicked open the file about the case. "Live it up," she said, handing me the tab. I accepted it with the solemnity of a samurai being handed a hara-kiri knife.

Myra drove back onto the road as I read the files. The first computer entry featured Swann Baumgarten, a punk-goth type with spikey white hair. She owned a boutique called Chix Rule, for which she designed and sewed all the clothes herself. A fanatical clubber, Swann seemed the type who enjoyed designer drugs. But she had no criminal record, not even a parking ticket. Despite her hip urban posturing, I sensed a sweetness about Swann—she called her mother every Sunday evening—and I found myself hoping she didn't do it.

But wishful thinking had little place in a murder investigation. I noted that at twenty-seven, Swann had been single for nine years. A week after graduation, she married her high school boyfriend, a bass player in a garage band, and he died on their honeymoon night after falling down a flight of stairs. Maybe she killed guys who reminded her of him, to feel in control of their deaths. Or maybe she thought no one compared to her first love, so other guys didn't have the right to live.

Another suspect, Willow McBride, used her maiden name, Willow Vance, at speed dates. You could call her attractive, but in an unsexy way, like the host of a children's TV show. She had an MBA and worked as chief loan officer at a downtown bank. At thirty, she'd been married for eight years, had two kids, played golf and tennis, and stayed active in the PTA and her church. Her husband, Chris, served as deacon, and she led the Sunday School.

She presented herself as one of those I-have-it-all types whom other women envied for her boundless energy. She even had oomph left over to cheat on her husband through speed dating, which deception held promise for solving the murder. The picture-perfect life stopped working. She belonged to a conservative denomination, and Willow needed more venues to express herself. Murdering men who found her attractive could've been one such venue.

A plain, unsmiling woman with big, round, tortoise shell glasses summed up the third person of interest, McKenzie Schultz. A brief video clip revealed that she walked with her arms crossed, her shoulders hunched over. It looked like she apologized to the world for taking up space. She came from old money but never spoke to her family. She also never touched her considerable portfolio of investments. Instead, she worked for low pay as a research librarian and lived in the smallest of studio apartments. When people became estranged from their families, it didn't take a genius to wonder if there'd been serious abuse of some kind. As it happened, she had an eccentric uncle with long hair who lived in a teepee on the grounds of the family estate. A happy coincidence, from a profiler's point of view.

McKenzie also had serious mood swings, with the pendulum seldom landing on happiness. She once had to leave work over an argument about the coffee pot in the break room. And on three occasions she got arrested for mouthing off to a cop at a tree hugger protest. A fanatical vegan and an environmentalist, she burst into tears when a coworker refused to save paper by making two-sided copies.

To be frank I found it odd that the murder victims contacted her, let alone asked her out, but maybe they knew about her money. Still waters ran only so deep.

"Quite an assortment," Myra said, as I switched off the tablet. "Any guesses?"

"Willow," I said, without hesitation.

"Really? Willow? I'm surprised. To me, Willow is the least likely. She seems like such a nice person. Just a little. . . you know, confused or something. I'd put my money on Swann. She strikes me as a very unstable person."

"I guess we'll have to see." I thought about telling a story about how I once tailed a suspect who turned out to be nothing more than a professional dog walker, but I felt too tired to share the pointless anecdote.

Myra turned on her conference phone to confirm our plane reservations. She had a special voice for the telephone, peppy yet businesslike and over-annunciating her consonants. When the airline phone attendant said, "Have a great day," Myra answered, with a lilt in her voice, "You have a great day, too." She turned to me and said, "Such nice people work for airlines. I'm always so impressed."

After a minute or so of quiet, she tapped my knee again, only this time harder. "C'mon. We're having an adventure. Let's show some enthusiasm."

Annoyed, I looked at my knee and looked at Myra and said, "I gotta pee." I didn't have to, but I couldn't think of any other way to respond.

"Uh, do you have to do it really bad? The nearest rest stop is ten more miles."

"Jesus Christ, Myra. Pull the car over like any idiot would do. I'll walk into the bushes. Millions of people do it every day." I rubbed my forehead. Out of nowhere, I got a bad headache.

"Okay, okay. Sorry."

She acted frazzled, like I kidnapped her at gunpoint to drive the car and here came the final blow to her sanity. After she pulled over, I walked into a thicket near the shoulder of the road. I found a patch of bare ground and sat there, listening to a cacophony of sounds: the whizzing cars, the leaves, the birds, the wind. I put my head between my knees, as if about to be sick, but nothing happened. Though not a very religious person, I prayed to God from the depths of my heart: *Please let me die. My family needs me. I'm sorry for being so mean to them.*

I heard Myra honk her horn. I sometimes saw spots when I first opened my eyes, but this time the spots were like balloons, each one containing the face of Swann, Willow, or McKenzie. I could tell they were making fun of me; I almost heard them chuckling. I thought I'd get an encore visit from my family at such a moment, but they were nowhere to be seen.

After the third honk, I stood up and walked back to the car. The door closed on the seat belt, and I had to open it again. Nothing's ever simple in civilization; every little thing went wrong. The second time the door closed okay, but the seat belt became tangled.

"Are you okay, Joe? You look like you've seen a ghost."

"I thought you didn't believe in ghosts. But I couldn't be better. Just takin a shit." (Not true, but I couldn't resist grossing out Myra.)

"You don't have to put it like that. What did you—oh, never mind."

"Relax, I found a creek," I lied some more. "Plus I always carry antibacterial." I turned the tablet back on to keep perusing for leads. I saw that Myra received an e-mail marked urgent.

"Read it to me," she said. "In case you hadn't noticed, I'm driving."

I took this as her way of getting back at me. "Well, let's see. . . 'Myra, your cunt stinks. Sincerely yours, The Speed Dater.'"

For about a second, the car swerved into the opposing lane. The driver of the lone car honked and gave her the finger. But Myra recovered her steely, professional demeanor.

7

"Maybe it's a man after all," Myra said, driving with a tiny bit of road rage. "No woman would say that to another woman. Only a man would think someone pointing out that she had one of those weirdo vagina things would humiliate a woman."

Before I could respond, another e-mail came through. "Myra, the guy you're riding with is psychotic." I tried to make light of it. "I could've told you that," I said with a chuckle.

"You're not psychotic, you're. . . just forget it. We'll trace the e-mails, though I doubt it will do much good."

"But how did this person know you were driving with someone? There must be a mole in the agency. Unless you told someone else."

"My kids know where my case is, but that's it. And anyway, would an agency mole be so stupid as to give us such an obvious lead?"

"The thrill of the chase. Or hey, could it be that maybe this serial killer is crazy?"

We stopped in the nearest town to eat, and for me to get what Myra called cleaned up. "Let's take care of you first," she decided. "I'm embarrassed to be seen eating in public with you the way you are now."

Desperate with hunger, I raised no objections. I felt like a dog obeying commands to get fed.

First she took me to the local hair salon. The woman stylist shaved off my long beard. She showed me my face in the wall-sized mirror. "Wow, what a difference," she said. "Why have you been hiding such a handsome face?"

Myra glowed with pride. "My sentiments exactly."

"You look ten years younger without that silly gray beard," the stylist said.

"Fifteen years," Myra corrected. She always enjoyed getting the last word.

I looked. . . well, I looked what I used to look like, only with long hair. Since I didn't have a mirror in my cabin, I only saw faint glimpses of myself in the windows, almost like a ghost. Since I hadn't bothered to take notice of myself when she first started shaving me, I never did fully see myself with the long beard before she shaved it off.

"Now the hair," Myra instructed. "Get rid of the gray. Keep it on the longer side, but style and shape it. Hip professional. That's what we're after."

The stylist studied my hair with concentration, as if nothing in the world mattered more. "I can match your natural shade perfectly."

I didn't know I'd say this, but the words came out of my mouth all the same. "If you're going to dye my hair, make it some other color. I don't care what, just something unfamiliar."

She turned to Myra. It was obvious the stylist assumed Myra and I were a couple and that I yielded to her dictates about these things.

"That's fine," Myra said. "Use your own judgment."

When the stylist finished, I saw a stranger in the mirror—a dude who looked like he had all the confidence in the world. He bore little resemblance to Joe Hilario.

Myra said, "I can't get over the new you. You look like— oh, I don't know, maybe an astronomer. Or some billionaire who invented something."

"But not a cop," I said.

"No, not a cop."

We happened upon a closed antique shop, though Myra stood at the windows for what felt like an eternity, sharing information I did not understand on the various items. At a local department store, we bought a selection of jackets, pants, shirts, ties, and shoes for me. The width of neckties, jacket lapels, and shirt collars changed over the past couple of years, which information Myra assumed I'd find interesting.

But even in the old days, I could not care less about the latest fashion nonsense. It served no purpose other than forcing people to replace all their functional clothes.

Decreeing that I looked respectable, Myra found us a local eatery. I liked diner food, but Myra saw this frou-frou place that better suited her pretensions. The décor of the restaurant imitated that of a French country inn. Though, at the bottom of the menu, I found a listing of good old American hamburgers.

"Would you like to hear about our specials today?" asked the table server.

"Please, I'd enjoy that very much," Myra replied.

The table server launched into a list of foods I never heard of, but Myra made her choice. After all but inquiring as to the amount of rainfall the grapes received, she added a glass of wine to her order.

I said, "I'll stick with a cheeseburger and fries. Burger well done."

"What kind of cheese, sir? We have Chèvre, Taleggio, Gouda—"

"American," I said.

Myra all but had a stroke. "American? That's not even real cheese."

I shrugged. "I like it. And I'll have a Coke."

"Very well," Myra permitted with the profoundest tolerance.

Her food turned out to be a tiny saucer of rice or pasta glop. "This is so filling, I can only take a couple of bites," she said. "But it is out of this world."

I tore into my burger like a starving dog and shoveled in the French fries with my hands.

"My God, you're going to have to relearn how to eat."

I looked down at my unfamiliar silverware. "It's true. I haven't used a fork in two years." Living alone in my cabin made me realize how much I always hated table manners, among so many other things. What enjoyment could be had in remembering to keep your elbows off the table or to set the butter knife a certain way? I failed to see the fun in doing what other people expected me to do. I looked around the restaurant, and the people reminded me of ants, waving their skinny little arms about to do this but not do that.

"You're right, it's a restaurant, so no one is supposed to like to eat. I forgot."

She set down her fork, wiping the corners of her mouth with her napkin. "Manners make eating a pleasant experience. Otherwise, we're no different from animals."

"We are animals, Myra. We eat, sleep, and shit. We live and we die. We fuck, we fuck each other over, and sometimes we kill."

"Joe, believe whatever craziness you want. But you're likely to have many a date to catch the murderer, and you'll have to do better. You must blend in with dozens of other well-to-do singles and not stand out like someone who schlepped in from the wilderness."

"Okay, fine. I'll slow down." And I did. I even used my fork to eat the fries, though last I heard the etiquette assholes declared them to be a finger food.

"Don't look now," Myra told me, "but you see that guy at the far end, talking to the other guy? See how he's undressing me with his eyes?" She arranged her legs, so that more of them could be seen.

"Huh, FBI profilers hit on strangers. Learn something new every day. And incidentally, don't we have a plane to catch?"

"I'm just having a little fun. If some guy gives me trouble, I can handle him." She gave what she thought to be a subtle open-mouthed smile to the guy in question, implying that he'd find a barrel of laughs in her company.

"Oh damn," Myra said. "Pardon my French. But the other guy is coming over, the one my guy talked to. Wouldn't you know, I attracted the wrong one."

"Good afternoon," he said. "My partner and I are happy together, and we'd appreciate it if you stopped coming on to him."

Myra's face turned tomato red. "You must've misunderstood me. I'm here with my date. But I'm glad for both of you."

During the course of the meal, another guy appeared that Myra insisted had the hots for her. But her theory proved wrong when, moments later, his wife or girlfriend showed up.

An elderly man with thick bifocals came to our table and said, "Excuse me, Miss. I live right upstairs. If you'll come to my room, I'll make it worth your time."

I said, "If you're talking about a financial arrangement, sir, you need to go through me."

Myra narrowed her eyes, threw her glass of ice water in my face, and hurried to the ladies room. She departed for a while, and I relished using my fingers to pick up my fries.

She rejoined me just as our plates got taken away. "Well, Joe, maybe next time you'll think twice before having a joke at someone else's expense."

"You mean throwing the glass of water? You did it, not me."

Myra sighed, as if a martyr worthy of sainthood for tolerating my irreverent attitude. "I did it because of what you said, but never mind. Let's forget it happened."

Back in the car, we took an exit to the nearest airport.

"The murderer . . . I think she has a romance novel idea of love," said Myra. "Very twisted, mind you. But she fits the profile of someone who thinks a dashing pirate with a waxed chest will sweep her off her feet. Thank God I'm not that type of woman. I have my parents to thank for that. They were incredibly supportive of me. Mom and Dad raised me to have a career that made a difference. 'The road to happiness is paved with excellence,' they always said. I never believed that Prince Charming fluff. Besides, men—" She stopped herself. "Well, never mind."

"No, go on. I insist." I thought about mentioning that she just got mistaken for a prostitute but decided not to antagonize her.

Myra sighed. "Men resent powerful women. I don't mean to get all women's lib on you, but I'm sorry. It's a sad fact of life."

"Uh, yeah. Sure." I scratched under my unfamiliar, stiff collar. How did I ever wear neckties every day? I felt like someone being choked, but choked to life instead of death, like when a torture victim passes out and then is doused with water to be revived. Everything about my unfamiliar, scratchy clothes and brittle dyed hair seemed to say, 'Welcome back, sucker.' As for Myra, if she thought of herself as a powerful woman, then good for her. But in the end, no one had more power than death.

"That's my problem in a nutshell. I scare men off by being me. Even successful men. Or should I say especially the successful ones? They hate competition. For years I've been told, 'Myra, you have so much to offer, but it's not for me.' Or words to that effect. My husband, bless his soul, died before I hit my stride. My job. My bestseller. Three straight-A children. Did you know my collection of Victoriana is insured for two million dollars? I wonder what would've happened if he lived. My husband, that is. Would he take my achievements in stride, or would he resent me like other men do?"

As we approached an airport car rental, I watched a plane take off and wondered if it would crash; it didn't. "There's all sorts of reasons for not wanting to be with someone," I offered. "People may say it's one thing, but there's always more to it. It's like saying there's only one reason why someone commits murder. A lifetime of nonsense leads up to the big moment."

Myra eased the car into a parking space. "How odd to liken dating to murder."

"Isn't that exactly what this case is about?"

"Yes, I imagine you're right, but I certainly didn't mean me, or the intimate things I told you. Which, by the way, never leave this car." Myra waved an authoritative finger as she stepped out of the vehicle. "I'll be back in a minute. Get up and stretch. We'll take the shuttle to the terminal. You know, I liked renting this car very much. It never gave me any trouble." She patted the roof, as though the car were a cute puppy.

I climbed out on the passenger side and realized I needed my new sunglasses. The sun radiated on the concrete and hurt my eyes. Or, to be precise, my whole body. For just a flash, I saw the Sun People dancing on the beach, only it also looked like Caitlyn and the kids. The vision evaporated as quick as it appeared, like when you nod off for a few seconds and start to dream, but then wake up.

Through the tinted office window, I could see Myra signing the routine paperwork and turning over the keys as if handing in evidence to the Attorney General. I had a passing thought to do something disruptive, like piss on the car. But I decided it wouldn't be worth the hassle.

She walked out with her usual bouncy step. "We have to wait at the shuttle stop across the way. The counter person's very helpful. She said it should be here any time."

I tried to remember if Myra always squeezed every little life-affirming statement out of every little thing she could, or if she only did it now for my benefit. She fed me one moral lesson after another: people were kind, society so worthwhile. I figured it to be some of both—she acted patronizing to begin with and now even more so.

Everything she said and did convinced me all the more that life sucked. All her perkiness seemed to come from an alien species. Her presence somehow kept my spectral apparitions away, but even that felt unsafe. A curious phrase occurred to me: Myra lacked the life needed to know the dead. Maybe that's why she enjoyed collecting antiques. She didn't see the death that surrounded a given artifact. Even in my zombie-like state, I had more juice than she did.

If all else failed, I wondered what it would take to get Myra to kill me. It might be the one honest thing she ever did.

8

Myra nudged me awake when the plane landed. "Here we are. In paradise."

Departing the terminal took almost no time, so within minutes we were outdoors in the thick, slow heat of the afternoon. It felt like all the oxygen in the world evaporated, and the sun looked so big and bright it seemed impossible to hide from. Still drowsy from sleeping on the plane, I saw one of the Sun People lean down into my face. After pointing at me and laughing, he thumbed his ears and stuck out his tongue.

The conventional perception was people who lived here loved the climate. Yet I could tell that everyone pretty much went from air-conditioned car to air-conditioned room and back again, like lab rats trained to go from one cage to the next.

Even the airport sported palm trees, and everyone wore skimpy but expensive summer clothes. Though touted as a laid-back and relaxing place, it made me feel self-conscious and inferior. You know the type of city I mean—expensive, and full of show-offs who aimed to prove how rich and problem-free they were with every movement and word.

"This is where I'm retiring," Myra declared, as she waved her hand in the air for a cab. "In Jamaica, I never kept busy enough. But here, you have it all. A tropical paradise *plus* the many cultural benefits of a city."

"I barely have time to get ready," I said, changing the subject. "My first speed date is in two hours." The FBI arranged for the three suspects to be invited to the speed date for free. And all of them accepted.

"You look fine." Myra fixed the collar on my shirt. "And you have your new wallet and phone. There's a weapon waiting for you in your beach house."

I assumed calling it a "weapon" made it sound more genteel than calling it a gun. As for the wondrous beach house, I reminded myself that the Sun People only happened in dreams and could not harm me.

"Sounds like a plan, Myra."

"You'll meet the other agents tonight, or maybe tomorrow morning." She kissed my cheek again. "Be careful, and if you end up bringing a date home, remember to turn on the hidden cameras immediately."

"What about fucking?" I asked, with an earnest look on my face.

She frowned. "This is nothing to joke about. You know perfectly well what the professional decorum would be."

"What is it again? I've been away so long I can't remember."

Myra ignored my comment. She looked on the verge of tears, which seemed strange since we were only working together. "I'm glad to see you again. Please be careful."

I never knew how to respond to mushiness, and wanted to change the subject. "Remember, my new name is Carlo. Carlo Rizzo, swinging real estate developer."

She tried to hug me, but recent years rendered me all but unaware of the custom. I turned away from her to board the airport shuttle to the car already leased for me.

The GPS in the fresh-smelling, upscale sedan led me straight to the speed date. It transpired in a conference room of a hotel chain, famous for reasonable prices. I observed the usual nondescript wall-to-wall carpeting, stackable metal chairs, and tables with pitchers of ice water. A big sign with the name of the speed-dating service hung from the back wall, featuring the slogan: *Your Time is as Valuable as Your Love.* As people took their seats, they engaged in small talk, but I made a point of sitting at the aisle and putting my program on the seat next to me so that no one would sit in it.

The slime ball who ran the thing smiled like invisible hands stretched his lips open. His teeth were glow-in-the-dark white. He made some bullshit speech about how finding your true love would happen with the right attitude, and how everyone in the room deserved happiness—she or he only had to believe it. Everyone applauded with great enthusiasm, as if to insure good luck. I forced myself to join in the applause.

Because I had to pass myself off as a genuine speed dater, I met with a lot of women. I felt sorry for some of the ladies whose time I wasted. A sincere person talked about the challenge of raising three boys as a single parent. She showed me their pictures in her wallet.

Another woman—beautiful and intelligent—explained how much trouble she had getting anyone to understand her unhappiness. At the same time, I met a woman who never brushed her teeth and another who told me why the Supreme Court stopped running her favorite TV commercial.

But finally, I met Swann Baumgarten, the punk fashion designer with a heart of gold. Damaged loser Joe Hilario needed to go on indefinite hold. Until further notice, I had to be Carlo Rizzo, uncomplicated winner.

"Swann—that's a lovely name," I said, as we seated ourselves.

"I've always hated it." She scrunched her nose to suggest we shared a conspiracy. It's awkward to meet people through speed dating, and I appreciated her effort to bypass the usual first questions: What do you do for a living? Have you ever been married? And so on. Of course, her ability to establish an instant rapport with a stranger could've meant any number of things.

I played right along. "What name would you like to have?"

"I think I'd make a good Felix," she replied. "I like the sound of it."

"Then Felix it is. Let's start over. How do you do, Felix?" I extended my hand, and she clasped it.

"Fine, Carlo. But I want to call you Joe."

Uh-oh, did someone slip up? Did she know my true identity? I tried to appear relaxed. "Why Joe?"

"Because, you goofball, you remind me of a ferret I had as a kid. I named him Joe."

"Why would you name a ferret Joe?"

She shrugged. "Why not? Joe is a common name, right? I wanted him to feel like a normal member of the family."

"How am I like a ferret?" I could feel her legs moving closer to mine under the table. I responded in kind.

"Oh, mischievous, kind of naturally oblivious, but always rummaging through things. Like you're not looking for anything, but you don't know what else to do."

I laughed. She didn't know it, but in a way she pinpointed why I wouldn't miss life once I sacrificed myself for my family. "Yeah, that's me, all right."

"Plus you seem—you know, cuddly."

I looked down in modesty. "It's true, I'm a big cuddler," I lied.

"God, me too. Nothing in life feels as good as wrapping yourself around another person who squeezes you back. And it doesn't cost a thing."

"Actually, sometimes it costs quite a lot." I crooked an eyebrow.

She laughed and pinched my cheek. "You are so adorable." She handed me her business card. "Call, text, e-mail, whatever. Let's have fun. Somehow I feel I've known you forever. I know that's corny, but I'll let you in on a secret. Underneath it all, I'm a cornball. I cry at beauty pageants and old Shirley Temple movies."

The bell sounded to switch partners.

"I think the world could use a few more cornballs." I smiled at her and tucked her card into my jacket pocket with a finesse I didn't know I had. "You'll be hearing from me."

She shrugged. "I already know that."

I noticed a strange phenomenon. When talking to Swann or any of the women, they seemed like real people, sometimes almost too real. But then when we were done talking, they appeared flattened out in the background, like they were cardboard cutouts. Twice I had to blink away the bloody images of my family. When no one was looking, I put my fingers in my ears in case I started to hear Caitlyn's soft voice.

After a few more five-minute meetings, I sat across from Willow McBride, married mother of two, who introduced herself as the single and available Willow Vance. In person, she had a sexual vibe that didn't come through in her bland photo. She had loose, full hair that dipped down over one eye. You could tell she enjoyed swinging her hair out of the way. She wore an intense perfume, and her dress clung to her curves. Willow reminded me of a sexy Myra, oxymoronic though the concept may have been.

Coming on to a married woman bothered me, but it had to be done.

I went right to the point, or rather the dishonest point: "Explain it to me, Willow. You're a beautiful woman. Clearly, you have so much to offer. So why are you single? I hope you don't mind my directness, but after all, we only have five minutes."

She smiled like a flight attendant or someone who worked at Disney World. "Thank you, Carlo. I've asked myself the same question a million times, but you're the first man with the courage to ask it yourself. I like that."

"Well, what's the answer? Don't keep me in suspense." I hated idiot-flirty talk, but it worked with her type.

Willow laughed, shaking her hair in the process. "The answer is that most men are duds. They don't know what they want. Or what they want is nothing original, if you get my drift."

"At the risk of betraying my sex, I have to say I agree with you."

She looked impressed. "Gee, Carlo, where have you been keeping yourself all this time? And by the way, Mr. Question Man, why are you still single?"

"Question Number One, I just moved here. Question Number Two, I'm single because I've been stung a few times myself."

She reached across the table to hold my hand. "It's always the nice guys who get hurt."

The more she held my hand, the more claustrophobic I got. Though hard to explain, I could see how this woman might commit murder.

"Well, I certainly hope I'm a nice guy. Since we haven't much time, tell me about the real Willow. What kind of books do you like to read?"

"How refreshing to be asked that instead of my favorite—oh, never mind. Promise you won't hold it against me, but I like romance novels. Getting swept off to sea by the man of my dreams."

"Hey, don't knock it. At least you're a woman who knows what she wants." I hated it when Myra guessed right.

"Amen to that. What's the point of falling in love if there isn't any. . ." She floundered for the right word.

"Love?"

Willow threw her head back in merriment. "Exactly. Love is romance and passion. Not coming home from work and seeing some boring, sickening man who makes your skin crawl." She feigned a cough. "Anyway, do you like to read, too?"

"Spy novels, espionage. Guy stuff, I guess you could say."

"A real man." She narrowed her eyes in admiration.

"Last time I checked," I joked. "Here's my card."

"And here's mine."

We traded calling cards just as the bell rang. She never mentioned her career, and I never had a chance to ask about it. She made me think of someone with hiccups trying not to hiccup—only rather than hiccups she hid something much worse. Unless, of course, as a super-religious person she flipped out over how much she enjoyed being a sinner.

My next speed date partnered me with the bland McKenzie Schultz. In the near future, I'd discover much more to her than met the eye, to put it mildly. But at the time, my eyes were all I had to go on. Though the speed date would only be five minutes long, I wondered how to fill the time. Her huge glasses seemed to dominate her entire being, as if a girl with glasses summed up her identity. The lenses were big and round and housed in thick tortoise shell frames.

I'm no beauty expert, but she looked like she picked the style that would make her as unattractive as possible. She had a Prince Valiant haircut, and wore a long sleeved white blouse pinned at the collar with an inexpensive brooch that depicted a sad kitten with big eyes. Her humorless brown skirt stopped just below her knees; despite her dark stockings, she seemed to have a rash on her legs.

"Hello, McKenzie." I pretended to read her name tag. "I'm Carlo."

She blushed as she looked away from me. "How do you do, Carlo?"

"Fine, and yourself?"

"Uh, I don't know. Okay, I guess."

This led to one of those excruciating pauses, the kind Joe Hilario excelled at. But dashing Carlo Rizzo rushed in to fill it. "I'm a real estate developer. But in my spare time I like quiet things. You know, staying at home, maybe reading or listening to music." I figured this would be less intimidating than saying I liked to hang glide or something.

"What kind of music?" she asked. I could see a glint of hope in her face.

"Classical mostly," I said, hoping that was the correct guess.

"Oh really?" Her face brightened. "Do you like Mozart?"

"Of course. Especially *The Magic Flute*." I happened to know Mozart composed this particular opera or symphony or whatever they called it. But I wanted to change the subject before she caught me in a lie. "I like to read nonfiction. Architecture books, things like that."

"I read about health foods, and organic gardening," McKenzie said. "Everyone should. It's the only way to save the planet."

"Oh, so you have a garden?"

"No. But I think about having one. If I ever moved into a building that allowed it. Only organic vegetables, though. I'm extremely allergic to flowers. I have a lot of allergies." She clasped her brooch. "I like cats, too. I don't have any because of my lease. But I have the Internet. There's a virtual garden I tend every morning, and a virtual pet cat I feed twice a day. The cat matches my brooch." In touching the object, she caressed it.

I knew from her file that despite her millions socked away, she lived at her current address for almost a decade. I wondered what that must be like, keeping yourself from having such simple, ordinary pleasures for no good reason.

Yet I understood it somehow. In fact, I had a passing thought that I rejected because I found it too depressing: while I liked to think of myself as some wild mountain man toughing it out in the woods, I had much in common with McKenzie. In effect, I lived in fear of everything and pampering my red nose with a tissue for my thousands of allergies. Not in a literal sense, but on the inside, life scared the crap out of me.

"Well, looks like we have many things in common. I've gardened all my life. And I'm a total cat person."

"Dogs scare me," McKenzie said. "They're so. . . militant."

"I see you're a woman with a fragile quality. Very feminine."

McKenzie flustered. "Do you have a cat?"

"I'm afraid not. I just moved to town, I'm busy with work, and I. . . well, I'm still getting over the loss of my last cat."

She brightened and almost seemed happy. "What kind of cat? What was its name?"

I said the first thing I thought of. "A tabby. I called her Caitlyn. She died of old age."

She blushed some more. "What a sweetheart she must've been. Maybe. . ."

"Maybe what, McKenzie?" I smiled for the utter safety of my being; I didn't want to frighten her away.

"Maybe, if you'd like, I can show you how to get a virtual cat online. But only if. . . I mean, I know you're busy."

"That sounds like fun. I'd like that very much."

Her attractive smile was a big surprise. "My online cat has a name. I've never told anyone before. I know it must sound silly."

"Not in the slightest," I said. "Please tell me what its name is."

She frowned, as if in apology. "His name is Tofu. He has very pale fur, you see."

"'Tofu.' How sweet. How imaginative."

"Would you. . . um, would you like to have my card?" she asked.

"I'd be delighted."

As our five minutes ended, I thought to myself, *Jesus, what the hell happened to her?*

I saw all three women as I prepared to leave but didn't say anything more to them or to anyone else. I noticed that even McKenzie smiled as she talked to another woman on her way out. I alone had no one to talk to.

Peculiar though McKenzie may have been, I didn't think her the likeliest suspect. Murder is, in its way, an intimate act, and even the gentle manner in which the victims died would've been too much for her. No matter how objective I tried to be, I kept coming back to Willow. The way the victims were arranged with their hands on their chests and grinning—it seemed like something Willow would've done. She'd find it important to seem nice.

The next likeliest had to be McKenzie. Serial killers were not the most well adjusted people in the world. So I couldn't rule her out with certainty. I found Swann to be the unlikeliest suspect. However, since life consisted of many a cruel joke, the unlikeliest could turn out to be the opposite.

Still, a decision had to be made. I took out my new cell phone and texted Willow:

*Sorry 2b impatient a drnk 2nite U pck bar Carlo*

She responded back within a matter of seconds:

*Yes Ariels at 11*

My watch read five past ten. I figured she wouldn't kill anyone in the next fifty minutes.

9

Until my drink with Willow, I forgot about an age-old problem with meeting people at a certain time and place. At work, I had a reputation for always being the first one there, which people took as proof of my dedication. But I harbored an acute fear of being late, like a dream where you have to go someplace but never get there.

Despite my dangerous life as a cop—or maybe because of it—I worried that if I gave myself only just enough time to get to wherever, something would go wrong, and I'd end up being late. I knew that you were supposed to arrive late to parties. But this unwritten rule made me more befuddled.

Sometimes I pretended that my watch must've stopped or I had the time wrong, so that's why I arrived upwards of an hour early. Caitlyn used to tell me to relax, which only made me more nervous. It used to drive her crazy when we went somewhere as a couple, but I tried to joke my way out of it or tell her how pretty she looked.

Doubting the accuracy of the GPS in my car, I drove from the hotel straight to Arial's, arriving at 10:40 p.m., twenty minutes early. It's amazing how twenty minutes drags on when you're sitting at a bar hoping someone shows up. The time might've gone faster if I drank, but I figured I should hold off until she arrived, since I hadn't touched alcohol in such a long time. I made do with tonic water and a twist of blood orange. It tried my patience to take periodic, miniscule sips of something I could drink in one gulp.

I didn't know what Willow told her husband about being out so late—maybe that she had work at the office, or maybe she said nothing because she knew he didn't care. She wouldn't go down in history as the first person to cheat on a spouse.

Ariel's proved to be an upscale singles bar filled with anxious people in expensive clothes pretending to have fun.

The owners must've dropped at least six figures on the décor. The bar had a shiny grand piano in back, and a woman in a tux played high-rent Frank Sinatra songs. The club featured a small dance floor, where two or three couples showed off the fact that they took lessons in swing dancing. I watched people spend hundreds of dollars on single malt scotches or a vintage bottle of champagne. But people liked flaunting how much money they had—or pretended to have. Looking at all the desperate, pretentious singles, I wondered how any of them expected to find love.

Maybe the answer grew out of my growing suspicion that love did not exist, only acting did—acting and fucking. In a way, had my marriage to Caitlyn been anything more than a drawn-out speed date?

At one minute past eleven, I grew nervous that Willow intended to stand me up. I also worried over having to decide how long to wait for her. She arrived at ten past eleven, the moment I began to text her. She wore the same clinging dress, but with a matching wrap thrown over her shoulders, which, with considerable drama, she removed upon entering. It had these complicated ripples sewn into it, which told me it cost a lot of money. When her eyes met mine, she smiled, running her fingers through her hair for the billionth time since we met.

"This is the 'in' place to go." She air-kissed my cheek. "Isn't it exquisite? Let's get a table, shall we?"

I crooked my arm to escort her, and she accepted it. I knew she'd go for old-fashioned stuff. I also pulled out her chair for her. A server took our orders. Willow ordered a Pink Lady. Tired of worrying about drinking, I told myself I needed to make the right impression and ordered a Jack Daniels straight up. I knew that women, or at least her sort of woman, didn't want a man with chi-chi tastes. They liked men who used nothing fancier than Old Spice and drank good, solid liquor.

Willow cupped her chin. "So, who is Carlo Rizzo?"

"I've often asked myself the same question." I thought it wise to appear introspective; it signaled a sensitive man beneath my assertive countenance. "Carlo Rizzo likes what he does for a living," I said. "But Carlo Rizzo is lonely. He has more friends than he knows what to do with. But he can't meet the right woman."

Our drinks arrived; Willow didn't offer a toast, so I didn't, either. "At the speed date, you mentioned being hurt, Carlo. I'm sure you'd rather not talk about it. It's hard for me to talk about it, too."

"Thanks, that means a lot to me. But I don't have any secrets. I've been engaged twice. The first girl left me for someone else the day before our wedding. The second one—well, let's just say I should've listened to my friends. A good-time girl who liked too good of a time, if you know what I mean."

"How awful." She looked at me as though I deserved all the sympathy in the world. "You've never lived with anyone?"

"Only my college roommate. Not my type. He never used deodorant."

Willow laughed. "What about kids? Do you want any?"

I drew my eyebrows together in sincerity. "You know, I'm not sure. I enjoy other people's kids. I'm like a big kid myself. But sometimes I think I wouldn't want to give my attention to anyone but my wife." Since it was probable her fantasies involved a man who wanted no one but her, I thought it best to be evasive about kids.

"You're honest, I could tell that about you right away." She nudged her chair closer in. "Honesty is hard to find, as I imagine you already know."

"Yes, all too well." I took a minuscule sip of my drink, letting the liquor leave a faint flavor on my lips. "Light social drinker," I explained.

"That's good. Some men, when they drink. . . never mind."

"Willow, forgive me for getting so personal, but did a man ever—I mean, have you known any mean men?"

Her mood switched and a slight craziness came through. "Certainly not. You think I'd let something like that happen to me?" Her protest did much to convince me that someone indeed had been "mean" to her—I assumed her husband. Did he beat her? Rape her?

"I apologize. Please tell me you accept."

She thought for a moment, looking perturbed. "Sure, okay, Carlo. You do like to be called Carlo, I assume? It's such a nice name."

"Thank you, Willow." I took another sip. "But I'd like to know more about you, to whatever extent you feel comfortable."

I learned over the years that while women wanted to know "everything" about a man right away, they often were not as forthcoming about themselves as they thought. Or at least not with the men they dated or married. How strange that people didn't have to say much to the people they had sex with. Maybe it's like that old saying about 'don't eat where you shit'.

Moody Caitlyn seldom shared with me but would get on my case for reciprocating. People told me, "Can't you see she's hurting?" But I couldn't. I just thought she hated me.

Willow took a contemplative swallow of her Pink Lady. "Gee, the story of Willow Vance. Where to begin? I guess I should start with 'Once upon a time.'"

"Sounds like a good way to begin. Once upon a time...?"

"There was a beautiful little girl," she said, in absolute seriousness. "She had so many dreams. She wanted to be a great actress and win an Oscar. She wanted to be a doctor who cured sick people in Africa. She wanted to be the first woman on the moon. She had the most wonderful parents. She always got everything she wanted for her birthday. Every summer the whole family went someplace beautiful. Rome. Venice. Paris."

I wondered if what she said contained any truth whatsoever, but I pretended to believe the whole story. "That sounds wonderful. Did you—did she have any brothers or sisters?"

"No," Willow answered. "I'm an only child. No matter how much my parents gave me, they wanted to give me more. But one day I got older. No more kid's stuff."

"What happened? It's important that I know."

She finished her drink and signaled to the server for another. "I met a guy. Bet you never heard that one before."

"Maybe once or twice."

"Well, if it didn't end so horribly, I'd laugh."

"So I take it you're divorced?"

Willow sighed. "I don't know why I'm doing this, but I don't want to lie to you. So here goes nothing. I'm married. I have two kids. There, I said it." Her second Pink Lady arrived, which she wasted no time drinking. "Are you angry? You'd have every right to be."

"Not at all. I admire your honesty. But why are you—"

"We met in a Bible class. We bonded so well I got pregnant. Talk about a miracle. My parents. . . well, it's true I got to travel, but they were missionaries. They said God works in mysterious ways, and before I started to show, I got married.

"I had very little say in the matter. I went to night school and got an MBA. And you want to know something? That bastard of a husband never changed a single diaper. I look back and wonder how I did it all. The nicest thing I can say about my husband is that he never beats me when I'm pregnant."

I moved my legs in closer to hers. "He beats you? Why do you stay with him?"

She rubbed her leg along mine. "Oh no, I'm kidding. But he's. . . I can't look at him. He's repulsive. I'm always working late at the office. Or at least I say I am."

I reached across the table to clasp her hand; I ignored the odd feeling it gave me. "Speaking of which, I have a house right on the beach. Maybe you'd enjoy a drink? Or taking a walk?" I'd never understood the big deal about walking on the beach but for whatever reason, it occupied a high position on the list of romantic things to do. Sometimes, as a detective, I searched through dating websites, and people said how much they liked walks on the beach.

"I love walking on the beach," Willow said. "Especially at night."

"So what are we waiting for?"

"I. . . I guess you're right. What are we waiting for?" She stood up and started to put on her wrap.

"Allow me." I rushed over to place it on her shoulders.

"We're both adults," Willow pronounced, as if to reassure herself. I realized that for her, I represented true adultery, since I knew of her marriage. I wondered if she'd done much with her other speed dates—assuming she didn't murder them.

"I'd like to know more about you. Your job, your kids."

"I'd just as soon not," she said. "I mean, not tonight."

"Gotcha."

"What about my car?"

"Follow behind me." I thought this would show how honorable my intentions were, though at the same time I attempted to show how honorable they weren't. Dating made no sense. No wonder that marriage didn't make sense, either.

Sitting in my car, I texted the FBI that Willow would join me at home. This meant the surveillance would begin. Directly across from the beach house, the FBI planned to park an unmarked van with a TV monitor. I'd turn on hidden cameras for the agents to watch me with Willow. If she snuck Roofies into my food, the agents in the van would signal me through a tiny, near-invisible earpiece I wore. I didn't ask for assurance. Nonetheless, Myra told me that at worst, I'd be given the Roofies, which so far, anyway, never got administered at a toxic level.

However, I kept a minor detail from the FBI: I planned not to turn on the hidden cameras. My death would be ruled the product of a technical malfunction. And if Willow proved not to be the killer, then no foul no harm. Of course, it also meant I'd have to think of other ways to work around the inane cameras in the future. But one thing at a time.

In my rearview mirror, I saw Willow's signal that she was following, as she blinked her SUV headlights at random intervals.

As I pulled up to my driveway, with Willow's SUV right behind, it occurred to me that I hadn't yet been inside the beach house. But the layout couldn't be hard to figure out, as one dwelling looked pretty much like the next one.

Besides, something more pressing captured my attention. My wife and children appeared before me again. In their bludgeoned state, they did a mocking reenactment of the kids being born. Caitlyn lay with her hacked up open legs before me. First Joe Jr. and then Stephanie pretended to emerge from her body.

They cried out, "It's a boy!" and "It's a girl!" and each of the kids took a bite of their mother's thigh, making fresh rivers of blood.

Caitlyn tried to blow me a kiss, but her lips were chopped off. "This is it, my darling," she said. "Soon you'll be with us. Think of it, Joe. Together. Free. Forever."

Willow stepped out of her SUV. "Carlo, the ocean—isn't it breathtaking?" She hugged herself as she took in the salt breeze. She had a small purse I hadn't noticed before.

"I like that it's private," I said.

Indeed, the nearest neighbor lived a half mile away. I didn't stop to look at the ocean, and instead typed in the security code I memorized to open the front door.

"Well, here we are." I held the door open for her. Then I locked the door behind me and guessed where to flick on the light.

"What exquisite taste," Willow marveled.

I shrugged with modesty. "I'm a real estate developer. I know about these things."

The living room looked like one of those TV designers had put it together, with everything color coordinated and well-placed. As a bachelor pad, it sported brown and black furniture with lots of leather. A small wet bar in a corner of the room featured rough, dark wood. The deck, I could see, went around three sides of the beach house, including, of course, the ocean side.

Static blasted in my tiny earpiece. I supposed they were telling me to turn on the cameras. I figured since in fact I couldn't make out what they were saying, I'd proceed as planned.

"Leave your things on the sofa," I said. "I'll be right back. Help yourself to the kitchen and the bar, and if you don't mind, make us a snack. Surprise me." I wanted to get a sense of where the bathroom and bedroom were. I also wanted Willow to be flattered that I trusted her—that is to say, I gave her every opportunity to drug my food. I didn't know what the FBI stocked in the cupboards or fridge, but I knew there'd be a bunch of food to make the place look lived in. Myra said they bought "romantic foods," though I had no idea what that meant.

"Sure," said Willow. "But there's one thing I need to do first."

I pretended to be bashful. "Oh, and what's that?"

"This." She put her arms around me and kissed me long and hard. It reminded me of something out of a movie—a very bad movie.

"I'll be right back," I said. "I'll drink whatever you're drinking."

I checked out the bedroom, which had an ocean view. The room featured a large master bath with a sunken tub. A gun lay in the nightstand, and I left it there. A Photoshopped portrait of me, with what were supposed to be my parents, stood on the dresser. I wore a cap and gown, and the parents looked pleased with me for graduating from wherever.

I toyed with the computer tablet the FBI provided, which had a touch screen and other handy features. To signify settling in, I took off my jacket and tie and threw them on the floor. Then, on second thought, I picked the clothes up and hung them in the walk-in closet. I wanted to take off my shoes since they were stiff and uncomfortable, but that seemed too forward, even as Willow knew where things might be headed.

I walked back to the living room. Willow sat on the dark leather sofa with her legs crossed, and her dress hiked up to her crotch.

"Anything look appetizing?" She gestured toward the wooden cutting board on the oblong glass coffee table. On the board were apples, grapes, French bread, and an assortment of cheeses. She also opened a tin of smoked oysters, which she arranged on toothpicks. Like a proud domestic goddess, Willow provided a serrated knife to cut wedges of food as we saw fit.

She took a black vase of these Asian stick things—I did not know what they were—and placed them beside the food arrangement. I also saw two carefully placed clear drinks in long-stemmed glasses. "Two vodka martinis, as dry as can be," Willow explained. "Stirred. I hope you like them that way. I couldn't resist these beautiful glasses. Such delicate crystal. Yet so proud and tall. They're like you, Carlo. A real man, yet so in touch with your feelings."

Her purse rested on top of her wrap, on the arm of the couch. When the slippery wrap slid off by accident, the purse went with it. I handed both back, and she straightened out the wrap, which had fallen into a heap, and placed both items next to her.

"I like simple foods," I said, kneeling at the coffee table. "I'm in the mood for bread and cheese. Would you like some?" I figured if she claimed an allergy to cheese or something, that meant Roofies. She kissed me some more in reply, and eased me onto the couch. We made out for a few minutes, and I pretended to be into it when she nibbled my ear, but I wanted to eat what might prove to be my last meal.

She could kiss okay, yet it's hard to care about how someone kisses when you think she's going to kill you.

She sat up and looked down on me. "Let's walk on the beach first. The food isn't going anywhere. I want. . . I want tonight to be extra special."

I smiled. "Sounds great. When we get back I'll feed you some grapes." I moved to stand up, but she kissed me before I could. She kicked off her high heels and made a big production out of taking off her panty hose, turning it into a kind of striptease. Then she insisted on unlacing my shoes and pulling off my socks. "I like a man with big feet." She rolled up my trousers a little. "It's always so silly when men have tiny little feet." She blushed and giggled.

"Or when woman have tiny little hearts." I winced for having to talk this way. I became glad the cameras were off for an additional reason—no one could see me in action during this ridiculous pseudo-date. The FBI's goal had nothing to do with my scoring a home run with Willow, and I'd have to keep things from going beyond PG-13.

"Poor Carlo. You deserve so much better." She mussed up my long, shaggy hair. "A man with hair. It's so virile. It reminds me of olden times. Some men. . . never mind."

As we stepped outside, I assumed the van across the street could see us, so I gave a subtle thumbs-up. I figured they'd take it as a sign that I had my act together, despite the fact that the cameras weren't on. (Later, I found out that they wanted to abort the whole thing, but Myra convinced the other agents in the van to trust me.)

We stood on a beach at night, but being in a city made for hardly any stars to be seen. Wisps of clouds ornamented a full moon. A long stretch of smooth wet sand shone in the dark, only to turn dry again until the next wave hit, as if the water and sand engaged in an endless battle of wills.

We walked holding hands, near enough to the waves so that they made our feet wet. Even at night, the water felt warm. I remember thinking, *So this is a walk on the beach.* Though not as torturous as I expected, I still didn't get what the big deal was. Twice in the one direction, and three times on the way back, Willow stopped us to make out. We were about to turn back up to the beach house when she stopped again, this time to put her hands to my face. Her hair rippled in the breeze as a forceful wave drenched our ankles.

I heard Caitlyn call my name as Willow stared at me with wonder.

"Everything is beyond beautiful," Willow whispered. "We're in heaven."

"I thought you had to be dead to go there."

She frowned. "Carlo, why break the mood when everything is perfect? Besides, the life after death—that's when real living begins. I believe that with everything in me. Think of it. In heaven, no one has a broken heart. Everyone just. . . lives."

"Yeah, I guess."

She turned away from me and put her face in her hands. "There's something I want to tell you," she murmured. "But I can't."

Since I already knew the marriage angle, I wondered what her big fat secret could be. Maybe that she wanted to kill me?

I touched her shoulders. "When you're ready you can tell me."

"Oh, Carlo. You are so sweet. And I'm so sorry for. . . for what I can't help being. Life is strange. You don't even know the people you affect the most. Total strangers want to be just like you, while the people you know. . . the people you know. . . "

I looked deep into her eyes. "Willow, whatever it is, I forgive you." This time, I kissed her first. I thought of it as kind of a blessing—that I approved of her murdering me.

"Smart boy," I heard Caitlyn hiss in the salt wind.

"Wait," Willow said, right before we stepped back inside the house. "I don't want us to get sand all over your beautiful floors." She sat down on her knees and wiped the sand off my feet. "I can wipe yours," I offered, but she replied, "That's okay," and wiped her feet herself.

"Now, on to our banquet." I led her by the hand to the sofa, thinking to myself, *I am leading death and not the other way around.*

Everything, of course, lay right where we left it. We sat down on the smooth leather sofa, and she handed me my drink. "This is a form of love, isn't it?"

"I should say so."

"Kiss me some more before we eat."

She set down her glass and toyed with a throw pillow on the sofa. I wondered if it would be the pillow she killed me with.

"All right." I set the drink aside, and as we kissed, she led my hand to her breast. My eyes were closed, but I felt something tugging at me.

I opened my eyes. A man I never saw before stared with pure hate. His bald head shone in the lamplight. He wore a business suit and smelled like a case of whiskey. I figured he'd been drinking since he left work.

"What the hell are you doing with my wife?" he shouted. I recognized him as Chris McBride, Willow's husband, though of course I couldn't say this.

"How did you get in here?" I asked him.

"Who the fuck cares? I climbed up the deck. I broke in the back door."

This told me that the FBI across the street hadn't seen him enter.

Chris pulled out a gun and pointed it at Willow. "I've been having you followed, you dumb twat." He packed an S&W black stainless, a popular choice for getting the job done.

Then Chris pointed the pistol at me, so I, too, experienced the gun's intent. "Buddy, go stand next to your whore. My wife, the whore of Babylon. The motherfucking mother of my children. The woman I sit next to in church every Sunday. In *church*, damn it."

"Look, it's my fault," I said. "Kill me, but don't kill Willow."

I heard Caitlyn sigh. "You're my hero, Joe. I can't wait to kiss you."

Willow said, "No, kill me, you prick. Hell is better than one more second of looking at you."

"You fucking cunt." He pointed the gun at Willow.

I couldn't let Chris kill her.

I charged at him, knocking him down. His head hit the coffee table, shattering it, but he stood back up and took aim at me. I grabbed the serrated knife and stabbed the arm that held the gun. He dropped it, howling in pain. The gun landed on the sofa, and Willow screamed as if it were a snake. Chris reached for the gun, but I punched him in the face hard enough to make him lose his balance. Though he resisted, I managed to pin him to the floor in a half Nelson.

The food lay scattered in the chaos of broken glass. I had cuts on my hands and bare feet, and Willow's husband had a triangular sliver of glass wedged into his face. Willow huddled in a corner of the sofa; her wrap and purse fell to the floor again.

"Willow, give me the gun," I said in a calm voice. I wanted to hold it over her husband and call in the FBI. But Willow sat there, trembling.

Her husband dripped with sweat as he squirmed to loosen my hold. "Crazy bitch," he hissed. "Next time I'll lock you in the basement."

Her hands quivering, Willow reached for the gun. She pointed it at Chris, though her aim suffered for her shakiness.

"Willow, stop," I said. "Give me the gun."

Despite my hold on his chest, Chris laughed. "You can't fire a gun, woman. You know you can't. Give it to me. See? I have a free hand." He wiggled his fingers in freedom.

"You mean the hand you beat me with?" Willow breathed hard as she tried to steady herself. "Yeah, Chris. I've seen it every day for years."

"You fucking lying whore," Chris hissed. "I never touched you." He looked at me as if we were old friends. "Dude, she's lying, you have to help me."

"Willow, give me the gun," I repeated. "Please. Your kids need you."

She started crying. "I. . . okay, here it is." Her hands trembled as she moved the gun in my direction.

With great relief, I reached as far as I could without losing my arm hold on her husband.

She needed to get the gun maybe six inches closer to me.

I heard a gunshot, and Willow fell on top of me, bug-eyed and open mouthed with surprise. I grabbed the gun and slid out from under her. A red puddle oozed from below Willow's heart. It looked like she had a punctured aorta. She was dead.

Caitlyn shouted at me, "Can't you do anything right?"

The shooter stood by the doorway. An FBI rookie, I thought to myself. You can spot them from a mile away, blustering and nervous at the same time. As for Willow being dead, it pissed me off that she didn't get a chance to snuff me out, assuming she planned to. Also, I had grown to resent people who died fast and prematurely, so in a weird way I also envied her. My cop instincts were to prevent murders. But since they happened anyway, I wondered why the same never happened to me.

"What the fuck?" Chris stood up and stared at the bloody corpse. A well-mannered guy, he turned his head away to puke on the floor.

"FBI," the stranger said, his voice cracking. "Hands on your head."

"FBI? What does the fucking FBI want with my wife?" Chris looked at the agent and then at me, as if our faces would answer his question.

"I said hands on your head," the agent repeated, with more force this time, yet failing to understand he did not have as much control over the situation as he assumed.

"You murdered my beautiful wife. And for what?" Chris rushed toward the agent, his hands poised to strangle him.

I did not think it wise to point out that minutes ago he attempted to kill the same beautiful wife. I jumped in front of him, and aimed the gun at its owner. "Don't move," I warned.

Chris made a motion that suggested he wanted to shove me out of the way. But I'll never know for certain, because the trigger-happy agent shot him from a different angle. This time, the bullet went through the victim's head, entering in front and coming out clean in back, like a toy peg going through a hole. His lifeless body fell on top of Willow's. In my state of shock, I thought he looked like a little boy, nuzzling his head in his mommy's lap.

I wondered if the rookie would shoot me next, to round out his evening.

## 10

The look on my face must've communicated to the rookie agent my disgust over how events played out. "The lady aimed a gun at you, sir," he said. "My duty is to protect."

"She was handing me the gun." I wanted to say much more, but couldn't. I felt too much of some things and not enough of others to have made sense.

He gazed at the bodies with a blank expression, like a kid who knew he did something to anger the adult but he couldn't figure out what. "Like I said, I had a split second to decide."

"So you shot a woman not trying to shoot me, and then shot an unarmed man when both of us had guns." I long believed that two types of people went into law enforcement: those who considered shooting people a last resort and those who couldn't wait to kill someone legally. I had no difficulty deciding which camp this agent fell into.

"He charged at me, sir. He didn't listen. I couldn't let him get my gun. I had to—"

"You had to shut the fuck up." The unfamiliar voice belonged to a man who bore a slight resemblance to Denzel Washington. He walked into the anarchic room with a grim confidence. I guessed him to be a senior FBI agent from the van. An entourage of people followed in after him, including Myra. "Not another word," the senior agent said to the rookie. "What's done is done." He looked at me. "Are you all right, man?"

"All right" could've meant a hell of a lot of things. "That's one way of putting it."

The man laughed. "You have a dry sense of humor, Joe. I like that." This happened to me sometimes. People thought I made a joke when I didn't. He extended his hand and introduced himself as Josh. "Joe, I'm really sorry. The cameras never came on."

"Are you serious? I heard some static in my earpiece. That must've been what you were telling me."

Myra said, "I'm so glad you're all right." She moved forward to hug me, but I pretended not to notice as I stepped a bit nearer to Josh.

"I wanted us to come in sooner," he said. "But Myra insisted we give you a chance. And when we saw your thumbs-up, we figured you had everything under control. And then this idiot over here—" He looked at the rookie agent. "Excuse me, I'll be right back."

Josh pulled the rookie agent aside. In the gaggle of people talking on their phones, taking pictures, bagging evidence, spraying chemicals and dusting with powders, I couldn't make out everything Josh said. But in essence, he told the rookie agent what he could do with a long blunt object in regard to his ass.

From what I could hear, the rookie started out in the van across the street with the other agents. When they heard the commotion of the fight, he ran out to play hero. Josh called for him to come back, but he disobeyed. When he saw Willow, the murder suspect aiming the gun, the rookie shot her to save my life. When Josh asked why he shot the husband through the head, the agent replied that in the moment it seemed the right thing to do.

Josh told the rookie he hadn't the authority to be making such judgment calls. His goal should be to follow orders, not save the day. Only Josh's method of expression was far less diplomatic. Josh concluded by telling the rookie to get the fuck out of the house, which he did.

"He's up to his neck in hot water," Josh said to me. "He disobeyed my direct order. He's still green, but he insisted he could handle it. Shannon, our boss, is very fair, so he'll get what he deserves. The important thing is that you're still alive."

"Yeah, I'm alive."

Josh laughed again, as if I should've been a stand-up comic. "You kill me, man," he said. "That deadpan look you get when you let out those zingers. Let me see your phone."

"Sure." I handed it over.

Josh turned the phone on and toyed with the buttons. "Looks perfectly fine. Maybe the cameras jammed. I'll have them checked out." He gave the phone back to me.

"Whatever," I said. "We need to analyze every crumb of food. Check her purse for drugs. The purse." I pointed near the sofa. "I last saw it there on the floor." I wanted to know if I lost my big chance to die when Willow got shot to death, though of course I didn't say this.

Josh's phone rang. "I gotta take this. I'll be right back." He hurried to the bedroom and closed the door.

"Gee, this went well," remarked the one person in a local police officer's uniform, sealing an airtight plastic bagful of broken glass mixed with bloodied cheese. "You federal fucks sure do know what you're doing. Good thing you stole the case from us know-nothing cops." He put his hand on my shoulder. "Call me Stu," he said. "Though you could also call me fucked."

I inferred that Stu started the case, and when the FBI took over he became the token local cop. He reminded me of my army drill sergeant, a big, outspoken guy. They were both men that scared the crap out of other people, yet were always kind to me.

A woman named Tish, who looked like a younger version of Myra, gave Stu a dirty look. As Myra's protégée, she hung on her mentor's every word, and never let anyone else get close to her. I felt a little sorry for Tish. Imagine believing the sun rose and set because of Myra.

"Myra was right as always to put you on the case," she said. "You must feel like you've been brought back from the dead, what with being back in the thick of things."

I replied, "So far, all I've done is make a mess."

"These things happen," said Tish. "At least you're okay."

Josh sauntered back into the living room. "The big shots," he explained to me. "I wouldn't describe them as happy."

"You mean about them?" I pointed to the dead bodies.

"Bingo. Our orders are to arrange the bodies in a park and shred a file or two. Hell, maybe a hundred, who knows?"

The look on my face must've displeased him because he added, "Yes, that's right. The federal government covers things up. I'm sure you're shocked to hear this—not."

"Josh, do you mean to say that—"

"Look, Mr. High and Mighty, the alternative is blowing our cover. The lovebirds are dead, and it sucks royally. We can't change that. But we can save other lives. This is kid's stuff. I've worked on cases where I had to say things that should've won me the prize for Best Actor."

"What about their kids?"

"We'll make sure they find a good home."

"I'm really sorry, Josh."

"For what? It's not your fault the rookie went ape shit."

Still, I could tell Josh felt worse than he let on. The cover-up appalled me, and later it would be put on display for the world to see. But for the time being, I let it go. I still had a mission to fulfill. Besides, I of all people couldn't afford to play holier than thou.

I stared at the cuts on my hands; a thin line of blood trailed down my right arm. "Their kids are never going to be normal. Even if they get a few insurance bucks out of it, what are they supposed to do with the rest of their lives?"

"They'll grow up to be very good or very bad people. What can I say? Shit happens." Josh shrugged as he took out a pack of mint gum and put two sticks in his mouth at once.

I assumed the mint settled his stomach at a crime scene.

"Anyway, you have to go to the hospital."

"It's only a few scratches. But I respect protocol. Remember, look in the purse."

Josh grinned in a melancholy way. "You're all right, Joe. You tried to save them."

"You'd have done the same thing."

Protocol further dictated that I ride in the back of an ambulance with an attendant. He kept insisting that I lay down. "Don't worry, I won't die on you," I said.

The ambulance guy answered, "This may be a joke to you, but there's nothing funny about it. It's important that we do this."

"So I don't sue anybody?"

The guy laughed. "You got it."

As we pulled into the emergency wing, he took out a wheelchair and placed me in it. "More of the same," he said.

Talk about hard luck. The first person I saw when I entered the emergency waiting area was none other than Myra, who took it upon herself to leave the beach house ahead of the ambulance. She appeared everywhere in my life now, like a hex.

"What are you, a leprechaun?"

She patted my head in sympathy. "Poor Joe. You're in shock."

"Make sure they check Willow's purse. It fell on the floor someplace."

"It's all being taken care of. You're not paid to worry, that's my job. Speaking of which, my kids are in town—or two of them anyway. Lisa's still on her way. I thought they deserved a little break from school. Only for a few days." She scrunched her nose. "They're staying at my hotel, and I'm sure they'd love to see you again."

Again? When had I ever met them? Maybe Myra had her wires crossed. Or maybe I met them after the murder of my family, and I blotted it out. But I didn't remember them. I had a terrible memory for non-professional acquaintances.

"Why do you want me to see them so bad? So I can teach them to drop out of society?"

"That's not who you are anymore. And deep down inside, you know it's never been the real you. The Joe I want them to see is the distinguished homicide detective."

Before I could reply, a nurse appeared to wheel me into an examination room. I did nothing but sit there and wait for a couple of hours, after which some doctor whose jokes weren't as funny as he thought looked me over for about fifteen minutes.

He took my blood pressure and temperature, checked my eyes with a flashlight, listened to my pulse and heartbeat, and felt around my body, asking if anything hurt. Nothing did. He hit my knee with a rubber hammer, he asked me for today's date and the name of the president and to count backward from 100.

"You have some minor cuts," he pronounced, which of course I already knew. He ordered a nurse to tend to my wounds; only one required a Band-Aid. I could leave the hospital standing up.

I found Myra sitting in the waiting room. She insisted on driving me back to the beach house. Once there, she asked several times if I wanted her to watch over me while I went to bed. Each time I told her that I felt fine, the last time raising my voice.

"Why are you taking your hostility out on me?" she said. "I'm helping you."

I stepped out of the vehicle without saying anything else.

"Check in with the lobby guards tomorrow," Myra told me, "and they'll direct you to Shannon's office."

As she drove off she appeared to be crying. Even the taillights on her car seemed to make a mournful expression. But if she had a bug up her ass, I knew she could deal with it.

Entering the house, I couldn't believe the FBI cleaned up the mess so fast. Having tile floors instead of carpeting no doubt made it easier; no bothersome bloodstains to blot out. They put in a new, identical sofa, and a new wooden coffee table to replace the glass one that shattered. I checked the floor for a minute or two and found not the tiniest shard of glass left behind. The entire place smelled of disinfectant. You'd never guess a double murder just happened.

I left voice messages with Swann and McKenzie, saying how I enjoyed our meeting, and hoped to hear from them soon. I tried not to sound pushy.

I hadn't watched TV since moving to my cabin, so out of curiosity I turned it on. But it looked and sounded so strange, I turned it right back off. I fell asleep and dreamt that I opened the bedroom French doors, and Sun People peered in on me. I kept waking up and going back to sleep, trying to get rid of the dream.

I gave up at the crack of dawn. The gun that I left in my nightstand now appeared on the pillow next to me. I had no memory of putting it there.

"Chief Hilarious," I heard my children call out in unison. They had only the right half of their heads; snakes poured out of the cavities on the rotted left side. Still, the twosome kept calling me Chief Hilarious. Some loud rock song they used to like and which I hated blared in the background as they danced.

"A gun on your pillow, how sweet," Caitlyn purred. She seemed to mistake the blood dripping from her body for sexy red silk. "A gun's like a teddy bear for grown-ups. Play with the nice Teddy, Joe."

"We broke your heart," Stephanie said in a sweet voice. "Isn't that what you told us when that guy tried to shoot us?"

"You said you couldn't even look at us," Joe Jr. said with a laugh.

"You stormed off to work," Cailtyn said. "Work, work, work, work, work."

I picked up the gun and stared at it.

"Don't hurt the gun's feelings," Caitlyn whispered. "A gun should be treated like a gun. It's like Ralph. A dog's gotta bark."

"He barked so loud in the bedroom with the ax," Joe Jr. recounted. "So cute."

## 11

I stared at the wall for three hours. I thought my family might come back, but they didn't.

After a listless shower and forcing down some coffee, I left the beach house and drove to the local FBI headquarters. A security guard gave me my nametag—an old passport photo and the title of "Special Consultant." As I waited for the elevator, someone tapped me on the shoulder. When I turned around, he punched me in the jaw.

"Thanks a lot," he said. "Next time I'll remember not to save your life."

I recognized the trigger-happy rookie. So much for the FBI screening the emotional stability of its agents.

"A six-month suspension without pay and for what?" He landed another punch, this time on my chin. I didn't even try to fight back. I couldn't jeopardize my role in the case.

"My wife's pregnant," the rookie said. "You motherfucker. How am I supposed to support my family?"

An armed FBI security guard approached. "Hey, everything okay here?"

The rookie raised his hands. "Don't worry, I'm going." The guard moved forward, but I restrained him. "It's okay, let him leave," I said.

The rookie walked backward toward the main doors, looking at me as if we were having a staring contest. "I hope you die," he said. "I hope you're the next victim." Then he spat on the floor, turned, and left.

As I rubbed my jaw, the guard said, "What a dumb ass thing for him to say. Are you sure you're all right?"

"I'm fine," I said, walking toward the elevator. I pushed the wrong floor for Shannon's office and had to survive the minor irritation of the elevator making an extra stop. For some reason, I found it difficult to forgive myself when I made these small mistakes.

Shannon's secretary greeted me and walked me to her boss's office, a healthy distance from where the secretary sat. I assumed this spoke to Shannon's high status. Big bosses always get privacy.

"Welcome aboard," Shannon said as she led me to a plush chair in her office. "Myra never shuts up about how great you are, so it's nice to finally meet you."

"I don't walk on water, but thanks." She had a picture of herself with what I took to be her husband and three kids. They all made goofy faces for the camera.

Shannon laughed. "You're clever. I like that." She moved some folders on her desk to see me better. "I just finished having a conversation with Agent Brizinski."

"Who?"

She fiddled with a pencil. "You know. The agent who shot two people to death."

"I saw him on my way up here."

"I hope he didn't upset you. He's extremely agitated about getting suspended for insubordination. I almost called security."

"I'm fine," I assured her. "But what if he—"

"That's why God made contracts. He'll never work again in law enforcement if he doesn't keep his mouth shut. Just because you have a whistle, doesn't mean you should blow it."

"Can I ask a personal question?"

"Maybe I can answer it without it being asked. I made the decision. And pragmatically speaking, it's for the best. If you're wondering about Willow's kids, there is no conclusive longitudinal data that indicates one can predict how a child will turn out solely on the basis of having parents."

"So you're okay with everything?" I asked.

"Okay is not the point. If I wanted to be okay, I'd be a kindergarten teacher."

It never occurred to me before, but how odd that any cop or federal agent would rather deal with murder all day than teach little children. I wondered what sort of people that made us, though of course I didn't share my curiosity.

"Let me bring you up to speed," said Shannon. "There's bad news, bad news, and really bad news."

"Nothing new in that. Let's hear the bad news first."

"The bad news is that we traced those vile e-mails Myra got to a sample computer in a high-tech shop here in town. No login required— it could've been anybody. The next bad news is that preliminary tests on the bloodied food were inconclusive. The really bad news is that you said Willow had a purse. It's gone. I could make a speech about how such careless work never happened before on my watch, but it wouldn't change anything."

It's always pissed me off when the simplest things got botched up. I sensed the hurt and frustration starting in my belly, then working its way through my body, until I found it difficult to think of anything else. I used to feel this way on a daily basis. "By 'gone,' I assume you mean someone accidentally threw it away or lost it?"

She grinned, with the corners of her mouth turned down. "Those are your words, not mine."

"Jesus, I told about a million people, 'Check the purse, remember the purse.'"

"I already know. Josh asked about it at three in the morning. They pulled an all-nighter. They looked through everything, but no such luck. They did find a bloodied silk shoulder wrap. It's in a plastic bag. But not the purse."

"So in other words, we have to wait to see if the perp strikes again to rule out Willow. Unless, of course, the murders stop now that Willow is dead."

Shannon leaned back in her chair. "Don't get your hopes up. Since when is life easy?"

I liked Shannon right away. I considered myself a quick study of other people, and I could see that leadership brought out her best qualities. She commanded respect, and she suffered no angst about being a boss and a woman at the same time.

I saw the mangled Caitlyn stand behind her, laughing and pointing. Then she swerved around to make faces at Shannon.

Shannon received a beep on her computer; she read what I assumed to be an e-mail and rolled her eyes. "Anyway, I'm very sorry, Joe."

"These things happen." I tried to sound sympathetic.

"In all honesty, we get most things right. Still, sometimes, the egos, the immaturity . . ."

"I know. You're talking to an ex-police chief."

"I know you know."

Our eyes met, and for the first time in years I felt a natural connection to another person. Then, all at once, something occurred to me. "Shannon, let me see that wrap or shawl or whatever it's called."

"I think I know where this is headed. Let's go together."

A short while later, we found ourselves in a conference room with Myra, Tish, Josh, Stu, and several other agents whom I recognized from the night before.

"Go ahead, Joe," Shannon said. "This is your show."

For all my superiority about the missing purse, I found myself in a state of pure terror. I felt way out of practice with these meetings, and the various agents might as well have been aliens from a sci-fi movie. An angle of sunlight poured in through the blinds, and everyone looked lit up and gigantic, like the Sun People.

I swallowed back the urge to puke, and when I spoke, my voice wobbled and my hands shook. But I managed to shift into automatic pilot mode. Feeling like a stage magician, I put on plastic gloves, removed the bloodied silk wrap from its bag, felt around in the textured ripples, and—as if having made a new discovery—slid my fingers down the edge of the garment, where the seams were open. My hand emerged holding a thin vial filled with a powder that I was confident would test positive as Rhohypnal.

"Voila," Shannon said. "One vial of Roofies, courtesy of Willow McBride."

There were gasps of admiration. But of course on a deeper level, I cursed my luck. It seemed obvious that Willow planned to kill me. Did she savor the inevitability of it by keeping me from eating? Or did she like me a little (or like Carlo Rizzo a little) whereby she had some ambivalence about doing me in? Either way, if only her crazy husband hadn't followed her, I might be with my family now.

Myra put her hands to her astonished face, as if she witnessed a human landing on Mars. "Didn't I tell you we'd get our money's worth with Joe?"

"Great work, Joe," said Stu.

"That's weird, I could've sworn we checked the shawl," Josh said. "But does this mean we can we all go home now?"

"I'm afraid not," said Shannon. "I just got word about Victim Number Eight. Smiling face, hands across his chest. Hispanic attorney. Cell phone records indicate he called all three suspects, along with half a dozen other women from the speed-date service. Died about two this morning, after the Willow incident. So she didn't do it, unless anyone had any ghost sightings recently."

Everyone laughed.

Tish said, "So assuming it's not a coincidence that Willow ever so happened to be hiding Roofies in her shawl, there's two perps. Or even more."

"Sounds like you studied arithmetic," said Shannon.

"I don't buy it," Stu said. "My cop instincts tell me something's off."

Tish wanted to respond, but Shannon beat her to it. "Joe, do your cop instincts tell you the same thing?"

The entire roomful of people looked at me, as though my answer would resolve something of epic proportions. "I, uh. . . I don't know."

"He's being polite," said Stu. "But something's wrong."

"This thing you have about cops versus FBI," Tish said. "It has to stop. We're all on the same page."

"And you just proved we're not," Stu replied. "Cops don't say things like, 'We're all on the same page.' This

Willow person. . . If her husband had her followed, why didn't he know she bumped people off?"

"I don't have an answer for that," Tish admitted. "But what do you think, that the vial of Roofies flew into her shawl by magic?"

"The FBI is full of magic," Stu answered. "Last night, for example, the FBI said, 'Abracadabra,' and two dead people suddenly appeared in a park."

Shannon looked agitated. "Stu, you signed a confidentiality statement when you got appointed to this case. You know it's for the greater good."

"Give me a break. 'The greater good.' What a joke that is."

"Stu, please. Need I remind you yet again—"

"Okay, Shannon. I get it, I get it."

Josh said, "Okay, so we're looking for another perp. I still can't wrap my head around McKenzie as a femme fatale. I know she's got M-O-N-E-Y, but let's face it, she isn't exactly *Playboy* material. How could she reel in all these upwardly mobile dudes? Unless she has a double life or something."

"These men were also single, so they may've had problems, too," Tish said.

"So single people have problems, but married people don't?" Stu asked.

"You know what I mean," said Tish. "Perfectionism, commitment phobia. Maybe a little OCD thrown in for good measure."

"Yeah, but let's not forget they've all been good-looking guys," Josh said. When a couple of the men in the room chuckled, he added, "What? A man can't say another man is handsome?"

Tish said, "So in other words, you're saying a handsome man can't see something in a woman who's. . . you know, somewhat plain-looking?"

"More or less," said Josh.

"In point of fact," Shannon interjected, "some men like their wives or girlfriends to be less attractive than themselves. One theory is that the woman will be easier to control because she should feel lucky he's interested. And when they go out together, everyone notices him, not her. People may even assume he's a sensitive guy for not judging a woman by her looks."

"Were any of the victims that type of man?" asked one of the other agents.

Shannon considered the question. "Possibly Mr. Domestic Violence. For that matter, possibly any or all of them."

"I still don't see Swann as a murderer, either," Josh said. "Remember? After the killings started, she actually saved the life of a guy she met speed dating. He keeled over during dinner in his loft—a bad drug cocktail he made himself—and she gave him CPR and called 911."

"Plus let's not forget she calls her mother every Sunday, like an obedient daughter," said Stu. "You people are unbelievable. Have any of you ever seen a murderer or talked to one? A fucking saint could be a murderer."

"Stu has a point," Shannon said. "Though he could have made it in a nicer way. When Swann saved her date's life, it may have been a diversionary tactic. Or for some crazy reason she wanted him to live instead of die."

"Swann could be a split personality," said Stu.

"There's no such thing as a 'split personality,'" Tish said. "It's always much more complicated than that. Besides, it's called dissociative identity disorder. Learn your terms."

"I don't care what some hoity-toity shrinks say," said Stu. "They change their minds every five minutes, anyway."

"The thing is," Josh interjected, "we still don't even know everything about Willow. Assuming she did it, why did she do it?"

Shannon sighed. "Josh, you're absolutely right. But we have to move forward. Do you honestly think we should go back to square one?"

Josh reflected. "No. But I'm kind of with Stu. Something isn't adding up right."

"Thank God this isn't a jury," Shannon said, which made everyone laugh some more.

"'Swann and Willow,'" Stu contemplated, leaning back in his chair. "Whatever happened to normal names? Mary or Susan. Now everyone is named Willow or Pillow or Ocean or Gladiola. Or Tish, for that matter. Is that your actual name on your birth certificate?"

Tish held her head high. "Yes, as a matter of fact it is. What's wrong with that?"

"What do friends call you for short? Ti?"

"That's enough, Stu," warned Shannon. "Apologize to Tish."

"I'm sorry," Stu said with a mean smile.

"I don't need your apology," Tish replied. "I have a case to solve."

Shannon's cell phone rang. I recognized her ringtone as the theme from *Star Wars*, which I took to be tongue in cheek. I liked that Shannon hadn't lost her sense of humor. But she didn't look too happy.

"Victim Number Nine," she told us. "Actually, this one's been dead for a few days. African American—a plastic surgeon. But otherwise, the same MO. And yes, a speed dater."

Josh stifled a yawn for having not slept all night. "Well, let's start digging. Again."

Stu said, "Before we do, I think we should thank my fellow police officer Joe Hilario for how he's handled things so far."

I panicked as all eyes gazed toward me. "That's okay, don't bother."

But Stu stood up and applauded me. With reluctance, so did everyone else. I never knew how to receive compliments, so I smiled at the floor as I left the room. I felt my heart beating faster for its discomfort but had no idea how to slow it down.

"Great job running the meeting, Joe," said one of the agents.

In truth, I had said next to nothing. People assigned all sorts of qualities to me I didn't possess.

Stu wanted to check out Willow's home and office, and Shannon asked an agent to go along with him to get clearance. I'd go with Myra, Tish, and Josh to the two latest crime scenes, both in upscale condos in a trendy neighborhood. As we waited for the elevator, Myra pulled me aside and said, "I suppose you're going to say, 'I told you so.'"

I knew what she meant but didn't want to get into it.

Myra added, "Don't pretend. I can spot a liar from a mile away."

"What are you talking about?"

"Willow, of course. You said she did it, while I thought her innocent. You must be gloating."

"I don't know what you mean."

"Remember, in the car?" she said, raising her voice. "You said Willow, and I said Swann."

"Oh, that. Well, we don't know much of anything for certain."

"You seem to. You're always going on about how innocent Swann is."

Shannon stood a few feet away, and from the look on her face I could tell she knew how to handle Myra when in a super-Myra mood. "C'mon, you two," she said as the elevator door opened. "Save it for later." The four of us stepped into the elevator as Shannon wished us luck.


We went to the older crime scene first. The high-end apartment seemed more like a funeral home. Everything appeared clean and neat, and the victim with long dreads looked serene on his living room sofa, which reminded me of a coffin. His hands were folded on his chest, and his pale lips wore a smile.

I thought to myself, *I can do this for my family. There's really nothing to it.*

"How horrible," Myra said. "What a waste of a young life. Joe, how are you holding up?"

"I'm okay," I said.

The next crime scene—a beachfront duplex—had nothing new to offer.

But just as we were leaving, I noticed something.

"Myra, look at the guy's hands."

"Okay, what about them?"

I scanned through my cell phone of photos of the other victims when first discovered.

"The fingers," I said. "This guy here . . . the index finger of his right hand just barely overlaps with his middle finger. And the one we just saw had his left thumb extended a tad away from the fingers." I handed her my phone. "Look, there's always some variation in the arrangement of the fingers."

I could tell Myra experienced embarrassment for having never noticed this herself. "Wow, that's what I call a sharp eye. And you know I'm your biggest fan. But I doubt it means anything. If it did, someone would've caught it by now."

"It could be a code. Something Willow or whoever made up. Or maybe the finger angles mean something. Maybe they take turns with the killings and leave messages for each other. Or us."

She smiled at me as if she patted the head of a small boy. "When hands are folded across someone's chest, the fingers may fall however they fall."

"But we know these killings have been staged meticulously."

Myra sighed. "I want you to do something for me right now. Fold your hands across your chest."

As usual, when told to do something in a scolding manner, I obeyed.

"Now do it again."

I started to repeat the gesture, but Myra stopped me. "No, I can see you trying to stiffen your fingers so that they fall precisely the same way. So you can argue that the murderer moved them around."

"But—"

"You're a genius, you truly are. But even geniuses are stupid."

Tish and Josh, who had been looking around on the second floor, walked toward us. "Are you debating the existence of God?" Tish joked.

"Not exactly," Myra replied. She proceeded to give a convoluted version of my ideas. It seemed impossible to interject anything while she gabbed away. I knew Myra to be a defensive person (to say the least), but the extravagance of her protest caught me off guard.

As expected, Tish agreed with Myra and said though my idea was "sweet"—her actual word choice—it would be a waste of resources to pursue. Josh agreed with Tish and Myra.

I had no idea how to respond and experienced considerable relief when I got a call on my cell phone. "Is this FBI Special Consultant Hilario?" asked the man at the other end of the call.

"Yes."

"Good. This is Agent Santiago of Internal Affairs. It is important that I meet with you ASAP. What are you doing now?"

"Uh, I'm on my way back to headquarters."

"Don't. Let's have. . . we'll call it a working lunch. I know a good restaurant."

"May I ask what this is about?" Though I had a feeling I knew.

"The McBride murders of last night. Do not, repeat not, say anything to anyone about our meeting. Unless you want your life to become a never-ending mess beyond anything you ever imagined."

## 12

The simple act of getting to the restaurant to meet Agent Santiago of Internal Affairs became complicated, courtesy of Myra. She claimed I promised to meet her kids for lunch, and went on at length about how disappointed they'd be to come all this way without seeing me. She acted even nosier than I expected about my mysterious appointment. I told her I had a banking matter involving transfer of one of my accounts to the new city. That sated her, but she still made me promise I'd see her kids when I finished.

For a law enforcement person, meeting with IA was scarier than a shootout. Soon, I'll be dead. None of this matters, I tried telling myself, when my stomach grew sick with panic. But I knew it did matter. How could it not? Though cops had a love-hate relationship with the FBI, I still felt I'd be crossing the thin blue line if I finked them out to Internal Affairs. The cover-up sucked big time, but IA sucked even worse. If the truth came out, then that's how the cookie crumbled. But I'd do nothing to help it along.

Besides, I was not the exemplar to blow the whistle on anyone else's shenanigans. I had plenty of my own.

The remnants of my kids appeared. "You're gonna be in trouble," they kept singing, louder and louder. Caitlyn's severed head rolled around like a ball while she said, "Joe, I've never been more ashamed of you."

Agent Santiago knew what I looked like, so he nodded at me when I arrived at the trendy café across town at which we agreed to meet. It was rare that someone arrived at a destination before me; maybe he had an even worse problem with being late. His humorless dark suit and crew cut communicated that he meant business. You couldn't imagine him not working for the government.

"Thank you for agreeing to meet me." He extended his hand. "Esteban Santiago."

As we shook hands and I sat down, he added, "If we met anywhere at headquarters, everyone would already know. It's hard to find privacy in a building full of professional snoops."

I forced a polite laugh. "I never thought of it that way."

The agent did not share in my amusement. "Among other things, I don't want to make life harder for you. I am aware of your past. It must be difficult for you to be back."

I knew this to be IA trying to ingratiate itself—they weren't the bad guys and all that crap. "Thank you for saying that."

"This meeting is totally off the record," Esteban said.

I said, "I figured as much," but I had no doubt he wore a wire.

The table server arrived to take our orders. "The curried turkey with horseradish is good," Esteban said. "In fact, that's what I'll have. With an espresso and ice water."

"Cheeseburger and fries. American cheese, well done. And a Coke."

The arrival of our food was so prompt that one might've thought Agent Santiago supervised the café's operation. There were a few token minutes of excruciating small talk before Esteban took his first satisfying bite of his sandwich and began asking me his no-nonsense questions.

"Have you heard of Christopher and Willow McBride?"

"Yes."

"How did you hear about them?"

"The news. They got murdered last night."

"How were they murdered?"

"They were shot." I took a bite of my cheeseburger, and then another.

"And who murdered them?"

I paused, so that I didn't talk with my mouth full, and also to bide for time. "The news didn't say for certain. According to the report, it might've been muggers. A neighborhood gang. By the way, how's your lunch? Mine is quite good."

He ignored my inquiry. "I realize the awkwardness of your position. You didn't come to town to get put in the hot seat. But we've been working on a case for the better part of a year. From time to time, a number of higher ups do what is easiest rather than what is honest. They find the law a terrible nuisance. They're lazy. They're criminals."

"I wish you the best of luck." I tried to pick up my fries with a fork, and then decided to use my fingers.

He shoved his plate aside and looked at me without blinking. "Mr. Hilario, your adroitness will not help you in the long run. This isn't a chess game. I am offering you immunity in exchange for the truth. Remember what that is? It's when you tell something the way it happened."

I took my hands off the table, so that he didn't see them tremble. "Immunity from what?"

"How did the McBrides die? I mean the real way. Not the cover story."

"I already told you, someone shot them."

"Give me the name of the person who shot them."

"I don't know it."

"Chief Hilario, you may think you've won. But very soon you're going to be sorry you gave the answers you gave me."

"I think that very soon I should talk to a lawyer."

"Because you're hiding something."

"No. While lawyers occupy the lowest position in the hierarchy of living and nonliving things, there are times in which a bottom-feeder comes in handy. Sort of like having a catfish in an aquarium."

"I'm warning you. I have information."

"Then why trouble me?"

"Ever hear of corroborating witnesses? Look, you've known these people a day—excepting for Myra, whom I presume you have not fallen head over heels in love with. Are you really that loyal to them?"

"No, but at least they aren't IA."

He slapped the edge of the table. "Damn it, I'm a good person. I do good things. I perform a necessary job."

"Keep telling yourself that. Someday, you might believe it."

"Set us free, Joe," Caitlyn murmured. "Be with the people you love."

Esteban opened his wallet, and handed me a business card. "Take it, should you change your mind. Think long and hard. Remember, I can protect you. And if you think people like Shannon won't throw you under the bus if you give her a hangnail, think again"

I took the card. "It's certainly been a pleasure to meet you, Esteban. Have a great day."

"Go fuck yourself, Hilario."

On that cheerful note I departed the café, only to be called by Myra.

"Please come to my hotel room. The kids are practically crawling out of their skin to see you again."

"I should get back to work, Myra. But I'll come over for a few minutes."

"I just got a raise, did I tell you? Now I make almost as much as Shannon."

Caitlyn stood there with her arms and legs plummeting out of her stomach. "It's so simple, Joe," she cooed. "Come back to me, and you'll never have to worry again."

"Congratulations, Myra."

"That early retirement bored me to death," she continued. "This is where the action is. Just by showing up to work every day, so many people are helped."

"Yeah, I guess."

I drove to the valet parking area of the hotel and rode the elevator to Myra's room with all the enthusiasm of a swatted fly. Like a child experimenting with his basic senses, I noticed that if I did not blink, everything turned blurry and moved around. It made me dizzy, like I stepped off a carnival ride. I almost tripped over myself as Myra let me in.

Inside the bland hotel room, two young people sat on a bed. The maid hadn't been in yet, so someone pulled up the bedcovers to give them a place to sit next to each other. The boy and girl both bore a resemblance to Myra. They were college age and squeaky clean enough to be the kids of a politician. Or at least the way politicians' kids used to be. Despite the beach setting, the girl wore a skirt, nylons, and high heels, and the boy sported a coat and tie.

Myra said, "Joe, I am so, so proud to present to you again my two oldest children, Laura and Lonnie." The twosome stood up; the girl paused to flatten her skirt. Then they walked toward me, smiling, hands folded in front. "Kids, you already know Joe Hilario, the bravest and sharpest detective I've ever known."

"Chief Hilario, it's always an honor, sir." Lonnie extended his hand; I shook it in return.

"Chief Hilario." Laura nodded at me, as if too fragile a flower to shake hands.

"Please, call me Joe."

"As you can see, my children have manners," Myra said, trying to prove some obscure point. "And as I believe you already know, Laura is a straight-A graduate student at Georgetown, studying early U. S. history, and Lonnie is a straight-A second-year at U of Penn Law School."

"Criminal law," Lonnie elaborated, as if trying to please me. "I want to be a federal prosecutor."

"He's already interned at circuit court," Myra bragged. "Next year he hopes to intern with the Supreme Court."

"That's great," I said, while wondering if it would be appropriate for me to leave this early into the little gathering.

"Laura was valedictorian at Choate. Did I tell you that?" Myra bragged some more. "She's going for a PhD. Her dissertation will be on the Constitution."

Laura blushed. "Well, sort of."

"My." I smiled at Laura, but she looked away in modesty.

I said, "It seems to me I'm the lucky one. Someday I'll tell people that I met two such distinguished individuals back when they were college students."

After a long pause, Myra said, "Well, kids, I need to take care of things. Work, you know. But the three of you sit down and have a nice chat. I'll be back before you know it."

It came as a total surprise that Myra elected to leave us alone together. It reminded me of someone playing matchmaker, though I couldn't imagine what sort of match she hoped to achieve.

For maybe thirty seconds after Myra left, none of us said anything, though we all sat with polite smiles.

Joe Jr. and Stephanie called out, "Hi Dad!" As they smiled at me, they each vomited up a rat, covered in bile and blood.

Breaking the silence, Lonnie said, "It's nice to see you again. I took your advice about Philosophy of Law. Everything worked out great."

I, of course, had no memory of any of this, but I said, "I'm glad."

Lonnie laughed with discomfort. "Mom gets these crazy ideas sometimes."

"Which is a nice way of saying she's a control freak," Laura said. "She wants us to discuss her birthday. Not that she came right out and said it. But she told us you're one of her best friends and that you knew a lot about her and wouldn't it be nice if we all got together before the end of the week?"

One of Myra's best friends? I always knew that beneath her sad, fake confidence lived an outsider, but she must've been much more of one than I realized.

"I take it the end of the week is her birthday?"

"With a surprise party," Laura replied. "Only it isn't a surprise. Mom thought of it. I can't explain how she does it, but she talks you into things without talking about them."

"I know what you mean."

"Oh, and by the way," Laura added, "just get her something at a thrift shop that looks old. She thinks she's like the world's leading authority on all that Victorian junk she collects, but she's pretty easy to fool."

Lonnie said, "One time I got these dumb paper flowers for a couple of bucks, kind of crunched them up, and included a fancy calligraphy note saying they were from a gown worn by Princess Alice, Queen Victoria's daughter."

"Mom nearly fainted from joy," said Laura.

"You two are pretty smart." I leaned forward, and my book fell out of my jacket pocket. They all saw the flaky title, *Supernatural or Psychotic?* It embarrassed me that even people as inconsequential as Myra's kids would know I owned such a book.

"A little light reading." I picked up the book and put it back in my pocket.

"Are you into ghosts and things like that?" Lonnie asked.

"A friend asked me to read it," I lied.

"Is it good?" Lonnie asked. "I saw a ghost once."

"You did not," Laura interjected. "You have to forgive my brother. He exaggerates."

"All I know," Lonnie said, "is that the wind doesn't blow open a locked door."

"So maybe it wasn't locked. We've been over this at least a million times."

"I distinctly remember locking it."

Laura bent her wrist in a dismissive gesture. "Yeah, you remember, all right."

Big Sis had to keep her younger sibling in line. I forced a short laugh. "I haven't had a chance to read the book, yet. But I'll let you know if I learn anything. As for your mom's birthday, yeah I guess I'll be there." Though I hoped to get out of it. I hated parties.

The three of us sat there, again saying nothing. I saw my wife and kids on the small balcony behind the sliding glass door. "On the count of three," Caitlyn said, smiling at her children. "One, two, three." They joined hands, and as they did so, their bodies broke in half. Blood spurted out from each of them like geysers as they laughed in merriment.

"This is bullshit," Lonnie said. "You seem like a nice guy. You deserve to know the whole story."

"Lonnie, what will Mom say if she finds out?"

Lonnie addressed his sister's concern. "Joe, can we trust you to keep a secret?"

It struck me as a loaded question, but I found myself intrigued, so I played along. "Sure."

"What Mom wants," Lonnie said, "is for you to get to know us. Plus our sister Lisa, when she comes."

"I already know she does. She talks about you every other minute."

"You're not quite getting it," Lonnie continued. "She thinks. . . I know this is going to sound stupid, but she thinks it's good for you to know us."

"Good for me? In what way?"

Lonnie sighed. "It's so simple but I can't say it. We don't know each other that well."

"You brought it up," Laura said. "You should be the one who tells him."

Her brother looked out at the ocean, not facing me. "She thinks that you'll find us so wonderful that you'll start another family. You know, given what happened to you. We asked her if she wanted to marry you herself. She burst out laughing and said the idea never crossed her mind. We know she's very worried about you. She said that if you didn't get reconnected with society soon, you'd be. . . you know, like a crazy person or something."

Stephanie said, "You already have a family." She kept pulling out her eyeballs and popping them back in.

"That's right," Joe Jr. agreed, reaching into his head to pull out his brain and bite into it. I could see the brain matter squirt.

"She means well," Laura interjected. "But when Mom gets these strange ideas. . . what I mean is, we end up humoring her."

Lonnie turned to face me. "Mom walks a thin line. We're afraid what would happen if we said she made a mistake." Then he reached into his jacket and revealed a prescription bottle. "Xanax?" he offered.

"No thank you," I said, not knowing what else to say.

"Don't worry, I have a prescription." Lonnie laughed. "I only take them when I feel stressed. You know, finals week, stuff like that."

Or now, I wanted to say, but didn't.

"Mom doesn't know. She'd be upset if she did." He popped a small yellow pill into his mouth and swallowed it. "She says meds are a cop-out. If you're unhappy you should take up a new hobby."

Laura grimaced. "It's so gross when you swallow pills without water."

"As you can see, my sister has a very low threshold for gross," said Lonnie.

"Anyway," Laura said, rolling her eyes, "please do come to the party. I've invited my steady guy. You'd like him."

"He's an amputee from the war in Iraq," Lonnie added. "He lost both his lower legs, but he walks seamlessly with prosthetics and is the nicest guy you'd ever want to meet."

"Lieutenant Colonel Jasper St. Cloud," Laura said with pride, as if to concur with her brother's opinion. "And he looks as good as he sounds. Mom is crazy about him."

Joe Jr. and Stephanie were playing a kind of game in which they took turns stabbing each other. It looked as if whichever stab made the most blood would determine the winner.

The door opened, and Myra entered, wearing her usual pleasant expression. "Is it safe to come in now?" she asked, not waiting for a reply. "The hotel has such flavorful cappuccinos," she informed us. "I got a skinny decaf vanilla. Delish."

"We had a nice talk," Lonnie assured her.

"Yes," Laura agreed. "Very pleasant."

"Definitely," I chimed in. "As nice a talk as I've had in a while."

"I expected you'd have an enjoyable time," Myra said, looking a little confused.

"And you were right," I said.

Myra glanced at her watch. "Have fun, kids," she instructed them. "Joe and I have work to do. Remember to go easy on poor old Mom's credit cards. See you at dinner."

As soon as the kids closed the door behind themselves, Myra asked, "What did you talk about?"

"What to get you for your birthday. I said you'd be happy with anything."

She clapped her hands together in glee. "Oh, that is so like them. They're the light of my life. Lisa's the same way. A jewel."

"You must be very proud."

"Proud isn't even the word."

"No, I guess not."

She took my hand, in the manner of someone making a speech in a movie. "Do you see how beautiful life can be? You're still young. Start a family."

"Or maybe just buy one at the store. With a free set of batteries included."

Myra shook her head in disappointment. "I thought it would be good for you to visit with Laura and Lonnie, but I can see it went right over your head. You refuse to see the good in life. I'm not dumb. You feel guilty because you think your kids died without knowing how much you loved them. And I'm here to tell you that they did know. The love between a parent and a child is the strongest bond there is. And children expect their fathers to be at arm's length. It's mothers who get close to kids. My children know they can come to me with anything, and I won't judge them."

I felt kicked in the stomach about a hundred times over, and only a few words could've devastated Myra right back. But I decided to save it for another time, like an ace up my sleeve. I said, "I never want to have this conversation again," and let it go at that.

"But Joe—"

My cell phone rang. For the first time I noticed the ringtone—that stupid old song, "Feelings." I wanted to change it to something else, anything else, but it took a form of concentration that eluded me.

"Howdy," said the cheery voice on the other end of the call. "Is this Joe the Ferret?"

It took me a moment to remember. "Swann, I'm so glad to hear from you. I mean, Felix."

She laughed. "Swann is fine. I'm not feeling the Felix vibe today. Sometimes I think of each day in terms of a different name. Instead of a Monday, it's Mabel. Instead of a Friday night, it's Veronica." She paused. "God, there I go, blathering away. You must think I'm nuts."

I heard myself laugh. "Well, in a good way maybe. And it's easier if you call me Carlo. No offense to ferrets."

"Anyway. . . why did I call? Oh right, do you want to go drinking and dancing tonight? I know all the good clubs."

I remembered being shocked as a kid when grown-ups said they didn't watch cartoons. Being such a party animal, Swann had yet to consider that some people weren't. Still, I had no choice but to accept. "Sure, sounds great."

As I ended the call, Myra said, "I think I caught the gist of that. So tonight it's Swann. If you'd like, I'll help you get ready. I know what the kids are into, courtesy of my own."

"I'm sure I'll be fine. But thanks."

"You have to stop refusing help. Remember, you're back in the real world. People do favors for each other all the time. What if I hadn't reached out to you in the first place? You'd still be back in your cabin, pretending to be Davy Crockett."

"Good-bye, Myra. I have things to do."

As I left her room, Myra shouted, "Things? What things? Come back, Joe. . ."

## 13

When I arrived at the beach house, I thought I'd study up on Swann, or maybe talk to a lawyer about Agent Santiago, just to be on the safe side. Instead, I went straight to bed and stared at the ceiling. As it became time to get ready for the date with Swann, I forced myself up, stepped into the sunken tub, turned the shower water to a comfortable coolness, and sat down under the spray of water, wondering if I'd have the energy to stand back up.

After a while, I turned off the water but continued to sit in the tub. I don't know how I managed it, but I climbed out, dried myself off, and even dressed. A pretend date didn't sound at all appealing to me, but I reminded myself I had a job to do. I had a day or so of stubble on my face and decided to leave it.

The doorbell rang, and in a stupid move, I opened the door without asking who was there. My visitor turned out to be none other than Myra.

"I don't care what you say. I need to make sure you're dressed correctly." She stepped into the foyer like a door-to-door salesperson.

"Myra, why do you care?"

"Swann is trendy. If you don't look exactly right, she'll never trust you." She gave me a critical once-over and insisted that my clothes needed what she called "joojing." She crinkled up the sleeves on my blazer and slightly loosened my necktie. She also pulled my wet hair back into a small ponytail, with the hair in front hanging loose.

Myra stood back to study her creation. "That's more like it." She all but oozed self-congratulation. "Now you're a with-it guy."

I thanked her, lied that I had to attend to personal business before dinner, and all but had to shove her out the door for her to take the hint that I preferred to be alone.

As soon as her car drove off, I repaired my jacket and tie
and undid the ponytail.

I drove to the swinging singles part of town, where
Swann sold her cutting-edge clothes at Chix Rule. I expect
that every city has at least one shop like this. The storefront
featured clothes in loud colors and bizarre shoes against a
Goth background. They were clothes a female rocker would
wear, to show she had attitude.

I opened the door and entered, feeling kind of shy.
Swann stood at the other end of the shop, talking to a
customer, tape measure in hand. She wore this shiny black
something that featured short shorts on one leg, and skin
tight long pants on the other. Swann's punkish white hair
now sported tips of black on its spikes, in the manner of one
who changed her hair color whenever she felt like it. She blew
me a kiss to say hi.

I waited until she finished with the customer, who acted
like she had all the time in the world to talk about what she
wanted. I thought about leaving and coming back. But after
an agonizing few minutes of incomprehensible details about
something being on or off the bias—I forget which—Swann
and I were alone.

The moment the customer closed the door behind her,
Swann put her arms around me and engaged us in a deep,
long kiss. "If you told me you were busy tonight, I'd have
totally freaked," she said, breaking away. "Not to seem too
forward. But modesty is such a waste of time."

"So, Swann. What name would you give to right now?"

"You mean like giving each day a name? I'm tired of
doing that." She folded a piece of fabric that had sparkles all
over it and then started going through her racks of clothes,
looking for something.

"Carlo," she reflected. "I realize now that's such a
perfect name for you. Your parents must've seen into your
inner essence when they named you."

"I don't know what to say."

"I know. That's one of the things I like about you. Your spontaneity. People who always know what to say are boring." She pulled out a dress with rivets and removed it from its hanger. She pinned a note to it and set it on a black painted box that I assumed doubled as a chair. "Speaking of boredom," she continued, "I'm bored right now. Let's do something different." She walked to the door and displayed the "closed" sign in the window. "I live here, too. In the back. Wanna see?"

"Sure."

A door at the end of her shop opened to a spacious studio apartment with a loft bed, large throw pillows, big feathers everywhere, and all sorts of messages and images painted on the walls. "I add to the walls whenever I feel like it," she said. "It keeps my home a living thing, always changing."

"An interesting concept," I said. "I never would've thought of it." We went back into the store.

"Where should we go? It's way too early to hit the clubs."

"Gee, I don't know."

"I don't like zoos," Swann said, in answer to her own question. "It breaks my heart, seeing animals all caged up, everyone gawking at them."

"I don't like zoos, either," I said.

"Now why did I already know that?" She had a way of doing busywork around the store—scrutinizing fabric, putting receipts in a drawer—without making you feel left out.

"Would I be correct in assuming you are not opposed to going to a movie?" I tried to get into the spirit of things, pretending to be what she wanted.

"I love movies," said Swann, as if it were the most original idea she'd ever heard. "There's some stupid action movie playing. I think they're hilarious—all the explosions and everyone beating up everyone else. I know it's politically incorrect, but I love violent movies. They make me feel. . .

satisfied, somehow. Gooey romance movies piss me off. So go figure."

In truth, I knew a lot of women who liked violent action movies, though they were cops.

"It sounds like we have a plan. And later tonight we can go to my place, if that's okay. I enjoy showing off my ocean view."

"Sure." She grabbed her big black shoulder bag. "I assume you have wheels?"

As we drove to the movie complex, Swann kept changing the radio station, trying to find something she liked. Yet she'd sing along with the songs she didn't like before changing them. I found her tuneful singing voice to be a nice surprise.

In the theater lobby, Swann bought a huge tub of popcorn, and two extra-large drinks. After what seemed like an hour of coming attractions, the movie started. Entitled *Guerilla Justice 7*, it starred a bunch of people I never heard of, though the audience cheered at one of the names. It had something to do with a rescue mission in the Middle East, but after about a minute I couldn't concentrate on it, so I spent two hours waiting for the two hours to end, pretending to be engrossed.

One vivid explosion inspired me to see the severed heads of my wife and children as part of the destruction. Swann acted wild throughout the film, clapping, stomping, hooting, and shouting things like, "Kill the bum." She kept nudging me, clasping my hand, and kissing me.

"Wow, talk about great. I love stinky movies. The stinkier the better." Swann took my arm and leaned her head on my shoulder as we made our way out of the theater. "Only phonies say they like movies with all sorts of deep characters and things."

"What about comedies?"

"They never make me laugh, isn't that weird?"

"So how about grabbing a quick bite at my place? Then you can show me the town."

She took my hand. "Are you a good cook?"

"Not in the slightest."

"Cool. You talked me into it. God, the disasters I've made in the kitchen. You know what I should do? I should write an un-cookbook. There'd be ridiculous ingredients and none of the recipes would work. Have you ever had a peanut butter and jelly fight?"

"No, I can't say that I have."

"It's hysterical. One person is peanut butter, and the other is jelly. Then they start throwing globs of peanut butter and jelly at each other."

"Who cleans up afterward?"

The question didn't capture her attention. "Gee, I dunno. Whoever."

The movie theater sat near the beachfront, so in a matter of minutes we were at my place. During the brief ride, Swann pointed out what she felt were nerdy people, as if even a short car ride required a game to make it interesting. You could be a one, two or three "N" nerd. When we arrived at the beach house, I noticed the FBI van parked across the street.

The second we stepped out of the car, she kicked off her spiky black high heels and grabbed my hand. "C'mon," she said. "Let's run down to the water."

"We should change first." I still had on my suit and tie from the morning meeting. "I have a woman's bikini, just in case." (And I did. The FBI thought of everything.)

Swann looked defeated, as though conforming to the social dictate to not run into the ocean fully clothed removed all enjoyment from life. But she recovered. "Okay. But we only have five minutes to change." She took out her cell phone to get the time. "Starting now."

Playing along, I led her inside, found the bikini, tossed it to her, let her change in my bedroom, and changed into my swimming trunks in the living room.

"We made it with eleven seconds to spare," Swann told me. "Now, let's go." Holding hands, we ran down to the surf,

Swann hooting and jumping along the way. She dove in first, and I followed after her. An excellent swimmer, she did the backstroke with ease, and bodysurfed the waves. As for myself, I thought that maybe, just maybe, I'd be happier swimming in the water than drowning in it.

When we came out onto the beach, Swann said, "I know a great game. We stand up to where the edge of the tide is and when a wave starts rolling in, we run away from it and scream."

Even in the best of moods, I'd have struggled to keep pace with Swann. She left me breathless.

"I need to slow down a little. Remember, I'm significantly older than you."

"That's a bunch of shit. But I'm starving to death, so let's go inside."

When people invite themselves into your home, it can seem rude. But with Swann, it came across as natural.

As we entered, I said, "You can take a shower if you want." I thought about the cameras and decided to leave them off for at least awhile. I could always say they didn't work again.

"Let's take one together, you moron."

"Swann, this is moving awfully fast."

She gave my face a teasing slap. "I take showers with people all the time. It saves water. I take them with boys, girls, whatnots. It's not that kind of shower."

It didn't sound completely repulsive, but I passed anyway. Swann sang as she took her shower, which she finished in something like one minute. She did everything in such a hurry.

"It's so stupid, the fuss people make about their bodies," Swann reflected, as she dried herself off. "I mean, okay, I get it. Now that we've established the existence of body parts, can we start learning how to live?"

I looked away from her to create some boundary of privacy even if she didn't think we needed one. "Are you bi?"

I heard myself ask, as I walked toward the shower in my swimming trunks.

"On some broad theoretical level, I suppose the answer is that I like to remain open to new experiences. But in real life I have this funny way of preferring men, though Lord knows they don't deserve it. I'm not into group sex, either, in case you're one of those guys who likes to see two chicks going at it. It's so confusing. I like to be with one partner at a time. It's much more Zen. What about you?"

The question floored me. No one ever asked me such a thing before. "I. . . I guess you'd find me pretty boring."

"You're so funny." She pinched my nose. "Have a splendiferous shower."

I didn't know about splendiferous, but it felt good to wash the sand off my body. I put on a pair of shorts and a T-shirt.

"We'll order a pizza," Swann said. "Let's put on music and dance while we're waiting."

"Uh, okay." Dance? Even as a teenager, I didn't like to dance and sucked at it. I had no sense of rhythm and I didn't understand it. Music is playing and you designate an area of space in which people move their bodies around in certain ways. I never saw the point. When I married Caitlyn, I insisted we forego the stupid ritual of the first dance or when this member of the wedding dances with this other member of the wedding. I hated those kinds of things. I never danced at my wedding.

Per Swann's dictum, I ordered an extra-large pizza with everything on it and a couple of liters of coke. I noticed I had a voice mail, and recognized McKenzie's voice:

"Thank you for calling, Carlo. Uh, call me back."

I could tell that even saying that much took major resolve on her part.

Swann put on a radio station that played songs that were sort of heavy metal, punk rock, and hip-hop all at the same time. It sounded loud, aggressive, and full of scorn for people who preferred some other, less disruptive kind of music. Yet, she moved to the music with the grace of a ballerina. She took me by the hands to join her in the middle of the room.

"I can't dance," I pleaded.

Swann closed her eyes in rapture as she gyrated. "Everyone dances all the time. Life is dancing. Feel it, Carlo. Let your body be free."

"I am your freedom, and you are mine," Caitlyn said. "Life is death."

I forced myself to move a little. Swann clapped and said "Bravo." Then she grabbed my hands again and said, "Maybe this will make it easier." She started spinning us around in the same spot. Swann laughed but I thought I'd get sick from dizziness. The world tilted from side to side. After a moment, she stopped, and we both lost our balance. Swann fell on top of me, still laughing. "Do you like to wrestle?" she asked. "I'll bet I can pin you down in nothing flat."

"Oh yeah?" I challenged, despite my queasiness. I slipped out from under her and pinned her down.

"Wow, Carlo—you can be a tough guy when you want to be." She smiled at me, out of breath. For a few seconds, we just looked at each other.

The pizza delivery person rang the doorbell. "Gotta take care of this," I said, standing up for a moment to regain my balance. It only took about a minute to set up the pizza and cokes on the coffee table. Still, I excused myself, wanting to call back McKenzie, but also, of course, wanting to give Swann a chance to drug my food. I felt ninety-nine percent sure she wouldn't, but I could not abandon my resolve to my family.

When I phoned McKenzie, there was no answer. I figured I'd leave a message. "Thanks for calling back, McKenzie, it's Carlo. Please give me another call, and we can talk. I look forward to it."

I fussed around in my bedroom for another minute or two, wondering how I'd feel about Swann if I could be the way people were supposed to be. She had a hundred times more energy than I did, but maybe that could prove mutually beneficial. I'd slow her down a little, and she'd make me laugh and feel younger. Though it's probable I'd weaken her spirit, and she'd turn into Caitlyn, always wanting something that I didn't know how to give.

"Pizza's getting cold," Swann called out. "You gotta try it, it's got a gazillion toppings." She burst out laughing for the sheer momentum she created, as if the next logical thing to do was laugh.

I walked back into the living room. Swann put a first slice on my plate for me, plus poured me some Coke on the rocks. For napkins, we used a roll of paper towels. There were these pale blue curlicues around the border of the towels, and I noticed that when I'd blink the shapes seemed to change.

"I always eat the crust first," Swann said, demonstrating this fact with the slice in her hand. "It's to get it over with because I like the other part better."

"I know almost nothing about you." I took a bite of spicy pizza; I could tell there were anchovies on it, which I didn't like, but I ate them anyway. "Are you from here? How did you get interested in clothes?'

"Yes to your first question. As for the second, my mother subscribed to *Vogue*, and I worshipped the ground her Prada heels walked on. I loved the beautiful pictures and started copying them with my crayons. In high school, I did all the costumes for the theater club. Then I went to design school. Then I dropped out. I got hip to the hippest neighborhood in town, and here I am.

"One thing you might as well know right off the bat is that my husband died on our honeymoon. He got wasted on about ten different things and slipped down a staircase. His parents were like living in the dark ages and couldn't handle the truth. I begged the cops to tell them he had an aneurism, and bless their hearts, they did. I've never gone near drugs again. But I drink sometimes."

"That must've been very difficult for you." I took another slice.

"It's still is. People don't get over things, not really. I accepted years ago that it would bother me the rest of my life. In a way, it inspires me to have more fun. Otherwise, I'd be morbid all the time." She poured herself a refill of Coke. "And what about you? How did Carlo Rizzo become. . . what is it that you do again?"

"I'm a developer. New houses, refurbishing neighborhoods, stuff like that."

"In other words, you destroy nature and make poor people homeless." She sounded nonjudgmental when she said this. For all of her quirky individuality, she seemed to pretty much accept people on their own terms.

"I guess that's one way of putting it."

She giggled. "I try not to judge. I live the best way I know how, and let the powers that be decide the rest."

"I don't like to talk much about work," I said. "For those very reasons."

"You must get lectured a lot," Swann offered.

"You don't know the half of it." I reached for another slice. "Not only my work but—"

I almost forgot that I couldn't talk about Joe Hilario. "But other things, too. Nothing worth talking about."

She reached for her second slice; I noticed she took one in the middle instead of one on the end.

"Carlo, I'm very drawn to you. I don't know why, since we're so not alike. But then, I don't think people are supposed to know why things happen. They just do. I'm also sensing some big secret you're not telling me. Like I'm going to find your dead wife in the freezer or something."

Caitlyn's face appeared like a growling tiger. "Ha!" she hissed.

"I don't talk much about myself," I said. "I'm not interesting. I'm not being modest. It's the truth. I work and then I work some more."

She moved in closer to me. "I don't think you know who you are. I think somewhere inside you is this stupid motherfucker who wants to fuck off, but you won't let him out to play." She amended. "I don't mean bad stupid, but good stupid."

I heard myself laugh again. "What is good stupid?"

She took my free hand and started massaging my fingers, which reminded me of my theory about the victim's fingers. "All kinds of things are good stupid," she said. "Not following advice of people who think they know everything. Not knowing how to build an atom bomb. Or sex. If you think about it, sex is stupid. But it's a good thing. Life is better when you let it make no sense. Because it never will anyway."

I prepared to make another speech about moving too fast, but Swann beat me to it. "Don't worry. I know you're a good boy. You eat your milk and cookies and never fuck on the first date. I assume you were raised Catholic?"

"Yes, now that you mention it. But I lapsed a few years ago."

"Maybe not as much as you think." She grabbed my face and kissed me. "That's cool. I go with the flow. To fuck or not to fuck, that is the question. It's all pretty much the same, if you think about it. The greatest sex in the world doesn't matter diddly-squat when you're getting a root canal or the electric company puts you on hold."

"I think you should write a book. The world according to Swann."

"It sounds like way too much bother. I'll leave it to people like you to pass along my pearls of wisdom." She stood up and stretched. "God, I have so much energy. I can't wait to go out. Did I tell you? I'm making costumes for this hip rock band out of empty beer cans. The band's called, 'Repurpose,' so I figured the beer cans would look cool. You should let me spray your hair different colors. Maybe put it in spikes."

I heard Josh's stern voice in my earpiece. "Damn it, Joe, turn on the cameras."

I told Swann I'd be back in a minute and locked myself in the bedroom as I called Josh in the van. "Sorry Josh, I guess they still won't come on. What do you want from me? All we've done is talk."

"Shit, they were supposed to check them," Josh said. "Well, be extra careful, and abort if you have to. We've done more digging on Swann. Her husband's death—the local police were sure she pushed him down the stairs but dropped her as a person of interest for lack of evidence."

"Why wouldn't we have known before?" I couldn't think of anything else to say.

"If you tell Stu I said this, I'll deny it. But the local police don't have their act together. The folder turned up in the cold-case basement, buried under some boxes."

"I don't think Swann would hurt anyone," I insisted, as much to convince myself as Josh. "Remember how she called 911 to save some other guy's life?"

"She had an insurance policy on her dear old hubby, an even million, which her daddy invested for her. She doesn't make two cents on her clothing store."

I pretended to sigh, disgruntled. "I promise to abort if anything even remotely fishy is going on. But she trusts me, and I need to finish what I started. At least Whatshisname the rookie won't be hanging around."

"What an asshole," Josh concurred. He started to say something else, but I told him I had to get back to Swann.

"So, what have you been doing?" Swann asked, as if she wanted to hear a magical adventure story.

I returned to my spot on the floor. "Just a phone call."

"You're upset, aren't you? Did something happen?"

"I. . . it's nothing."

She ran her hand along my cheek. "It doesn't sound like nothing. If something's getting you down, that means it's important."

I decided to go out on a limb and see what happened. "I heard about a double murder yesterday. The parents of two small children. They were supposed to meet with me this week. They sounded so nice on the phone."

Swann looked away from me. "A shooting, right? I heard about it on TV this afternoon."

"Yes."

"I take it you didn't know them?"

"No. That's what's so weird. But I feel sad. Especially for their kids."

Swann took a swallow of Coke. "Aw, fella. It's okay to care about people you don't know. If more people did, life would be. . . well, I hate to say it, but sometimes I think my husband lucked out. He doesn't deal with lousy presidents and dumb-ass TV commercials and everything fucked about the world."

"But murder. Why do people do it? What does it accomplish?"

She moved farther away from me and picked at the loose toppings that fell into the pizza box. "I don't know, having never killed anyone. I try not to think about junk like that." She licked her fingers. "And you shouldn't, either. What good can come of it?"

"You're right." I made a point of smiling. "These clubs you go to—are they loud and crowded?"

"Absolutely. What did you expect, someone reciting Shakespeare?"

"No, I suppose not." Somehow the lighting in the room made everything throb, as if every other second nothing existed. I started to sweat.

"Stop wasting time," Caitlyn said. There were beetles scurrying in and out of her mouth. "C'mon, Joe. Hurry up. The kids miss you so much." She laughed and laughed.

"Well, what are we waiting for?" Swann asked. "Let's go." She stood up. "Huh, that's weird. I thought I heard something. Someone talking."

## 14

We drove to a dirty alley downtown and went inside an old warehouse converted into a club called Foxglove. Low lights disguised the fact that almost nothing had been done to spruce the place up, other than paint it black inside and out. The live band looked derelict and full of anguish. There were so many people inside it took two songs to get from the entrance to the bar.

"Two boilermakers," Swann shouted to the shirtless bartender, whose entire torso front and back sported tattoos. I couldn't tell what the dark and detailed images depicted.

I shouted in Swann's ear. "Boilermakers. That's when they put a shot of whiskey in a beer, right?" I didn't know much about drinks.

"Oh, here they are," Swann's said, as if answering me. I followed her lead as she dumped a shot of whiskey into her beer. Then I watched as she drank hers down in only a few seconds.

"Here, have mine," I said. "Trust me, I'm more fun when I don't drink."

She looked disappointed. But after a moment she said, "Okay, Mr. Party Pooper." And she managed to drink the second boilermaker as quick as the first. I knew people whom "never did drugs" but drank themselves into oblivion. I wondered if Swan would prove to be one of them.

I hated being crammed inside the club, and I felt a peculiar shakiness in my arms that darted out through my fingers.

I did a double take when I saw Esteban Santiago flirting with a woman in a skimpy dress. Since it was rare for me to socialize with people I worked with, it struck me as odd that someone so rigid all day long could be so playful after dark. I became a cop because it suited my disposition. If I wanted this nightlife stuff, I would've been a bartender or bouncer. I wondered how someone like Esteban functioned. Did he still think about IA when he picked up women in clubs?

He looked around and then stopped, staring at me, as if I'd done something wrong by seeing him hit on someone.

"Okay, let's go." Swann held my hand as we moved to another area of the floor where, with close observation I could see something akin to dancing occurred. But the place became so crammed—surely in violation of the fire code—that dancers proved barely distinguishable from non-dancers.

Swann still managed to put on quite a show, shaking her boobs and crawling between my legs. I let things continue for a couple of songs, and then told Swann I needed to rest. "I keep telling you, I'm an old man," I said, reading her thoughts. "If you want to keep seeing me, you'll have to get used to it."

Swann's third boilermaker in about a half an hour appeared to be her limit. "I want air, Carlo. Let's go out back."

We squeezed our way through the crowd as if fleeing a burning building. I can't describe how relieved I felt to be outside. Being crammed in a small space with hundreds of people whom I didn't know frightened me.

Despite her three boilermakers, Swann spoke without a slur and moved in her feline way.

We sat on a concrete slab that housed the trash bins. Swann had a way of making silly things like this seem outrageous fun. She bopped around to the loud music emanating from inside. The oil stains on the cobblestones had a neon glow in the dark. "Look at the whatchamacallit—the moon." She pointed upward with her fingers spread apart, as if she could snatch the moon from the sky. A rainbow of smog encircled it.

"Some say the moon does things to people."

Swann laughed. "Ask a werewolf."

"No, seriously," I insisted. "Supposedly when you look into the moon, you become more honest." Since she had a few drinks, I hoped she'd confess anything she'd been hiding.

"Honesty is already part of everything," Swann replied. "I mean, everything is honest because it is what it is. A lie is honestly a lie. That's why nothing makes any difference."

I saw my mangled kids in a tug of war over who'd hang the birthday banner. I didn't hear what they were saying, but I could tell they were arguing. Pieces of Caitlyn hobbled over and said they'd all hang it up together. Everyone seemed happy, but as always they kept getting more and more broken. The word "dad" fell off the banner and turned into a heap of bones.

"I wouldn't say that. When I feel... I mean, if I felt like nothing mattered..." I didn't know how to finish the thought.

"See, I'm the opposite. If nothing matters, life is more fun." She flashed a naughty grin.

I slid off the concrete slab and stood up, looking at the night sky that disappointed me for its few stars. (There were so many stars back at my cabin that I could see the Milky Way.) "Have you ever felt guilty about something you've done? I mean, so guilty that you feel you'll never get over it? Like when your husband died. Did you wish you could've done more to save him?"

"Ugh. Why are you talking about that?"

"Because if we're going to keep seeing each other, we need to share what's real," I added, "I mean, it's not as though you pushed him down the stairs or anything."

"Oh yeah, right—I pushed him. I'm a murderer. In fact, I kill every man I date." She gave an arch, mock-evil laugh. "I have a picture of him in my wallet, if you want to see."

"Sure."

She took her wallet out of her purse. "Here he is. Or was. I think he looks like you, Carlo, only younger."

Other than the fact that he wore his hair on the long side, the smiling young man looked nothing like me at all.

With unexpected emotion, I put my hands on her shoulders. "I need to know I can trust you. I've never trusted anybody." I said this as Carlo, but I might as well have been Joe.

"Yes, you can trust me." She turned to walk back into the club, but I caught her arm. "Please let's not go back in there. I hate being around so many people. Can't we go to my place, where it's quiet?"

"Let go of my arm, you motherfucker."

I cupped her face in my hands and kissed her with all the horniness I could muster.

"You would have to be a good kisser," Swann complained, folding her arms and looking away from me. "Okay, what the hell. Let's go."

"Thanks, Swann. I, uh. . . I like you."

Swann found this comical. "Oh, my silver-tongued knight in shining armor. I, uh, like you, too."

In the ride to my place, she clung to my arm and hummed to the music on the radio. Then she stretched out a little, putting her head on my lap.

"When I was a kid," she said, "this lady lived next door with her son. This ancient hippie named Parker Barker. Isn't that dumb? He had like three strands of hair left, and he wore them in a ponytail. He never did anything—didn't work, drive a car, nothing. Nice job if you can get it, I suppose.

"Though I can't comprehend living with Mommy my entire life. I love my mom to pieces, don't get me wrong. But still, to live with her? Anyway, Mom used to gossip with the neighbors about him. They said he. . . I can't think of the word. Not a pediatrician—that's a doctor, right? What do they call it when you like kids, but in the wrong way?"

"A pedophile."

"Right. A pedophile, and he'd been to prison. A funny guy, though. I used to go over to listen to him play the guitar and sing. I remember once he played 'The Shadow of Your Smile.' Isn't it weird to remember that? Anyway, my mother like shat in her pants when she found out. I promised never to go over to his house or speak to him again. Once, though, I cut across his backyard, and heard a tap from the window.

He stood there with a big smile, exposing himself. The first time I saw a man's cheese doodle. Before that moment, I hadn't the slightest clue why they made such a fuss about being a boy or a girl. I was only like six or something."

"That must have been awful."

"Yeah, thanks, now will you let me finish telling the story? See, my older brother used to talk with his friends about pussy. I didn't know what it meant, but he'd gesture toward his crotch so I knew it had something to do with something major. So anyway, at the dinner table that night— with this new youth pastor from our church—I said to everyone, 'Parker Barker has the world's biggest pussy.'" Swann burst into hysterical gales of laughter.

I feigned a chuckle or so as she sat back up and nibbled on my ear.

Once at the beach house, we just sort of took it for granted we'd end up in the bedroom. "I need a snack or something," Swann said, kicking off her shoes. "Those drinks are starting to take up residence in my head."

"Help yourself," I said. "And whatever you find, please bring some for me, too."

I took off my shirt and pants and sat up on the bed in my boxers. A short while later, Swann returned with two bowls of ice cream. Each had two flavors—white chocolate chunk and dark chocolate raspberry. The bowl she handed me seemed to have more white chocolate than the other one.

She looked at the picture of my supposed graduation with my proud parents. "That's weird. You don't look happy."

"I'm smiling," I offered in my defense.

"But your eyes. No, you weren't happy. I don't think you're close to your family, am I right?"

"It's a long story. For another time."

"I know you want to go slowly." Swann stripped down to her bra and panties. "And I know it's because you're old and decrepit, like you keep telling me."

I couldn't help laughing. "Thank you very much."

She tickled me under the chin. "The thing is, there are so many ways of being close to another person. Every night we have the chance to lie next to someone. All that's important seems so near." She climbed into bed beside me.

"I've never thought of it that way before. You make everything sound like fun."

"That's because of dying."

"Uh. . . say what?"

"I want to be doing something happy when I die. Since I don't know when that'll be, I have to do as many happy things as I can."

"Oh."

Swann held a spoonful of glistening ice cream before my face; it came from her bowl. "Here, let me feed you." Adopting a playful mood, I tilted my head to gobble it down. It tasted so sweet and creamy, like ambrosia, the food of the gods. I ate another spoonful, and another and another, like a good, happy baby. I wanted to feed Swann in return, but I felt so sleepy I drifted off, hugging a wonderful soft pillow.

I remember a dream in which I flew across the galaxies, jumping from one star to the next. Swann drifted in and out of the dream, her body seeming to twist in slow motion, like a knotted-up bed sheet.

I heard Caitlyn calling out to me, and I said her wait was over. I could hear my kids clap and giggle.

## 15

When I woke, I found myself on the beach. I coughed a few times because of the damp morning fog. I had no idea how I ended up there. I saw no evidence of Swann, not even an imprint of her body in the sand.

The ocean seemed to be moaning, over and over, as if to remind me I couldn't do anything about its existence. I experienced a lingering sense of the Sun People, as if maybe I just had a dream about them. I couldn't see anyone else on the beach. Sometimes back in my cabin I felt like the only person left in the world, and the thought comforted me. But on the stark beach, I experienced a different kind of aloneness. Maybe the Sun People scared me because they made me feel abandoned.

I staggered to the house, feeling like shit. Once inside, I saw the bed was made. The bowls and silverware from our ice cream had been washed and placed back in the kitchen cabinet. Swann and I finished all the pizza, but I couldn't find the box. I called her, and hung up when the voicemail came on. I thought about leaving a text message but decided not to. I didn't want to say the wrong thing.

I took a cold shower and then sat around in a bathrobe, wondering what to do next. When Josh called, I experienced actual gratitude for having something to connect with.

Most of all, I hoped he knew how the hell I ended up on the beach or what became of Swann. I knew I'd have to wait for Josh to bring it up. Yet to my disappointment, he didn't. "Hey, meeting with Shannon in an hour," he said, as if nothing much happened since the day before.

"Can't wait," I said. Caitlyn appeared to imitate how I talked, and laughed at me some more.

I entered the conference room to the sound of Myra talking up a storm. I took a seat as far away from her as possible and felt the weight in my chest intensify. Everyone looked gossipy and full of secrets.

As Shannon took her seat, I figured I'd survive the meeting by saying as little as possible. It took one second for my goal to come to naught.

"Looks like you had a rough night, Joe." Shannon shuffled through her paperwork. "Do you need a break?"

Myra answered, "Joe is fine. He just doesn't know it."

"I'd like to hear from Joe himself," Shannon said.

Everyone looked at me, but in a strange way I felt ignored. They were like the Sun People with their opaque dark glasses and smiles.

Caitlyn and the kids laughed at me. The more they laughed, the more their bodies fell apart, but as always they didn't seem to care. At one point, Caitlyn knelt down and brought her face close to mine, like a human bending down to see a bug.

Myra's loud voice dominated the room, and for the first time she didn't stop my family from appearing. I took this as a bad sign. I felt a sour tingling throughout my body.

I tried to make them go away. I thought about Swann and other happy things. I even tried singing "Jingle Bells" in my head, but it made no difference. Maybe I'd gone Loony Tunes for keeps.

"I'm okay." I hated the unexpected crack in my voice.

I don't think I fooled Shannon, but she proceeded anyway. "Another victim," she began. "This makes ten. At five in the morning. A neighbor saw the apartment door unlocked and found the body. Again with the smile and folded hands. Computer hardware developer. This time Asian American. No confirmation yet on speed dating, but a copycat wouldn't know how to present the victims." She passed around the stack of new files next to her coffee mug.

Stu said, "The world's first affirmative action serial killer," but no one laughed, and Tish gave him a nasty look.

"It's interesting that it's so easy to stumble upon the victims," said Josh, glancing at the photo of the newest victim. "The perp is seeing how far she can push it. She likes attention."

"Probably doesn't get any otherwise," Shannon said. "Attention, that is. Not, you know. But anyway, that'd be McKenzie much more than Swann."

"Or maybe she can never get enough attention," Myra said, in a loud voice, to draw attention to herself. Myra hated to be left out for even a moment, which maybe explained her obvious irritability when she pretended to be happy.

"So that puts Swann back into the running," said Shannon.

"Yes, it certainly does," Myra agreed.

"Joe, what happened with Swann last night? Anything we should be watching for?"

I felt guilty, though I didn't know why. "Well, I'm still here, aren't I?"

Josh led the laughter to my response, though I didn't see the humor.

"Another camera screw up, but Joe is a real trouper," Josh said. "After she left the beach house at 3:14 a.m., Joe came out to the van and told us not to worry, she posed no threat. He laughed and carried on. She must've done something to put him in such a good mood."

Everyone laughed again with their no-eyes eyes and their unsmiling smiles.

"Nothing like that happened," I interjected, hoping my panic didn't show.

"She took a cab to the hospital," Josh continued, "and we followed her. We finally got the green light from the Bureau to tail her 24/7 because of the old file about how maybe she offed her husband. Man, I wish I'd seen the selling of that one to the powers that be. Anyway, Swann argued with the receptionist about wanting to see a patient, even though visiting hours were over and only relatives were admitted. Then she went home."

"Do you know who she wanted to see in the hospital?" asked Shannon.

"No. She's—she doesn't tell me everything. Or at least not yet."

I had no memory of Swann leaving, talking to the agents in the van, what I found so funny, or who straightened up the house, let alone how I ended up on the beach.

"Joe, is it too hot in here for you?" Shannon asked.

"No, I'm fine." But I could feel myself sweating.

"I'm not prepared to say Swann is so nice she's innocent," Shannon continued. "We don't even know conclusively if the murders always happen on the first date."

"What did you do with Swann?" Tish asked.

"Nothing. We talked."

"What about?" asked Josh.

"Nothing much. Just kind of getting to know each other. As a little girl she had a child molester for a neighbor, if that's any help."

Stu said, "I don't get you. A hot number like Swann, and you *talked?*"

"Pay no attention to Stu," Tish said. "I'm sure you did everything by the book. You have too much integrity and experience to do otherwise."

"How touching," said Stu. "Why don't we all sing, 'Kumbaya?' When we catch the killer, we'll say, 'Group hug.'"

Shannon said, "Stu, shut the hell up." In a nicer tone of voice, she asked, "Joe, does Swann get sexually aggressive?"

I cleared my throat and picked up a pencil, spinning it with my fingers; for some reason, I found it easier to talk while I twirled something. "She's hedonistic. She's young. But I wouldn't say aggressive."

Josh frowned. "Maybe she only goes after guys she's hot for. No offense, Joe."

"Which would be easier to prove if we had a little thing called evidence of sex from any of the victims," said Shannon. "Which could mean she's extraordinarily good at cleaning up after herself. Or maybe she's agraphobic."

"Agraphobia," Tish contemplated. "Probably a man came up with that one. I mean, who isn't afraid of sexual abuse?"

"But it's to the point when people don't have sex at all, dummy," Stu replied.

"All of a sudden you're Sigmund Freud? I thought you didn't believe in psychology."

"I never said that. It's only that I don't believe in you."

I saw Caitlyn again with my son and daughter. They held up the birthday banner, as if even the blood dripping from their mangled bodies became part of the merriment. This time the word "Dad" appeared from cut-up human hearts that still pumped.

Stephanie said, "The banner is crooked."

Then Joe Jr. said, "No, it isn't."

"Joe?" Shannon asked. "Are you okay?"

"Sure."

"Then please answer the question. What are your latest plans for Swann and McKenzie?"

Shit, how long had I been out of it? "I called Swann this morning, but no answer. I'm on the verge of hooking up with McKenzie."

"Make sure you note even the smallest thing that arouses suspicion," Shannon said, "We need another 24/7 tail."

"But remember to go easy with McKenzie," said Myra, suffering for not telling me what to do for a couple of minutes. "She can barely stand being around people."

Josh said, "Joe can handle it. You're the one who's always saying how great he is."

Myra pretended to be exasperated. "All right, already. Jeesh. No one can say anything without getting their head bitten off. Dare I also say that if Joe became more of a father figure to Swann, she might open up to him?"

Shannon covered her mouth to yawn. "The case is getting to us. It happens." She looked over at the clock. "Well, another incredibly productive meeting must come to a close. My God, it's lunchtime. And I have to go straight to another meeting."

What I experienced as about twenty minutes took over three hours. I had no idea where my mind went for all that time.

I chased after Shannon. "Make it quick, Joe." She smiled, but I could tell she didn't appreciate my stopping her.

"I, uh. . . I have kind of like a theory."

She looked puzzled by my hesitance. "Why didn't you mention it at the meeting?"

"Everyone says I'm crazy—not *crazy* crazy, but that it's a bad idea."

Shannon glanced at her watch. "Okay, you have exactly two minutes."

I told her about the different finger positions and showed her pictures on my cell phone.

"I don't have time to deal with this now. But we definitely should talk."

"When?"

"My secretary can set up an appointment."

She didn't act as amiable as when I met her. Maybe she was having a bad day. Or maybe like many people she acted nice when you first met her, but then turned snooty.

As I listened to Shannon's high heels click down the hall, it sounded like a reminder of my distance from other people. When she turned down a hallway out of sight, she might as well have been walking toward infinity.

Josh tapped me on the shoulder.

"Hey man, are you okay? I didn't mean to startle you."

"I've never been better."

"Maybe I shouldn't bring this up. But I heard a rumor you met with His Majesty Esteban from Internal Affairs."

My heart sank. I never expected Josh to say this. How did anyone know?

Caitlyn said, "Of course they know. Do you think you're smarter than the FBI?" She laughed until her head fell off backward.

Josh and I walked back to the now-empty conference room. He shut the door behind us.

I tried to smile and seem relaxed. I sat in the same seat I'd used during the meeting, hoping some lingering warmth would bring me comfort. Josh chose to remain standing.

"Sure, I had lunch with Esteban. Just a social thing. He asked about a couple of cases I solved, he told me that IA walked on water. Stuff like that."

"Nothing about the McBrides?"

"Josh, let me tell you something. I served as Chief of Police in one of the dirtiest cities in the country, and I mean dirty in every conceivable way. I never ratted out anyone and believe me, I saw plenty of dirt. Everyone stank with dirt. The building stank.

"My office had mice. I used to set the mousetraps myself. I never knew what to do with the dead mice. I flushed them down the toilet. One time a mouse got stuck and the toilet overflowed. I ran out of the men's room and got in my car and drove around the city for the rest of the day. I couldn't let anyone know I made a mess. After that, I put the dead mice in a plastic bag in my briefcase, and I threw them in a trashcan outside the building.

"My daughter wanted a pet mouse. I couldn't let her have it. She cried and I still said no and my wife yelled at me but I couldn't do it. I just kept saying no and they'd say why not and I'd say no. Do you understand?"

Josh said, "Joe, please. Let go of me."

I realized that I stood up, clutching his herringbone jacket by the lapels. He looked startled, as if a lunatic confronted him.

"Maybe you should take some time off. Maybe the case is too much for you."

I told myself I had to make a quick recovery. "I'm so sorry. You're right, I am under a lot of strain. But I'm fine, really. We all freak out a little sometimes, don't we?"

"No, not in the Bureau. We're professional."

I flashed a big, normal smile. "Well, us cops are quite uncouth, you know. Seriously, people go a little batty all the time. Look at . . . look at Stu. I'm cut from the same cloth. But I will never act like that again, Scout's honor." I hated the thought of being taken off the case for mental instability. I'd never get over the embarrassment. And anyway, I had to meet McKenzie, who almost surely would prove to be the other perp.

"Okay. Let's forget it ever happened."

"Thanks. And to answer your question, I would never, ever tell anyone from IA anything. I'm not one of them."

He put his hand on my shoulder. "I believe you. Get some rest, if you can."

As luck would have it, at that precise moment I got a text message from none other than Esteban Santiago:

*Only truth will help u*

"Anything important?" Josh asked.

"Just a promo ad from the phone company," I replied, deleting the text.

## 16

Just as I entered the elevator to leave the building, Myra stepped inside to join me. "Can you believe that Stu idiot? I swear, the happiest day in Tish's life will be when she never has to see him again. We're already talking about a no-more-Stu party. It'll be one of those no men allowed things, but if you play your cards right, we might be able to sneak you in."

"I thought the happiest thing about solving the case would be no more innocent people being murdered."

"Well, of course that's the most important thing," she admitted. "You need to stop taking people so literally. Learn to relax. Let people be themselves, and you'll find that if you let them into your life, some wonderful surprises are in store."

"I have to get to work."

"He says to the person who got him the job." She smiled at me, but I could barely bring myself to look at her.

"Is there anything else?" I had a feeling there would be.

"Your powers of perception are sharp as ever. My kids had the best time talking with you, and now Lisa, my youngest, is in town. Join us now for a late lunch. They'll all be there."

Lunch with Myra didn't occupy the Number One slot in my list of things to do. But in my peculiar frame of mind I couldn't think of how to say no. "Sure, unless McKenzie—"

"Why do you keep doing that?" Myra asked. "You act like I don't know we're on a case. Go on, call her right this moment if it makes you happy."

We drove in our separate cars to the restaurant and arrived at the same time. However, I took a few minutes to sit in my car. A stampede of mice ran over Stephanie's mangled body.

The eating establishment attempted to remind you of an amusement park, ingestion disguised as wholesome family fun. There were super-bright colors everywhere, like balloons intended to obscure real life from view. The plastic menus had as many pages as *War and Peace*. Table servers wore bright red bowties and treated you with more care than a mother gave her newborn. But I minded it less than those chi-chi places that served you a mushroom on a toothpick and charged you a hundred bucks.

Upon seeing me enter the happy-happy place, Myra waved and waved to make sure I wouldn't miss her. She couldn't wait to introduce me to Lisa—or rather, reintroduce me—so I stood a good ten feet away from the booth when Myra all but screeched, "Joe, you remember my baby, Lisa." Lisa looked away with self-consciousness. She could've passed for her sister, other than being a little taller. And she affected the same wholesome personality as her older siblings.

"Chief Hilario, how nice to see you again," Lisa said.

"Please, call me Joe." I sat down at the far end of the booth, opposite Laura.

"Yo, dude," Lonnie said, with a big grin that reminded me of how my dog Ralph used to look when he wagged his tail. Lonnie appeared much more relaxed than at our first meeting. Laura kept giggling but managed to say hello. I assumed they put Lonnie's Xanax prescription to good use. But maybe they smoked pot, too. Who knew what kids did nowadays?

Myra couldn't wait to tell me more about Lisa. "She's in her senior year at prep school, and, like all my children, has a straight-A average. She's been accepted at Yale, where she plans to major in chemistry."

"Pharmaceutical chemistry," Lisa interjected, with the same modesty her sister displayed when her mother sang her praises.

"You know," Myra continued, "I've been trying to convince Lisa that the Narcotics Division could use someone with her excellent training. But she has her eyes set on working in the corporate sector."

"What can I say? I love money," Lisa joked. Her discomfort was palpable.

I knew Myra well enough to recognize my cue to tell Lisa all about the deep inner rewards of a career in law enforcement.

"She hasn't even started college yet," I said. "Give her time to decide."

Myra said, "Well, I knew I wanted to work for the FBI by age fourteen."

"And I know I want to work for a private company," Lisa responded.

Myra touched her daughter's cheek. "I don't blame you for being confused, dear. It's the Internet. There's too much information out there. Young people can't make up their minds."

"Mom, I'm not confused. I know what I want to do."

"Stop yelling at me. I'm your mother."

Lisa looked down in shame. "I didn't mean to yell. Look, I'm sorry, okay? And I. . . I promise I'll keep the FBI in mind."

For some reason Laura found this comical and burst out laughing. Lonnie followed suit. Lisa didn't seem high. Sometimes, the youngest kid in a family grows up faster because she sees the mistakes everyone else makes.

My own drug experience consisted of once eating a grass brownie by accident back in the army. I didn't like it at all. I felt out of control and everything became silly, as if nothing meant anything. When I came off the high, I got depressed. I couldn't understand why anyone would want such an experience.

Myra smiled like someone who did not appreciate being left out of the joke. "Kids, what's gotten into you? You keep laughing, but I fail to see what's so funny."

"It's. . . it's one of those funny days." Laura caught her breath. When she looked at her brother they both laughed some more.

"Joe, as you can see, my children think their immaturity is amusing." Myra feigned exasperation by putting her index finger to her cheek. "One of the many joys of parenting."

I developed a thicker skin toward her thoughtless remarks, though I still resented them. Still, I thought it peculiar that Myra could profile murderers yet hadn't the slightest clue that right under her nose, her children indulged in the very narcotics she wanted Lisa to prevent. As people far wiser than me have said, denial is the strongest drug of all.

The table server arrived with the pep of a Dallas Cowboys cheerleader and explained that if we needed anything, anything at all, to ask for it.

"I'll have the summer fiesta salad," Myra pronounced, working hard to restore what she considered to be decorum. "With the dieter's delight dressing. And black coffee."

Lonnie said, "Wow, you can have anything you want, and she wants a summer fiesta salad." It took Laura and him a minute or so to calm down from his witticism. Myra cleared her throat as if clearing away her embarrassment.

"Is it okay to have the triple chocolate fudge cake for lunch?" Lonnie asked no one in particular. "With three scoops of ice cream. Papa Bear, Momma Bear, and Baby Bear." He and Laura found this hysterical.

"Lonnie," his mother scolded. "You had your goofy fun, but now it's time to have lunch like a civilized person. Honestly, at your age."

"Um, okay. I am twenty years old and I want a slice of the triple chocolate fudge cake with three scoops of triple chocolate ice cream."

"Okay," said the server.

"Can you make it two slices of cake?"

"I certainly can. Do you want ice cream on the second slice of cake as well?"

"Uh, can you give each slice of cake one scoop of ice cream, with the third scoop kind of half on both slices?"

This request led to more hilarity for Laura. "My brother is very OCD," she managed to say, which made Lonnie laugh some more.

"Really, Laura. That's not true, and if it were there'd be nothing to joke about." Myra turned to me with furrowed brows. "I apologize for my children's behavior, Joe. They might as well be toddlers."

Joe Jr. and Stephanie stood over the table, staring as though accusing me of something. They dismantled their bodies, one bone at a time.

"I can see this is a fun table," the table server said. "Who's next?"

"I'll have the same thing he's having," Laura said.

"Me, too," said Lisa.

Myra frowned. "Are you sure, girls? All that *fat and carbs*?" Her voice lowered to a whisper for the last three words, the way people do when saying something taboo.

Laura said, "We'll be fine, Mom." She'd stopped laughing.

"And you, sir?" the table server asked of me.

Succumbing to what you might call my devil nature, I said, "I'll have what they're having." I knew this would throw Myra off her game, as she expected me to take her side in this passive-aggressive battle over nothing. I also knew she'd be defensive about being the only person at the table eating something different.

"You're certainly setting a fine example," Myra commented. "You're all going to feel plenty foolish when people see me with my sensible, nutritious salad while the rest of you look like a bunch of pigs at a trough. To me, the fun of eating out is that everyone gets something different. But I guess I'm out of step with the times."

Laura and Lonnie lowered their heads in shame, which disappointed me. I guessed that whatever drug they took started wearing off.

"We'll try to remember next time, Mom," Laura said with contrition. "And we're sorry for how we've been acting."

"Yeah, Mom. We're really sorry," Lonnie added.

"I'm sorry, too," added Lisa.

Laura and Lonnie already told me how much they dreaded hurting their mother's feelings, yet seeing it in action pissed the hell out of me. I never knew much about parenting, but I believed kids should not live their lives around not hurting the parents' feelings. If anything, my kids had the opposite problem of taking me too much for granted.

Yet I felt proud in that moment. Whatever I did right or wrong as a father, at least I didn't do it like Myra. And neither did Caitlyn. If we had trouble getting along, at least each of us had a separate identity.

Joe Jr. and Stephanie faded away for the time being.

I couldn't remember the last time I pigged out on chocolate like this, and I had to admit it made a powerful argument for life as the preferred choice over death. Lonnie and I gobbled all of our food. Under their mother's watchful eye, Lisa and Laura ended up doing little more than play with theirs. They also declined doggie bags.

Most of the lunch became a rapid, impossible-to-stop monologue from Myra about how she had to shift gears to parallel-park her new FBI car. Lonnie, however, managed to get in a mumble now and then about his enjoyment of the cake and ice cream.

I received a text message. I hoped it would be from Swann, but instead McKenzie apologized for all the phone tag and said she had the day free.

I asked Myra if I could talk to her in private. Her kids offered no objections as she followed me to the vestibule.

"Looks like today belongs to McKenzie."

"We make a good team," Myra replied, apropos of nothing. "Oh, by the way. Nada from Willow. No leads from her home computer, nothing at her home or office. Agents went to every trendy place in town. A few people recognized Willow, but they couldn't ID any victims."

"That doesn't prove anything."

"True, but it also doesn't not prove anything."

I felt too exhausted to argue. "Anyway, I should leave. McKenzie beckons."

We strolled back to the table.

"Listen, everybody," I said. "I need to get going. I have to—"

"Excuse me," Lisa said. "Joe, would I be able to talk to you for a few minutes? I promise it won't take long." She exchanged meaningful glances with her siblings, and then looked at me.

"Let's go outside," I replied. Myra looked pleased, no doubt assuming we'd have a discussion about her birthday.

In the stagnant, humid air, Lisa and I walked to the side parking lot. I looked down and saw a large locust-type creature whose skin wore a dozen different colors. A smaller version of the same species sat on its back. Though I didn't know for certain, I guessed the big one to be a female, with the small male on top of her having locust sex. The twosome scurried into the bushes without losing balance.

Lisa said, "If my mom asks you—"

"I know, I know. You wanted to know what to get her for her birthday."

She smiled. "It must be fun, working so closely with her."

"A laugh a minute," I replied. "But what do you want to tell me?"

"I know it sounds goofy, but I had this weird dream about you last night. One of those super-realistic dreams that's hard to forget. I thought I'd feel better if I told you about it."

"A dream about me? Well, what do you know." In reality, I found other people's dreams boring, but I didn't say as much. "What happened?"

Lisa searched for the right words. "It's hard to describe. You know how dreams are. But you were trapped. You couldn't move. As I recall, nothing held you down. You were frozen, a statue. A woman stood over you. I remember her exact words. 'Katy won't wait forever.' She made it sound like it all depended on you. You made the mess. And now you had to make it better."

"Katy" sounded close to "Caitlyn," but on the other hand, who knew what dreams meant? Still, my curiosity sought satisfaction. "Huh. That's interesting. Did I act scared?"

"I wouldn't say scared. More like you were unhappy, but you had to deal with it."

"I see. Did anything else happen?"

"This is the nutty part. The woman said to you, 'I'm Katy, and you have to do it.' She. . . well, she gave you an ax. You aimed it at her, but then she grabbed it and turned it around the other way, so it pointed at your head. 'That's right, kill your enemy,' she said, which didn't make any sense. But the people seemed so real. At some point a gun went off, and I could sense the bullet going into your brain. Then I woke up. Pretty strange, huh?"

"Dreams usually are."

"Well, anyway, I just wanted to tell you about it. I've had a hard time shaking it off."

I pretended to laugh. "Maybe tonight you'll dream I won a million dollars."

But in truth, the story frightened me because I saw Caitlyn appear in front of Lisa, all but swallowing her in the shadows.

Lisa said, "How weird, I just got goose bumps."

I forced a smile. "Dreams will do that to you if you think about them too much."

Caitlyn, for her part, kept nodding her head up and down, over and over, like a broken doll. She kept saying, "Yes Joe, yes Joe, yes Joe. You can't keep stalling. We need you."

17

Having departed from Myra and her kids, I took out my phone and called McKenzie. She answered on the first ring, albeit in a tentative manner. "Uh, this is McKenzie."

"Hi there, it's Carlo. At long last we're not playing phone tag." I tried to sound unassuming and affable at the same time.

After a pause, she said, "Carlo, it's really you?"

"Of course. I said I'd call. Why wouldn't I? I want to adopt an e-cat. Is now a good time?"

"Now is. . . now is fine, Carlo. We can. . . I mean, I guess we can meet at my place."

"Sounds great. I'll need your address, though." I remembered driving in a state park that had a speed limit sign of three MPH, and wondering how the hell anyone could drive three MPH. In a way, that's how I felt talking to McKenzie.

I called Swann again, and again she didn't answer. I ended the call without leaving a message, in case I said the wrong thing.

I found McKenzie waiting outside her apartment building. The sun glared on the blank sidewalks, and the entire world turned into a giant ugly smirk. McKenzie wore jeans, which surprised me. She did something that millions of other people did. She also sported flat sandals, and a fresh white blouse buttoned to the collar with her cat pin. She didn't wear sunglasses, even though she had to scrunch her eyes to see me. Looking at her through my tinted shades, she seemed somewhat cartoon-like.

"Hello there, Tofu," I said to her brooch.

"You remembered." McKenzie smiled. "I always wait outside when I'm expecting visitors. I don't want to let the wrong person into my home."

"That's very wise. You can't be too careful these days."

"If a man approaches me on the street, I freeze," she elaborated. "Then I take out my police whistle and pepper spray."

I had an image of the dour McKenzie standing there on the street, blowing her whistle and spraying her pepper spray every other minute.

Her small studio surprised me. Colorful posters hung on the walls, which she painted bright yellow and green. Her many houseplants were in perfect health. The single-sized bed had lots of big pillows against the wall, creating a cozy, day-sofa ambiance. In her tiny kitchen were all sorts of grains and herbs on display in clear containers. She had a computer pad on her red desk.

"You have a nice home," I said.

She flashed a timid grin. "It's all the room I require. If people in this country were willing to live only in the space they needed, and if they didn't throw away reusable objects, our useable land space would do I forget what. Double or something." McKenzie picked up the one other chair in the studio—a piano stool painted with bright stripes—and set it up next to the desk. "Besides, I like to see everything I own at the same time."

"You mean like when you're a kid, and everything's in your bedroom?"

She turned pale. "No, not at all. Being a child. . . I don't remember anything about it."

They say people don't remember unhappy childhoods, yet I remembered every last Foster SOB I had to live with. But an unhappy childhood had proven to be a reliable old chestnut when it came to solving murders. "My father beat me and/or molested me," confessed countless killers, as if that explained it all away.

"Do you have brothers and sisters?" I asked, knowing well she did.

"Look, I don't talk about my family." She sounded forceful, as if exposing her shyness as a sham.

"Gee, I'm sorry."

"Don't mention them again. Ever."

"I promise, never again." My fingers made the Boy Scout oath, though it was probable she didn't know about things like that.

McKenzie didn't offer me any refreshments, not even a glass of water. "Have a seat, Carlo, and we'll get you a virtual cat."

She explained why the virtual pet site she worked with should also be my choice; it didn't cost anything, and every hit translated into a miniscule donation for animal rights causes. "Plus the graphics are the best," she said. "You can almost feel the cats kneading their paws."

I couldn't care less about my virtual cat, but McKenzie's bossiness caught me off guard. I checked "female" for the sex of the cat, thinking that would impress McKenzie for its lack of machismo. But she looked at me with creases in her forehead and told me, "You're a man, make it a male." It's hard to describe her belittling tone when saying this. But it sort of felt like she said, "You're a man, go eat shit."

"What do you want to name it?" She asked this in a manner that implied if I said a name of which she didn't approve, she'd punch me in the face.

"Gee, I dunno. What about Joe?"

My choice could not have been more absurd in McKenzie's view. "He's not a Joe. That's the name of a nobody. Use some imagination."

I could've been in grade school, the teacher calling upon me to answer a question I didn't know the answer to. "Um, Mr. Cat?"

She sighed and rolled her eyes, as if a lesser mortal than she would've run out of patience long ago. "Well, he's three colors all at once. Why not call him Trio?"

"That sounds fine." I typed in the name, and the computer took a moment to record all the info. The realistic animation impressed me. I found myself regarding Trio as a living thing with feelings. He purred, and the screen provided a translation for humans: "Thank you for adopting me."

"So, Carlo, there you have it. A virtual pet."

"It's pretty cool."

"It's a responsibility," she said, correcting me. "Now, if you don't mind, I should do some library referencing." She said this in a manner that implied I had diverted her from doing this long enough.

"Can't it wait?" I asked. "It's almost dinnertime. Why not come over to my place?"

McKenzie's eyes darted in surprise. "I suppose I could, but. . . The thing is, I'm totally vegan. What will we eat?"

"I'm sure we'll find something."

She thought some more. "Okay, I guess."

Back outside, I pushed the open button on my remote, and as the doors unlocked, we heard a brief honking sound. As McKenzie slid into my car, she said, "That honk served no purpose. There's enough noise pollution in this city." As she settled herself in, she asked, "What road did you take to get here?"

After I told her, she said, "I know a shortcut. It'll waste less gas."

"This car has a number of ecological features," I said, trying to impress her or at least pretending to try to impress her.

"I knew that," McKenzie said. "But we must stop all dependence on fossil fuel. It would change the world so much more than people realize."

"No doubt, but I worry about all the people it would put out of work."

"Are you kidding? There'd be more jobs than ever. Cheaper energy means cheaper production costs."

That sounded naïve to me, but I didn't want to get into it with her.

"Turn left at the next light," she said. When I almost neglected to do so, McKenzie snapped at me. "Left, left, I told you, don't you remember?" Then she said, "Sorry, I get upset when people don't listen to me." As I looked at McKenzie, it unsettled me yet again to think we had numerous traits in common. Everyone knew me as a glorified nothing of a person. And with the same short temper I tried to hide.

"Do you believe in God?" She asked this in a humorless, abstract way, as if ready to have an intellectual discussion. This could've signaled the presence of an interesting person, but in McKenzie's case, it made her seem all the more unfamiliar with common human customs.

"Do I believe in God? Yeah, I guess so. I don't think I've ever met anyone who didn't at least sort of believe in God."

"Now you have. There is no God. It's impossible that there could be. Look at the world. Look at. . . look out the window right now." We were driving past a cheesy chain restaurant that served lousy food. "You mean to tell me that that exists, and God exists?"

"McKenzie, I don't know everything. Let's give it a rest."

"Do you go to church? I assume you're Christian, right?"

"Sort of. I haven't been to church in a while."

"Any special reason for not going?" she asked, as if seeking a crack in my wall of faith.

"Haven't gotten around to it."

"Well, even if there is a God, I wouldn't be impressed. God allows people to do terrible things. So what difference does God make?"

"What am I, the Pope? How the hell am I supposed to know?"

McKenzie laughed—a strange, mirthless laugh, but a laugh nonetheless. "Okay, I'll give you a break, Carlo. For now, anyway."

She took off her glasses to wipe the lenses on her blouse. Like many people who wore glasses, she looked different without them, and the faraway gaze in her eyes made her far more attractive. But the glasses went right back on.

We pulled up to my driveway.

"It's very nonindigenous to build real estate along the oceanfront," McKenzie remarked, believing that principle here outweighed being polite. "One day a tidal wave will come and whoosh! Your home will be gone. You'll have no one to blame but yourself. You never should have lived here in the first place."

"I'll get a huge insurance check." I couldn't resist the little white lie.

"If you survive, that is."

"If I don't, then I guess it doesn't matter."

"Why Carlo, what a hostile thing to say."

She looked alarmed, as though what she'd been saying constituted pleasant small talk. I didn't find her cruel, just lacking whatever made you aware that how you treated people mattered.

I saw the familiar van across the street, filled with agents ready to come to my rescue if needed. When we stepped inside, McKenzie did not comment on the dwelling at all, other than to say she smelled a lot of harsh chemicals. "Or," she said, "It could be the air conditioning. I'm very sensitive to that as well. Also photocopy machines. They give me migraine headaches."

"I doubt that it's the air conditioning," I said. "But I did have the floors cleaned."

She rummaged through her purse. "I'll take one of my homeopathic pills."

"Would you like a glass of water?"

"Not if it's from the tap. But anyway, the pill dissolves under the tongue."

My cell phone rang, and I answered it without delay, hoping it would be Swann. In fact, I answered it with such haste that I did something awful.

I hit the button to turn on the cameras.

Caitlyn got so angry with me that her body exploded. Yet she could still speak. "How many times must you keep murdering me?" she hollered. "All I do for you is die."

Joe Jr. and Stephanie were crying hard, their tears made of bits of bone.

The lenses made a slight, almost undetectable whizzing sound as they came on.

"I heard something." McKenzie looked startled. "A noise. Like a machine."

I put on a puzzled expression. "I didn't hear anything."

"Carlo, who did you buy this house from? I swear, we're being filmed. I can feel it. I know when I'm being watched." She rubbed her temples. "He's not here. He can't hurt me anymore. That's what they told me to say. He's not here. He can't hurt me anymore."

I assumed the "he" to be her father or maybe her hippie uncle. I thought about offering her a hug but vetoed the idea. "McKenzie, whoever this guy is, you're right. He can't hurt you anymore."

"Easy for you to say. When have you ever been frightened? You, with your decadent beach house. You're probably only seeing me to make fun of me later. You're probably filming me to post it on the Internet, so other people can laugh at me, too. If that's true, Carlo, I swear I'll sue you for everything you have."

"That's not true at all. Not even the part about never being frightened. Why do you think I've been single all these years?"

I gave a meaningful look into the cameras as I turned them off with my cell phone.

"There. Didn't you hear it that time?" McKenzie said.

"No, I didn't. I only know that I'm with a refreshingly intelligent woman, and I hope I don't screw things up as always. I'm very shy."

McKenzie touched my arm. "You don't have to worry, Carlo. Believe me, I'm not hard to please."

"Same here. I don't judge people more harshly than necessary."

It could've been a moment for a kiss, but I imagine we both experienced relief when we let the moment pass us by. McKenzie said, after a pause, "We're here for dinner, so let's get started."

She marched into the kitchen, and opened the cupboards, pointing at various food items. "No, no, no, and no," she decreed. "Oh, wait. Peanut butter." She read the label. "There's no sugar or additives, though I doubt the peanuts are organic. I guess it will do. I'm going to cleanse my colon tonight, anyway. What kind of bread do you have?"

I opened another cupboard for her inspection. "Rye," she commented. "Not exactly whole grain, but I suppose better than nothing."

"That's it, just peanut butter sandwiches?"

"I like plain things."

"That's good to know."

"And I only drink pure or filtered water, so I'll pass and have nothing to drink."

"Same for me," I enthused, removing four slices of rye bread from the loaf.

"I'll do it," McKenzie corrected. "I eat mine a certain way, and you'll get it wrong. I like the thinnest spread of peanut butter, just enough to go into the little holes in the bread. Thick peanut butter makes me nauseous. Literally. I have a very sensitive digestive tract."

I didn't know if she planned to sneak me Roofies but watching her make the two sandwiches might've made anyone want to die. It took her a lifetime to spread peanut butter on two slices of bread and then put two more slices of bread on top. Then it seemed to take forever for her to put away the jar, and put each sandwich on a plate.

"Ready," she said, without enthusiasm.

She set up the plates at the small table in the kitchen. It took too much imagination to consider eating at the living room sofa. Or maybe she feared I'd come on to her if we did.

The plain peanut butter sandwich tasted so dry, I had to excuse myself to pour a glass of nonorganic cranberry juice.

"McKenzie, when you said he couldn't hurt you anymore, what happened?"

She set her sandwich down. "Why do you want to know? To tease me?"

"Please stop going there. I want to know more about you."

She picked at her sandwich. "My uncle. A worthless bum. The day before my eighteenth birthday, in the horse stables. Grooming my pony—how I loved him. 'Ponies are for children,' my uncle said. 'It's time you had a real man.' He punched me so hard in the face that I fell down. Then he. . . he did what he did. And I lost my virginity. Naturally, my parents believed him and not me. He told them he couldn't have done it because he only liked pretty girls. 'A real man.' That's him, all right.

"I planned to go to college. But instead I took a bus into the city, got my studio, and took a job. That's all I've done since. I. . . I went to the speed dates just to. . . to try, you know? Maybe I shouldn't have. I should've stayed home."

"I'm sorry for all that happened to you, but I'm glad you came to the speed date."

She laughed a little. "You're sweet, Carlo. Especially when you say nice things you don't mean."

"I mean it. I really do."

She fixed her glasses, which were sliding down her nose. "Let's change the subject."

"Whatever you prefer."

"It's not about what I prefer. It's about focusing on more relevant topics."

McKenzie walked such a thin line between the shyness she acquired from her family and the snobbery she likewise acquired from her family. If I wanted to be like Myra, I'd talk to McKenzie about being your own worst enemy. But since I didn't want to be anything like Myra, I said nothing of the kind.

"Do you ever miss your family?" I asked.

"No. I don't let negative energy into my life."

For someone who never let negativity into her life, she wouldn't qualify for the Miss Sunshine Pageant, but I chose not to point this out either. "I wish I could do that."

"You could if you wanted to. Anyone can. It's all about the neurons in the brain. It's about diet. Diet and attitude."

In her singsong voice, McKenzie proceeded to convey a long-winded story about how she became interested in natural foods. It began with a vivid description of how constipated she became after eating a candy bar, which incident proved to be her rock bottom, so to speak, from which point onward she sought to amend her dietary choices.

I frowned in a way that suggested serious interest as I gobbled down my dry sandwich. I did feel groggy, though it could've been because of McKenzie's tedious story or a lingering drowsiness from sleeping on the beach.

"Now, the important thing to remember about blue-green algae," McKenzie said, "is that less is more. I would say to start with one capsule a day . . ."

I didn't know what blue-green algae were, but I didn't ask.

Stephanie and Joe Jr. were arguing again about the birthday banner, as Caitlyn attempted to break up the fight. Mealy worms crawled over their rotting flesh. Caitlyn's face turned into moldy layers of dead skin, pustules bursting out with a body fluid that may have been blood but may have been something else.

"Ginseng isn't the lily white we once thought," McKenzie said. "I don't recommend drinking it more than once a week at the most."

"I love you, Joe," Caitlyn said. "When you love someone, it lasts forever. You love me right this second, I can feel it." She reached inside herself and pulled out her heart. Covered in foul-smelling mold, it did not beat. "This is for you," she said. "It's your birthday present."

"The corporations want everyone to take the same multiple vitamins," complained McKenzie, "without thought to the differences of each individual's body needs. It's easier to mass-market products for corporate profit. That's why we all have to work to stop the Christian white male racist ageist heterosexist, right-wing power-elite capitalist war machine. I happen to require extra vitamin D. If I don't get enough D in a given day, well, I guess you could say it's a day without a D. Of course, the sun gives off vitamin D, but I worry about skin cancer."

Caitlyn and the kids danced in a circle, holding hands. Their feet stepped into the sticky mess of their own decomposing bodies; I could hear crunching sounds of what I assumed to be brittle fragments of bone. They sang "Happy Birthday" to me, spinning in a circle, over and over.

McKenzie sat up with a start. Then she trembled. Every nerve of her body shook. Her teeth chattered. Her head moved from side to side. I wondered if she had a condition I didn't know about, maybe epilepsy or diabetes.

McKenzie sang "Happy Birthday" with the same carefree abandon as my family. She stood up and pretended to be holding hands in a circle, singing away.

## 18

It took a good half hour for the singing to stop, for my family to go away again, and for McKenzie to collapse on the floor. It constituted the longest episode I'd spent with them since leaving the cabin. McKenzie appeared to be asleep, and I thought about letting her stay there. But if she woke up on the floor, she'd be frightened and angry. Taking great care not to disturb her, I lifted her on to the sofa.

I sat in a chair nearby, staring into space for maybe ten minutes.

McKenzie opened her eyes and sat up. "I fell asleep? I'm so sorry. How rude of me."

"Don't give it a second thought."

I didn't want to look at her, let alone say anything. So much for it all being something occurring in my head. My crazy idea to get myself killed made sense. The spirits were real. What other explanation could there be?

"You are the most selfish man who ever lived," Caitlyn said upon reappearing. "You can't even help us when we're dead. You, you, you, it's always about you. You're a total egomaniac. You say you're shy but it's really that being with other people distracts you from your beloved self. It makes you unhappy to think about anyone else."

"Daddy, let's play," Stephanie said, her face flaking off to reveal raw layers of skin.

"How could you cheat on Mom?" Joe Jr. wanted to know, tossing his severed penis like a baseball.

Caitlyn got it right. I had to stop thinking about myself whatsoever. It occurred to me that in a way, nothing changed. I still couldn't show my affection except by working. Only my job now required me to die for them.

"Carlo, do you hear something?" McKenzie asked.

"Uh, no, but I thought I did."

"Did something happen?" She sat next to me on the couch.

I nodded my head in affirmation, but I didn't say anything.

She ran her fingers through her hair in panic. "Did I. . . did I do something strange?"

"Yes," I said. She couldn't meet my gaze and looked at the floor.

"It's happened before. Someone made a video of it, but I couldn't bring myself to watch. Were you having a bad dream?"

"Something like that."

"And did I start acting it out?"

"Something like that."

McKenzie started to cry. "There's something very wrong with me. That's why I keep to myself so much."

"How often does this happen?"

"I started doing it at thirteen. I'd say about two or three times a year since then." She covered her mouth with her hand. "This is terrible. I should go." She grabbed her purse and headed for the front door.

"McKenzie, wait." I didn't want her to stay; yet I also didn't want her to leave. "You're a medium. You connect with. . . with spirits, or whatever you want to call them. You could help people. Explain their visions. Find out what souls are asking from the other side."

"There are no spirits. There is no other side. It's something to do with my brain waves. The pollutants in the air have poisoned my brain cells."

"But McKenzie—"

"I should do some library referencing." She opened the front door to leave.

"Is this why you're an atheist?" I asked as she slammed the door.

Caitlyn said, "You let her get away on purpose. You're such a hypocrite."

I got a phone call; I earlier conjured up the energy to reset the ringtone to chirping birds, thinking it would be more soothing. Nonetheless I let the call go to voicemail:

"Joe, this is Esteban Santiago. I don't have to do this, but I'm still willing to give you a get-out-of-jail-free card in exchange for telling me what really happened. If you're smart, you'll call me back. If you don't, well, don't say I didn't warn you. Not just about you, but all the cute little hobbits in Homicide."

Esteban sounded like he could pick me up in his hand and crumble me like a piece of paper. But this could've been desperation trying to pass itself off as bravado. I believed he needed me more than I needed him.

I renewed my resolve to let it be. Besides, I received a text message reminding me that I neglected to feed supper to Trio, my virtual cat—a task I could execute without fear of the sky falling on top of me. On my smart phone I logged into the website.

A tiny GIF depicted a mournful Trio meowing. I gave him fresh food, water, catnip, and kitty litter. I rubbed the small screen to e-pet the creature, which purred. It even did a little cat dance of sorts, as if to please me. I felt genuine relief that I fed the cat in time. This dumb little computer animated thing made me forget about the whole ball of wax for a minute or two.

Next, I called Josh and the others in their van. "We got news about Victim Number Eleven," he said. "Same everything. Expect a meeting."

"Hopefully, we'll get to keep a closer watch on McKenzie," I said, telling him the story of McKenzie's uncle. For any number of reasons, I said nothing about her unusual little episode.

"The molestation bit should be enough to convince the higher-ups to give her the deluxe treatment as a suspect." I heard Stu in the background saying, "It must've been hard to keep your hands off her."

"Listen, Joe," Josh said. "I saw how the cameras freaked her out. They're more trouble than they're worth. Let's keep roughing it with the earpiece and phone."

"That sounds fine."

"On my word of honor, you'll be safe," Josh said.

"Okay," I replied.

"Here's hoping there's no new victims," Josh said.

"Yeah, hope. I guess that's better than nothing."

I lay in bed with a pillow over my face. I saw my kids playing catch with a sharp, bloodied ax, and thought if I covered my head it would go away.

It didn't.

For awhile, I made a childish game out of tapping the mattress a certain number of times with one hand and then the other. When you're a foster child, you don't own lots of toys, so I made up pointless finger games as a kid.

After maybe an hour, my ringtone of birds began its misbegotten chorus. I thought about not answering the call, but decided I might as well.

"What's with the calling and not leaving a message?" Swann said. "Didn't you think I wanted to talk to you, Carlo? Today might as well have taken place in a giant pile of dog shit. My friend is dying of cancer, and I can't even see her. Don't you think I would've appreciated hearing a kind voice?"

"You knew I went to the hospital. Why didn't you at least leave me a message? You know, 'I hope your friend is doing better,' or 'I'm thinking of you.' Thank God for my mom. She's always there for me. But I have this peculiar idea that I should be able to get support from people other than my mother. Silly me."

Since I had no memory of her leaving me to go to the hospital, I had to invent a convincing answer. "I thought you wanted privacy. If you wanted comfort from me, why didn't you bring me along in the first place?"

"Oh, so we're back to that, are we? Yes, how nice of you to want to come along. But when I told you thanks but no thanks, I didn't mean to shut you out. I just didn't want you stuck in the waiting room from like now until the end of time."

I thought it prudent not to get into how I woke up alone on the beach. "How's your friend?"

"Marvelous, I imagine. She's on her deathbed and has no family, but they won't let her only friend in town see her."

"Did you try going back during normal visiting hours? Or ask to talk to a supervisor?"

Swann sighed. "You would ask that, wouldn't you? Mr. Logic. Mr. I-Know-Everything. No, I didn't go back. I don't go where I'm not wanted. I spent the day crying into my pillow, if you want to know. Maybe you remember it from when you saw my place. It's the one with the embroidered elephant with yellow fringe all around."

"I'm sorry to hear that. About your friend, I mean." My body became imbalanced, like in a dream that you're a passenger sinking on the Titanic. Everything appeared too dizzy to be real. Then, from the pit of my gut, came the all-too-familiar despair that I had to push aside in order to talk to people. Only I couldn't keep pushing it aside.

"Joe, I'm still waiting," Caitlyn whispered, as a chunk of her face fell off. A rat nibbled the fallen wedge of nose, cheekbone, and eye socket.

"Tell you what, Swann," I managed to say. "I'll pick you up and we'll go to the hospital and I'll do everything I can for you to see your friend."

"Oh, sure. What are you going to tell them? 'I'm Carlo Rizzo, and what I say goes?'" She laughed at the absurdity.

"Swann, I want to see you. Is that so terrible?"

I heard one of those unbearable long pauses. "I don't know, Carlo. I like you and then I don't. When I see you I like you, but when I think about you afterward, there's something I don't like at all. It's like. . . it's like the only reason you're seeing me is because you're lonely or something dumb like that. I don't think you approve of me. Not really."

"I've had a lot of fun," I offered in my defense.

"I believe you. But if I didn't make it fun, there'd be no fun. If I said we should go stamp collecting, you'd go stamp collecting. Hell, if I said let's murder someone, you'd do that, too. I let people into my life because I like them. But you, Carlo, you let them in because you think you have to."

"I, uh. . . I don't agree."

"Who gives a royal-red-carpet-fuck if you agree? The truth's the truth. You're so extroverted, it's obnoxious. It's like you're scared to death of being alone."

My head hurt. I saw flashes of light. "Swann, please promise me you'll at least think about seeing me again."

"Fuck you." She ended the call.

I had no idea why Swann hated me so much. Yet it seemed fitting. A winner has no time for a loser. There didn't have to be any more reason than that. I tried acting like a normal person—or whatever you'd call it—and my attempt ended with obvious inevitable failure. The FBI would not be amused to learn that I lost my rapport with Swann, but I didn't have to worry about telling them for at least a few hours.

If I slept for the rest of my life I'd still be drained of energy. I felt embalmed.

I woke to the doorbell. Someone rang it over and over. I forced myself out of bed and walked to the front door. My head weighed a ton.

"She died," Swann managed to say through her tears. I put my arm around her, and led her to the living room. I sat us down on the sofa, and she cried into my lap for an hour. As best I could, I stroked her stiff spikes of hair. Since she knew hundreds of people, I thought it odd that she should pick me in which to confide, in particular after our last phone call. But I also knew that grief made people do all sorts of unexpected things.

I'd like to say that caring for someone else made me feel better, but it didn't.

Swann sat up. She took out a tissue from her shoulder bag and wiped the streaks of mascara from her face. "God, I must look awful." In spite of herself, she giggled through her wet, red eyes. "People need each other. It's so simple. Why does it get complicated? I deserted her. Sheila died alone." For all the talk about this unfortunate young woman, Swann at last told me her name, unless of course she told me the other night.

"I've seen many. . . I mean, I've seen a few people die. It's impossible to know what they're feeling. Maybe Sheila's at peace. Maybe she understood why you weren't there." I wanted to add that whether alive or dead, people were pretty much inscrutable, but chose not to.

"Thank you, Carlo." She kissed me on the mouth. "You're special."

"No, I'm not."

Swann burst out laughing, the kind of laugh that sounds a little like crying. "What is it about you? You always know how to cheer me up. You're like a cute little boy. Especially when you smile." She held my face in her hands.

"Do you have dinner plans?" she asked, as if the earlier phone call never happened.

"Just a pizza delivery." I figured this insured that she'd stay.

"I'll order it, if you'd like."

"I'd like that very much."

"Terrific. I'll get the same as last time and go fix my face."

An extra-large everything pizza to be eaten on the floor became a fun, guilty secret between us. We got more than halfway through the delicacy—in large part thanks to me— when my phone rang. "Sorry, Swann, let me turn off my phone." I felt a wave of drowsiness, but then it went away.

"Take the call, Carlo. I get calls all the time." She reached for another slice of pizza.

"Okay, but I promise to make it quick." I thought it might be McKenzie. But the caller ID indicated Myra's son, Lonnie.

"Joe," Lonnie said. "Thank God."

"Yes, Lonnie. This is Carlo."

"Um, Joe, what the—oh wait, I get it. You're like undercover. How cool is that?"

"Hang on, Lonnie." I silently mouthed to Swann, "It's nobody."

"Joe, are you there?"

"Yes. How are you?"

He laughed. "Considering I have a monster report due next week, and I'm nutso from too many Xanax, I'd say I'm fine. If truth be told, I don't even want to be a lawyer. All this heavy duty academic stuff. . . it's easy for my sisters, but not me. But it's yes-Mom-yes-Mom all the way. All I do is study."

"And take way too many Xanax. But I don't feel like lecturing you on the evils of prescription drug abuse. If you're flipping out, call 911."

"Every dumb fuck in the world knows to call 911. That's not why I'm calling." He laughed some more. It always bothered me when people finished what they said with a laugh.

"Okay, then. Why did you call? I have company."

Swann looked worried and set aside her slice of pizza. "Carlo, is someone OD-ing?"

"Uh, no. Someone is confused, that's all."

"Confused about what?" Swann asked.

"Trust me, it's complicated."

"Joe, are you there?"

"Yes, Lonnie. Now tell me. Why did you call?" I held out a restraining hand to Swann.

"It's about my mom. A couple of things."

Great, just what I wanted. More Myra in my life. "Is it that important? I'm sure—"

"She talked to this guy named Esteban Something. In the hotel bar. She couldn't see me from where she sat—Mom, I mean. Your name came up. Something about how Mom would keep you from being arrested as part of the deal. I know Mom can be a pain, but Joe, if you're doing something that's getting her in trouble, I'll—"

"Slow down, Mr. Prosecutor. Give me a second." I mouthed to Swann that I had to go into the bedroom for a moment.

"Can I help?" Swann asked. "Please, I'm right here if you need me."

At the time, I had no idea why carefree Swann wanted to get involved in my mysterious problem. I imagined the ghost of Florence Nightingale taking possession of her soul. Looking back, it should've been obvious that she felt guilty about her friend Sheila.

"Okay, Lonnie. I'm alone in the bedroom. Please tell me everything you heard them say. I promise, I'm not getting your mom in trouble. She'll be fine."

"He's so weak," Joe Jr. said. "He's not a real man. Why do you care about him?"

"You're sure?" Lonnie asked.

"One hundred percent sure."

"Okay, well, Esteban said how any time now heads would be rolling. Those were his exact words. Heads will roll. And Mom said, 'I want to help, but give us more time to solve the case. Then I'll deliver as many heads on as many silver platters as you want.' Plus how she didn't want anything to happen to you."

"Shit."

"What's it all mean?" Lonnie asked. "Is the FBI doing something wrong?"

"Not at all. It's not even about the FBI," I lied. "Your mom and I are involved in other things. It's for the government. I can't talk about it. And neither can she."

"Yeah, but if you know what's going on, why did you have to ask me about it?" As often happens when you're caught lying, I experienced annoyance with Lonnie for busting me.

"Hey, you called me. You brought it up. I just wanted to know what you heard."

"And everything's okay?"

I pretended to chuckle. "Good will triumph over Evil, I assure you. But now you have to promise me something. And that is to never, ever tell anyone about the conversation you overheard."

"If that's what's best for my country, I'll do it," Lonnie assured me.

"You never comforted me," Joe Jr. said. "You called me weak. You hated me, didn't you? I couldn't be the son you wanted."

"You never called me princess," Stephanie complained. "You always made me feel stupid when I wanted something."

"You owe so much to your children," Caitlyn said. "And to me." She started to whimper, though her tears were made of some strange body matter.

"Please join us," Joe Jr. said.

"We need you," added Stephanie.

"I trust you," I told Lonnie. "You're an upright young man. Except for one thing."

"You mean the Xanax?"

"Maybe I feel like lecturing you after all. Talk to the doctor when you get back to school. Tell him the truth. It ain't working like it's supposed to."

"Okay. I promise. But can I ask you something?"

"Sure. We're friends."

"But I'm not your friend, am I?" Joe Jr. sneered, scratching the flesh off his face.

"Why do you get out of bed every day?" Lonnie asked. "What motivates you?"

"Nothing. I just do it."

"But *why?*"

"Because I'm not dead. In fact, I. . ." I took a deep breath. "Do you think your mother is happy? I mean, really, is that what you think?"

"I never noticed. She's just Mom."

"Well, you're always saying, 'Don't tell her this, don't tell her that.' Isn't it because you know she can't handle anything too real?"

"Mom makes it so easy to lie. It's the only thing you can do to survive."

I said, "Don't blame your mother. Even if you're right, it won't get you anywhere. The point is that how you feel is sometimes beyond your control. All you can do is live your life the best you can."

"Or the worst you can," Joe Jr. chimed in.

"But what would you do if you were me?" Lonnie asked. "Would you drop out of law school? Would you tell my mom to flake off? Mental illness runs in our family. My mom's mom spent most of her life in a hospital."

So much for Myra's idyllic childhood, though I can't say the information surprised me. Desperate people are desperate for a reason.

Swann knocked on the bedroom door. "Hello? Do I still exist? Am I composed of physical matter?"

"I have to go now, Lonnie. It sounds like you have a lot to think about."

"'A lot to think about' should be my middle name."

I pretended to laugh again. "Well, have a nice—"

"Oh wait, I almost forgot. Another thing about Mom."

"Okay." I sighed and made a face at Swann to indicate my impatience with the phone call.

"Don't worry, this is good news. Today I went to some weird store full of old stuff, and I bought your gift for Mom's birthday."

"That's very thoughtful of you. I forgot all about it."

"I figured you did. It's this old book from like 1870-something. I'll drop it by your house. I already got your address from Mom."

"Lonnie, you're the greatest. Do it in the morning, though."

"Sure thing."

"By the way, what's it called? The book, I mean."

"*Shadow Language*, whatever that means. All I know that it's old and in excellent condition."

I ended the call, kissed Swann, and we walked back to the living room.

"So this person. Is she-he going to be okay?"

"I'm sorry, Swann. But there's things you don't know about, and it would be mighty fine to keep it that way."

"Who appointed you my legal guardian? There's things I haven't told you, either. But I'm no stranger to mental BS. I can help."

"That's nice of you, but everything's fine."

We returned to our pizza on the floor.

"I have kind of a nutty theory," Swann said. "Want to hear it?"

"I have a feeling I'm going to hear it whether I want to or not."

She gave me a playful jab in the ribs with her elbow.

"It's like there's only so much good luck a family gets," she began, "and sometimes it gets spread around pretty evenly, and other times one person gets almost all of it. But you see, the person who gets it all, that person also has the most bad luck, because they have to do all the living for everyone else. If someone's in denial, someone else has to carry on their back all the crud that isn't being faced."

In her goofy way, Swann struck me as one of the best examples of mental health I'd ever met.

"I can see how there's something to that."

I felt close to her, and I dared to believe she felt close to me, too.

My family put in a return visit. "Happy birthday, Dad!" they called out in unison, their flesh more rancid than ever. In a teasing voice, and with a snake slithering in and out of her abdomen cavity, Caitlyn said, "Who's the girl, Joe? Don't tell me this little twerp has replaced me." Something black as squid ink gushed out of Stephanie's mouth, but as always she kept on looking gleeful.

Swann frowned. "I'm hearing that noise again, same as the other day. Maybe there's something wrong with your pipes."

"I didn't hear anything." But I heard something I couldn't deny—a beep that told me I had another text message. It came from Esteban:

*last chance tomorrow 9 am same place*

19

Anticipation of the morning meeting put a considerable damper on my night with Swann. Lucky for me she took it like a good sport—sort of.

"Obviously you're in a crappy mood," she said. "But the reason I'm going home is because you'll never tell me why."

"Swann, please stay. I know you don't want to be alone tonight." After all, she just lost her friend, Sheila.

"Exactly. So I'm going home. My stuffed animal, Mr. Hippo, will be an engaging companion. We've had an on-again off-again relationship since my fourth birthday."

"Are you upset with me?"

"No, just not jumping-up-and-down thrilled." She kissed me. "Do whatever you need to do. I'm okay now, really."

She made one inaccurate assumption—that I had any idea what I needed to do. In the end, I spent the night in bed, rereading *Supernatural or Psychotic?* At times the ocean sounded like my family whispering, but they never showed up. I did however dream that the Sun People picked up the beach house and threw it into the ocean. Again and again I started to drown and then got to the surface only to sink again, as if even in my dreams I couldn't do anything right.

Come the morning, I had some time to kill, so I decided to sit on the beach. I told myself the Sun People were just a dream. I was sure I could relax for a few minutes on a beach that people would sell their souls to visit.

As I eased onto the velvety sands, I saw a family nearby, a mother with three kids. The two bigger kids decided to bury the smallest kid in the sand, and the little kid screamed. The mother looked up from her magazine to take a drag on her cigarette and say, "Now kids, play nice."

I sat there, doing nothing for a few blessed minutes.

Then I saw my family. "Every day's a birthday," they said. A hissing, bumpy lizard like a small tyrannosaurus jumped out of Joe Jr.'s hacked up mouth. Stephanie grabbed the creature and squashed it to death with her hand.

Then she ate it, licking her fingers.

I went back into the house. As if on cue, my phone rang.

"Hey, amigo," Josh said. "Still no evidence from Willow. Her kids will be living with their grandparents. I forget which side of the family."

"That's nice," I said. "Is there a meeting this morning for Victim Eleven?"

"Nope. Shannon is all tied up. Tish filed a sexual harassment whatchamacallit against Stu. Seems he liked her much more than we thought because he tried forcing her to kiss him in the break room yesterday afternoon. It's complicated because Stu works for the city. It's taking time away from the case. Lucky me, I walked in on him. He had her cornered and twisted her arm. I'll give my testimony this morning."

I could see why Tish would file a complaint, but I didn't want to be involved in any of it, not even the residue gossip. I pictured Myra having a ball, despite her sober countenance in the presence of Shannon or Tish. She had so much goo to play with.

"You sound strange," said Josh. "Are you feeling okay, man?"

"Sure."

"Oh, one more thing, dude. Our little party girl Swann. It turns out she's bipolar."

I felt as if a 20-story building stood inside me, and someone pushed a piano off the rooftop. Poor, brave Swann, lover of life, funny optimist. All just a glorified manic episode.

"How do you—"

"We know, and let's leave it at that. She's good about taking her meds, but still. . ."

I ended the conversation in a daze.

I understood nothing about life. But at least I knew I did.

I arrived at my 9:00 a.m. meeting with Esteban a full half-hour early. The restaurant didn't open until nine, so I sat in my car for a half hour, doing nothing.

Once inside, I waited fifteen more minutes before Esteban arrived. When he did, Myra tagged alongside him. This didn't surprise me. I assumed she already finked people out.

"Good morning." I gestured for them to join me at the table. As they got seated, I said, "I expected to see you, Myra."

"And I'm not surprised you agreed to meet," she replied. "You're like me, Joe. You always tell the truth."

The table server came to take our orders. Esteban said, "I already ate, so I'll have a latte."

"I never eat breakfast," Myra said, "So I'll have one, too. Decaf and skimmed milk."

"Coffee for me."

"We all have to get to work," said Esteban, "so let's be quick about it. Here's a statement I prepared. Read it, sign it, and we're done. I'll never trouble you again."

"And IA agrees to give us a month to solve the case before they do anything," Myra added with great enthusiasm.

The statement contained no surprises: the cameras didn't come on, and the rookie disobeyed orders, shooting to death two people. The orders to stage a cover-up came from Shannon. Tish, Josh, and a few other agents carried it out. Myra and I were listed as "witnesses" to the event.

I set the paper on the table and stared at it.

"As I said," Esteban reaffirmed, "Sign it and we're done."

"Unless of course I have to testify."

Myra leapt in before Esteban could respond. "Testify, shmestify. That's nothing. I'm sure you've taken the witness stand a thousand times before."

"You knew about the cover-up, Myra."

"Au contraire," she said. "I gathered evidence at the murder scene and went to the hospital to help you. I didn't know a thing until after the fact, when Tish told me."

I couldn't gauge the validity of her claim, but it alarmed me that Myra would sell out her protégé without a second thought. "I thought you liked Tish."

"I do. I hope she wins her complaint against Stu. I assume you heard about that? God, can you imagine? But anyway, it's nothing personal. It's only—"

"It's only the truth," I said. "Or at least one version of it."

"What do you mean?" asked Esteban, as our modest orders arrived.

"The cameras didn't come on because I didn't turn them on."

Myra laughed. "It's too early in the morning for kidding around."

"It's the truth. I didn't want them on."

Esteban took a sip of his steaming latte. "Why not?"

"Because," I said, "I wanted to die."

Myra laughed some more, but a sober-faced Esteban asked, "Why did you want to die?"

"I missed my family."

Myra looked flabbergasted. "I'm appalled that you'd joke about something like that. Damn it, you're happy now, and you know you are. I made you happy."

"Are you joking, Joe?" asked Esteban.

"Why would I joke about something so serious?"

"You didn't answer my question."

"Chill, Esteban," Myra said. "Everything in the statement is still true. Even if we were dumb enough to think that Joe meant what he said, the cameras didn't come on. And Joe had nothing to do with the cover-up."

Esteban said, "She's right. Sign it, Joe."

"Why? You just said I had nothing to do with this so-called cover-up."

"But you knew about it and did nothing." Esteban looked pissed off.

"Okay, fine." I took out my pen and signed the document. "I have work to do."

"Joe, you didn't even touch your coffee," Myra complained.

"Then you drink it. I'm sure you'll get a promotion, and you'll need all the extra energy you can get."

After I left, they had to have noticed that I signed with the name, "Batman." I dated it July 4, 1776.


I told Josh I'd try to spend the day with McKenzie, but I turned off my phone and went to the beach house to sleep. Less than an hour later, I heard the doorbell. I opened the door, looked down and saw a book in a shopping bag.

For a second I thought Lonnie rang the bell, but it appeared he dropped off the book and left. Instead I opened the door to Stu the cop, who looked pale and shaken. He wore his dress blues. My sense of smell did not have to work overtime to signal that he'd been drinking. I noticed the van had gone, maybe to get gas or something.

I didn't expect Stu's visit, but in a way it didn't shock me. People down in the dumps often singled me out as someone to confide in, even people who otherwise avoided me, though I hadn't the slightest clue as to why. Maybe my lack of interest came across as being non-judgmental.

"That fucking Tish," Stu said, inviting himself in. "After thirty years on the force, I'm suspended until further notice without pay."

I followed behind him, putting the shopping bag on the kitchen counter. "That's unfortunate. But I'm expecting someone, and you have to leave. Call me later." Of course, the only people I expected were my dead family.

He walked to the living room and sat on the sofa. "I didn't do anything. I swear that's true. It's all about the cover-up."

"Stu, someone said he saw you. He'd have no reason to lie."

"And would this someone by any chance be Josh? Don't you get it, dummy? I planned all along to tell the Attorney General's office about Willow and her husband."

I wanted to keep my nose clean, which meant I wanted to distance myself from Stu.

"Did you tell anyone you were going to report it?"

"Of course not. What do you think I am, stupid?"

"Then why would they frame you?"

Stu laughed. "Don't you pay attention? I'm a loose cannon. I kept bringing it up. I scared the shit out of them."

"Did you go to Internal Affairs?"

"Try inhabiting the universe for a change. I'm a cop. I never get within a mile of IA. Plus I'm not FBI. They think nothing of feeding me to the wolves."

Caitlyn and Stephanie were playing some kind of clapping game; when one of their hands fell off, the owner would reach down and put it back, as though nothing were the matter.

"It's always hard to know who to trust," I admitted.

"No one believes me," Stu continued. "Not even the cops. I have to go to some motherfucking anger management class. Plus some shit-sucking seminar on diversity training. And this asshole group for sex addicts, whatever that is. 'Suspended until further notice.' What the fuck does that even mean? How am I supposed to pay the goddamn mortgage? Tish—she should change her name to Shit."

"Maybe the classes will help you," I suggested, but Stu ignored me. "Shit is Tish spelled backward," he said with a chuckle. I saw no point in correcting his spelling.

"Again, I'm sorry, Stu. You have to leave."

Stu grinned as he took out a Beretta 92 from under his pocket.

"This is my beautiful gun," he said, kissing it. "The fuckheads took away my cop gun, but I always have a spare." He twirled the Beretta with his fingers. Then he threw it toward the ceiling and caught it. "People like you, Hilario, never have to worry about a goddamn thing. You're always so happy, so in charge. Nothing gets you down. That's why you're such a motherfucking worthless piece of shit."

"Stu, can I please see your gun? I've been thinking of getting a Beretta compact."

"This case. I'm telling you, there's something wrong. They don't know what they're doing. The truth will come out."

"Tell you what. I'll work on it with you in secret. No one has to know."

"Fuck you, Joe." Stu aimed the gun at me, then at himself, then back at me again. "Eeny, meeny, miney, mo." He laughed, his aim moving back to his head, then back at me.

I walked to about a foot in front of him, looking him straight in the eye.

"If you have to take out your frustrations on someone, kill me." I lifted my T-shirt. "Right here. Shoot me in my heart. Then run like hell."

For maybe a minute, the sound of the ocean became indistinguishable from my heartbeat. Stu appeared to be studying my belly as it breathed in and out.

He burst out laughing. "You think I don't know what you're doing?"

But I wouldn't know what Stu meant, nor would it matter, as he fired the gun into the side of his head. He wore a contorted, mocking face as he fell to the floor in a heap. I got a few drops of blood on my chest, as though it were a blessing from the god of suicide. The ocean continued bleating, like a Greek chorus.

Caitlyn stood behind him, a look of utter rapture on her decaying face. "See how easy it is?" she said, in her gleeful way. "It takes one second. Maybe even less." She used what remained of her thumb and forefinger to pretend to shoot herself in the head, and made a twisted face. "It's fun," she assured me.

I wondered if a normal person would feel something for Stu. I witnessed too many violent death scenes in my career to care about someone as troubled as him. All I felt might best be described as forbidden envy. He had the guts to do what I couldn't. Or did he have no guts, while I did? I squatted to get a better look at him. I couldn't tell if he seemed peaceful or tormented; maybe in death they became the same thing.

It occurred to me that the beach house had been the scene of three shooting deaths in a matter of days.

"Holy crap." The voice startled me until I realized it belonged to Josh, who let himself in upon hearing the gunshot. The van arrived; I later learned they had a problem with the starter wire.

"I tried to stop him." I stood up, feeling embarrassed, though I didn't know what about.

"Did you call for an ambulance?"

"No, I. . . I didn't think—"

"I'll take care of it." Josh extended his arm to keep a distance from me. After making the call, Josh put his phone back in his jacket pocket and said, "Tish will need everyone's support. In case she blames herself."

"That would be stupid," I said. "It's not her fault."

"People do stupid things." He squeezed my shoulder. "How are you holding up?"

"Fine."

We both stood still. It seemed like one of us should say something about Stu or death or suicide, but neither of us said anything. Something told me to wait on telling Josh about my meeting with Myra and Esteban.

"I'd better get my ass in the van," Josh said. "You handle the ambulance."

The ambulance workers arrived in a few minutes. One of them looked at Stu and said, "Hey, I knew this guy. I picked him up once before."

"Had he injured himself?" I asked.

"Yes and no. He suffered from chronic depression and said he wanted to kill himself."

Josh called a few minutes later from the van. There'd been another murder, or rather, a corpse several days old with the same MO had been discovered. This made twelve known victims. I had to report to headquarters at once. The blood would be cleaned up after I left.

## 20

Back at headquarters, Myra greeted me with her offensive false niceness. "Joe, it always brightens my day to see you." She hugged me, and I had no choice but to let her do it. She said nothing about IA or my lack of cooperation. But my relief over not hearing about it outweighed my interest in learning more.

We took our usual seats around the table in the conference room. I wondered if someone would talk about Stu, but no one did. Shannon didn't even say if another cop would take his place. If Tish harbored any unresolved feelings, she did an expert job of not showing it. At one point, she whispered something in Myra's ear, and they both tittered.

I didn't think it possible that I could like Myra less than I already did, but watching her act buddy-buddy with Tish just hours after she agreed to ruin Tish's career made me experience a new kind of hatred that went beyond anything I thought possible. A hatred that made me think I should be called Joe the Great.

Everyone grilled me over and over about Swann and McKenzie. I insisted that nothing personal or sexual developed between Swann and myself. "There's been a few kisses," I said, "but that's as far as it goes." I thought it better left unmentioned that we cuddled in our underwear, which would've humiliated me to say the least.

"What about McKenzie?"

"Not even kisses. Though she's an unusual person."

One of the agents asked, "What else have you learned?"

"That I need more time." I hoped no one knew how intimidated I felt.

"What does that mean?" asked the same agent.

"It's hard to get them to say anything that helps us. McKenzie told me her uncle molested her, but it didn't go anywhere after that."

Tish shook her head. "Such a friendless person. All she wants is a little happiness."

"A little happiness can be a dangerous thing to want," I heard myself say.

"What do you mean by that?" asked another agent.

Everyone looked wavy to me, as if part of an abstract painting. I wanted to say something about my family, but I didn't know what it should be. So I said: "Isn't that at the heart of every murder? Someone unhappy wants to be happy. This serial killer. . . all she wants is to know someone won't abandon her. For her, a dead man is better than none at all."

Shannon said, "You're certainly being very profound this morning. But you're right."

The meeting went on for another half hour, but I spaced out. It startled me when I realized the meeting ended. Shannon talked the entire time, but I didn't hear anything she said until the last moment, when she reiterated that now we all knew what we had to do. I could only hope I didn't have a new assignment.

On my way out the door, I heard Tish say to Josh: "I'm not happy he's dead, but I can't say I'm sad, either. I never knew I had a bad temper until this case."

It seemed to me that everyone had a bad temper. Some people showed it while other people hid it, and there you had the mess called life.

I trembled, like my brain caught the flu, and I hoped it didn't show.

I made it to my car and sped out of the parking lot. I didn't want anyone to see me. I almost ran someone over and made the sign of the cross when I didn't. I slid over to a loading zone—the only available spot—and closed my eyes. I began to hyperventilate. I forced myself to open my eyes and keep driving, as if I were drunk.

Back at the beach house, I lowered the temperature on the thermostat to fifty degrees. I needed to feel cold air. Breathing in the healing coolness, I turned off my phone again. I closed my eyes and fell into a deep sleep. I had a strange dream in which the Sun People danced on top of murder victims from my real-life cases. My dead family floated in and out of the dream, serving as page-turners from one murder to the next.

I opened my eyes to Myra and an irresistible urge to puke, which I proceeded to do, all over the front of my unfamiliar hospital gown.

"Can't you control yourself?" were the first words I heard. Myra found someone to remove me from the bed, sponge me clean, put me in a fresh gown, change the sheets, and put me back in bed. As I became cognizant of being in a hospital, I said to Myra, "What happened?"

"You're lucky to be alive," Myra decreed. "Both you and the girl."

"What girl?"

"Swann Baumgarten, who did you think? The two of you almost died."

I couldn't remember anything other than falling asleep in bed. Swann came over? News to me.

"Swann? Where is she?" I sat up in bed, even though doing so made my head spin.

Caitlyn and the kids waved at me. "Almost there, Joe," she said, with the vim of a tour guide. While waving, Joe Jr.'s head fell off, but his sister stuck it back on for him.

"Lie down." Myra eased me back onto my pillows. "You can thank Tish and Josh for saving you. From the van, they saw you and the girl"—for some reason Myra kept referring to Swann as the girl—"go into your house, after frolicking or whatever you did on the beach." Myra arched an eyebrow.

"When they kept not getting an answer from your earpiece they broke into the house. The two of you were lying in bed, unconscious. You were wearing your bathing suits. I suppose you could say they got there in the nick of time in more ways than one."

"Not funny, Myra."

"Oh, I heartily agree. Anyway, your stomachs got pumped. The ice cream contained a ton of ground up Zolpidem, a powerful prescription sleeping pill. About ten times the normal dosage of ten milligrams. Or about a hundred milligrams."

"I know what you mean by 'ten times,' Myra." She irritated the hell out of me. But I wanted to learn more about the ice cream. Had it knocked me out when I woke up on the beach? Why was Swann only affected by it the second time?

"I'm sure that sharp tone is the aftermath of the pills, so I won't hold it against you. We've taken all of the food in your house to the lab for testing. You both could've stopped breathing."

"Where's Swann?"

"At headquarters. They're giving her a polygraph. There's a cover story, in case you see her. A business competitor wanted to get you."

"I thought you said she got an overdose, too."

"She did, but she came to hours ago, fit as a fiddle. We brought her in for questioning. It's ten past three in the afternoon." Myra made it sound like I did something wrong by sleeping a lot from an overdose of sleeping pills.

"She's younger than me. She has a lot of energy." In fact, I could picture Swann finding it cool to be questioned by the cops, like on TV. "But if anyone's thinking murder-suicide, you're barking up the wrong tree. I'm sure of it. She's much too full of life. You spend five minutes around her and you feel like you drank an entire pot of coffee."

"Don't you know she's bipolar?"

"If she's bipolar, I wish I were, too."

For a flicker of an instant, I saw genuine hurt in Myra's eyes. "Well, anyway," she continued, "let's not forget that serial killers are often suicidal. You can't afford to lose your objectivity. It's no way to go through life, and it's no way to handle a case."

I sat up on my elbows. "How much do you want to bet that Swann is clean?"

"Nothing. Who's right and who's wrong—who cares? You should know me well enough to know I never play mind games."

As usual, I refrained from saying all I could. "If I'm so lousy at what I do, why didn't you let me be at my cabin in the woods? Alone and happy. Not getting on anyone's nerves."

"I don't at all care for where this conversation is headed. The important thing is that if Swann's cleared from suspicion, someone else doped up the ice cream. It's been sitting in your freezer, after all, and McKenzie could've done it."

"Plus the sooner we solve the case, the sooner IA can swoop down on us. And with Shannon out of the way, the kingdom will be yours for the taking."

"Since you brought it up, Esteban is furious with you. I'm sure you'll be hearing from him. Last time I do a friend a favor."

I ignored what she said, which had become second nature by that time.

"Help me get out of here so I can get to work." I sat up in bed. Though I wobbled, I did my best to hide it. "See? I'm fine."

"I'll tell the doctor you're awake. Oh, I almost forgot. The kids say hi."

As I put on my clothes (which Myra made a point of telling me she brought in herself), she took a phone call and ended it a short time thereafter. She told me that Swann passed the polygraph and left for home and that she fell for the cover story. After a doctor looked me over for about ten seconds, Myra offered me a ride back to my place so I could get my car, and I had no choice but to accept; the hospital wouldn't let me leave in a cab.

"I can hardly wait for my birthday," Myra said as she drove. "I'll act convincingly surprised by whatever the kids planned. I don't like not knowing something. But I totally understand that you need to keep your mouth shut."

In my imagination, I said to Myra, Speaking of keeping your mouth shut. . . But I said, "In all honesty, I have no idea what the final plan is."

"Lisa's a doll, isn't she? I think she's the one most like me."

"That's interesting."

"Why do you say it's interesting? What does that mean?"

I shrugged. "Nothing much."

"I certainly love all my children equally, if that's what you were getting at. I'm not saying Lisa is my favorite, I only meant—"

"Myra, I know what you meant. Christ, give it a rest."

After a few seconds of blissful silence, Myra said, "You never talk about your childhood. Were people mean to you? Were you abused?"

I couldn't believe she had the audacity to ask me this. "Myra, what's it to you?"

"Well, frankly, I've wondered if you grew up around a lot of bad examples. Children, you know, learn to behave by what they see adults do. I'm wondering if maybe it isn't your fault when you get so short with people."

"A pack of wolves raised me." Were that true, I'm sure the wolves would've done a better job than the humans who brought me up.

"Someday you may need someone to confide in. And maybe then you'll think back on how I reached out to you. But I won't be there for you. I'll have moved on."

We both were silent for the rest of the ride.

"Thanks," I said to Myra, as she pulled up at my place. I could tell she wanted to talk more, so I leapt out of the car as soon as it stopped. She drove off as I revved up my own car and hurried to Swann's without calling first.

I wondered how Swann would feel to see me again, but I found out soon enough when I knocked on her storefront door, and she turned the lock shut at the sight of me. Then, through the glass, she yelled at me to go away and never speak to her again.

As a kind of PS, she told me to go eat some ice cream, and that in the future she'd stick to what she called Mr. Vibrator, since at least no one wanted to murder him. I could've lived without this last remark in particular. But I seldom knew how to respond to hostility, and since I felt guilty for almost getting her killed, I went back to my car and drove home.

Yes, I liked her very much, but I knew I should never speak to her again. I'd put her in the unenviable position of restoring my belief in life. My future depended on someone with whom I'd never have a future. I needed to let her marry some rock musician or tattoo artist. She'd die of boredom back at my cabin, and I'd die of insanity if I had to go clubbing with her. I did the right thing by letting her go. Not that she gave me much choice.

Still, it surprised me how it stung to lose Swann. I forgot how much a break-up could hurt, even when the relationship never had a chance to develop.

On my way back to the beach house Shannon called me and said she needed to see me in her office, but not to tell anyone.

## 21

I wanted to talk to Shannon about the placement of the dead men's fingers, so it pleased me to have a private meeting with her. I was hopeful, too, she'd be nice again, like when I first met her. I felt somewhat attracted to her, and I dared to wonder what might've happened between us had she been single. In anticipation of her making herself available to me, in my mind I rehearsed a speech about how I had to refuse her, even though I didn't want to.

Upon driving back to headquarters, I looked both ways to insure no one saw me knock on her office door. Shannon did say no one should know about our meeting. We shook hands as she greeted me. I said, "Confidential meetings are the best kind. You never have to worry that anything will go anywhere."

Shannon laughed. "We understand each other. In fact, we understand each other so well you needn't have said that."

She seated herself behind her desk and gestured for me to sit in a chair.

"I'm very busy," Shannon began, "so I need to get to the point. Or should I say points? Point number one is that you have an impressive record of solving cases. Finding murderers—it's a talent, if you think about it. Those of us who have it can recognize it in each other. Myra, as we both know, doesn't have it. She's closed her share of cases, but she's like one of those kids who gets straight A's only because she's so fanatical about doing her homework. There's no mind there, no creativity."

I smiled. "I had no idea you felt that way about Myra."

"Oh, I feel all kinds of ways about all kinds of people. But that's exactly it. You are far too good at what you do to have done so little for us here."

"I've only been on the case a few days." I felt an awful weight in the pit of my stomach.

"That makes no difference. Numerous people who shall remain nameless wonder if you're on the level. They think that for some reason you're not telling us everything that happens. Or. . ." Shannon took a deep breath. "Or everything you're trying to do. They don't suspect you're the killer or anything idiotic. Just. . . other things."

I forced myself to act calm. "Such as?"

"I'll be honest. They think you're getting too personally involved with Swann—"

"I keep telling you, that's not true," I semi-lied. "It's all part of a larger strategy."

Shannon looked at me with skepticism. "I suppose that's one way of putting it. I got to where I am in the Bureau by developing immunity to bullshit. It's like getting a shot of smallpox to keep you from getting smallpox. But I can't figure out what the hell you're trying to do. You don't seem to care about the money, and you purposefully put yourself in precarious situations. When you almost died—not to sound unsympathetic, but it made us look bad. Someone went so far as to say you have a death wish."

"That's ludicrous. As a matter of fact, I even have a theory—"

"Yes, I heard. The fingers. I'll take that under advisement. I am far more concerned about you. According to Tish and Josh, when the ambulance first arrived you talked in your sleep. You said, 'I'm dead at last, Caitlyn.' Those were your exact words. And then something about bodies chopped into pieces. You've been lazy about using your earpiece. Then there's the problem with the cameras not turning on, when they work perfectly fine. I'm even starting to wonder about Agent Brizinski."

"Who?"

Shannon replied in a reproachful tone. "Remember, the agent I suspended for six months without pay? The one with a pregnant wife? If the cameras were on, he never would've done what he did. And then having to cover it up. There are no words."

"No one knows what may have happened differently," I said. "Once the husband showed up, all bets were off. And anyway, Brizinski shot a possible serial killer and a wife beater."

I thought it wise to make no mention of Esteban Santiago unless Shannon did first.

"What about procedure? Does that ring a bell? You may think you were brave, but true bravery would've been aborting when things fell apart."

Though not about to admit it, I felt sorry for Agent Brizinski. He did, after all, think he saved my life. "I would've had things under control if he followed his orders."

"Under control? Nothing you've done here indicates that you have anything under control. Your behavior is. . . well, it's off. Myra confided to me that you made a pass at her after a meeting. She wondered if you'd be able to handle the sexual tension that goes with the case but decided to give you the benefit of the doubt."

"I wouldn't take what Myra says too seriously." But I couldn't comprehend my anger toward her. I'd make a pass at a hamster before I'd make one at Myra.

Shannon smiled. "I am well aware that Myra exaggerates. But the list of do-nothing screw-ups goes on. Plus you act so nervous, no matter how much I try to reassure you. Years ago I worked at a bank, and we had a temp worker. We kept him on for a while. Then one day he started playing with paper clips and drawing pictures rather than getting his work done. So we let him go. You remind me of him. It's like we're trying to find a serial killer, and you're playing with paper clips and drawing pictures."

I didn't like where things were going. "Say it, Shannon. Whatever it is."

"Do I even need to? The duty has fallen to me to tell you that you're off the case, effective immediately. You did one good thing: finding the vial of Roofies in Willow's shawl. Although I must say, even there the dots aren't connecting the way they should. Looking back, what a terrible idea to put you on the case. You lived in the middle of nowhere, saw no one, and we had you date and drudge up all sorts of heavy-duty emotions. Even those five-minute speed dates can be stressful. Myra never should've come up with the idea, and everyone else, including myself, never should've agreed to it. The stakes are way too high to have anyone on board who isn't one hundred percent with us."

"In that case, it sounds like I'm not to blame, you are. You and Myra."

"Please let's not be childish, Joe. Be accountable for what you did."

I wondered if they fired me so that everything pointed to my incompetence, should IA keep snooping around. But then again, Shannon wouldn't do anything out of the ordinary while IA watched her every move. I wondered how Stu's death would be handled. Would they say he died a hero in a shoot-out? Did they blame me for that, too?

It pained me to admit it, but they fired me because I stank at my job.

After a moment, she added, "Please stop biting your knuckles, Joe."

I hadn't even noticed I'd been doing this. I looked at my tooth-marked hand as if I never saw it before. "Oh, sorry," I replied.

Hardly accustomed to being fired, it pained me to listen to Shannon. The humiliation tore my heart. Life made no sense. Getting fired hurt much more than being suicidal—for lack of a better word.

Caitlyn appeared and said, "It's still not too late. You don't need this stupid case. You're my one true love. I need you."

"What about money?" I finally said.

"You've scarcely worked a week," she replied. "But for your time and trouble we're paying you through to the end of the month. Stu wanted to keep you on, but obviously that's a moot point."

How incredible that so much happened in a few days. Everything got all mixed up. A year, a day, an instant, a decade—it all formed a jumble in my mind.

"I've enjoyed knowing you. It's nothing personal. But we can't afford any more setbacks or mistakes."

She extended her hand, and I shook it. Doing so flooded my heart with a stinging, acidic sensation, but I did it.

"How long do I have to get out of here?" I asked.

"You have seventy-two hours." Shannon frowned. "That came out wrong. We don't want to rush you, so you have three whole days. That sounds better. Numbers are funny that way."

"What about McKenzie?"

"We're on it. She's none of your business anymore."

I, of course, never considered telling her about McKenzie's hidden talents. "I guess I'll start getting my things together."

"That's a good idea. Deal with simpler things you can handle."

That struck me as an odd thing to say. "Does everyone think I'm crazy?"

Shannon laughed some more. "Far from it. If anything, you're too sane. You see too much into things. After what you've been through, no one can blame you. But . . ."

"Go on, say it."

"Well, when something like your family happens to someone, they don't get over it. I hate to say it, but your idea of living alone in your cabin may not be a bad one. I'm no psychiatrist, but it's possible you'll never again do things like you used to. Or at least not without becoming a drunk or an addict or a total shit."

"I've always been shy, though people don't seem to notice."

Shannon looked at the clock. "Interesting though this is, I need to get back to work. Go see my secretary. She'll give you forms to sign, including a confidentiality statement, which I trust you will not be foolish enough to question, given your own liability in things gone wrong. Your paycheck is there, too."

Back at the beach house, I sat on the bed for about a half hour, oblivious to most everything. Weird as it sounds, I thought about Trio, my virtual cat. As I fed the e-creature and it acted happy, I had to fight back the urge to cry. Existence is so fragile.

I stood up and organized my move back to the woods. I enjoyed putting all the suits and dress shirts and neckties and business shoes Myra bought for me into a pile. Next, I proceeded to walk everything to the beach dumpster. Let bums use the clothes. I kept only a pair of jeans, a T-shirt, and a pair of flip-flops.

Per the arrangement Shannon's secretary dictated to me, I still had to call a cab for a ride to the airport, where my ticket back to the cabin would be waiting for me.

I considered saying good-bye to McKenzie, but I figured she'd say something from outer space to show how little she cared. Then I thought more about Agent Brizinski—I didn't know his first name—and stared at the handsome check from the FBI.

Before I talked myself out of it, I called Shannon's secretary and asked her for Agent Brizinski's phone number. She put me on hold, and Shannon's demanding voice came on the line. I'd hoped to avoid talking to her again, but I took a deep breath and said I wanted to make amends with the suspended agent. Shannon sighed and said she shouldn't give me his number, but if it kept me from bothering her again she'd okay it.

I had something important to say but hadn't the nerve to say it out loud. So I texted Agent Brizinski that I got fired if that made him feel better, I'd be willing to testify as to what happened the night of the shootings to clear his name, and that I wanted to give him my check from the FBI. He texted back a couple of minutes later:

*Fk u enjoy yr sleazy $ but want job back & earn honest $*
*lucky13 victims r too many*

I hadn't heard there'd been Victim 13, though there
seemed a certain poetic justice to my leaving at that number.
Still, saying "lucky 13" meant he didn't make a typo. I called
Josh on the pretext of conveying how much I enjoyed
working with him, and all that other crap you're supposed to
say.

"I didn't enjoy working with you," Josh said. "You're a
cool guy. I think you should be a comedian. But the case is a
mess."

"I know. Wow, thirteen victims."

Josh paused. "No. There's only been twelve. You can't
even get that right."

"You're sure? Didn't someone say there were thirteen?"

Josh made a grunt that signaled the profoundest
annoyance. "Of course I'm sure. Is there anything else?"

"Nope."

"Well then, good-bye. Have fun in the woods, or
whatever it is you do."

The second I got off the phone, I texted Brizinski:

*How u know 13 victims? only 12 reported*

I paced the floors for about five agonizing minutes,
waiting for a response from Brazinski. It's frustrating when
inspiration strikes, but you have to wait for someone else
before you can make your move. Create your masterpiece, so
to speak.

I texted the message again, adding:

*I know everything*

Saying I knew everything bore little relation to the truth,
but I had nothing to lose by making the claim. This time, my
phone rang immediately.

"Listen, you fucker," said Brizinski. "You say you know
everything? Prove it. What do you know?"

When in doubt, fake it—that's my motto. "I know the
real reason you killed the McBrides."

"Oh really? And what might that be?"

Good question. I needed to think of something vague yet ominous. "You had to throw a curve ball into the case."

"And why would I do that?"

"Well, uh. . . To make Willow look guilty. With everyone running around like they knew what they were doing, you planted the vial of Roofies in her shawl. You took the purse just to confound things even more."

He laughed at me like a school bully would—to belittle me. "And why would I want to make Willow look guilty?"

"Because," I said, hoping I nailed it, "you're the serial killer. You knew how to clean up after yourself and create suspects. You doped up the ice cream. You knew how to get into the beach house."

He didn't respond.

"Are you still there, Brizinski?"

"Why in fuck's name would I be a serial killer? Why would I want to kill a bunch of dudes?" He said this as if it made sense if he wanted to kill women, which somehow seemed less gay.

"Why does anyone kill anyone? I dunno. You're a closet case. The first guy did something you didn't like, and you had to keep going. Maybe he raped your wife. Maybe he's the father of your baby."

"I don't know anything about Roofies in the shawl or a missing purse or any of the other bullshit you're saying. You are truly a psycho. If anyone's a cocksucker, it's you. And you shut your fucking mouth about my wife."

Murderers often confessed things in stages, so I didn't let his insults stop me. "But you don't deny the murders. You did them."

"Are you forgetting I'm FBI?"

"Well, you sort of are, at this point. And we only know of twelve victims, remember? What's this about a thirteenth?"

"Okay then, twelve. Have it your way. Who else have you told this story to?"

"No one."

"Then what's to stop you from spreading it around?"

"Nothing."

He paused. "Look, I don't have a lot of money. But my wife doesn't need any more bad news before our daughter is born."

"So you did do it?"

"I'm only asking what will shut you up?"

"Not money. But something else. I'm at the beach house right now."

"You mean if I kill someone for you, you'll keep your mouth shut?"

"No, I mean that if you mow my lawn, I'll keep my mouth shut. What do you think I mean? Meet me at the beach house."

Brizinski thought about it. "I'll be there in ten minutes."

In a short while, I could hear someone typing in the security code at the front door. I sat on the living room sofa and waited.

My family skipped in a circle, splattering blood like confetti while singing, "For He's a Jolly Good Fellow."

"Long time no see," I said as Brizinki entered. He wore a T-shirt that bore the logo of a local surfboard shop. He also packed a Smith & Wesson, which I assumed he hoped to surprise me with.

He stepped into the living room. "The door code is the same," he said. "Shannon and her Three Stooges never thought to change it after the McBride thing."

"I guess not."

Brizinski walked toward me.

I did not move. My breathing grew heavy, like after an orgasm.

"Go ahead. It's why you're here." I stared at him with my head held high.

"You really are a nut job. You want me to shoot you?"

"It's a win-win. You're clever enough to not get caught, and I won't be saying too much to anyone once I'm dead. Corpses are funny that way."

Caitlyn and the kids had a bloodied birthday cake with lit candles. They all cheered, "Hooray!"

Stephanie said, "Daddy, I knew you'd come back to us."

"You crazy dumb fuck." I could see his finger squeezing the trigger.

A loudness bore into me, a great force that pushed and then pulled, pain yet beyond pain.

I saw clouds trimmed in gold.

22

"Christ, it's hot," I heard someone say.

"He's awake," a different voice mumbled. "He just said it's hot."

"What the fuck?" My voice sounded like a cough or maybe demonic possession. Had I gone to Hell? What about my family?

"Easy now, Joe. Lie still." I looked up and saw Tish. Did she die, too?

Tish smiled. "Don't worry. Just as Brizinski shot you, I tackled him. He got you in the arm, but you'll be fine."

"You are one lucky SOB." Josh looked down at me. "A split-second difference, and you'd be wearing a toe tag. You owe Tish your life."

"You were right there, too, Josh," said Tish. "We're a team."

I looked around and with my free hand I felt my body. It wasn't Hell, just some damn hospital room. I expected Caitlyn and the kids to appear any moment to call me stupid and worthless, but so far they weren't there.

"Aren't you going to thank Tish?"

"Let him be. He's on a morphine drip, for Chrissake."

"Thanks, Tish," said my hoarse voice, though I wanted to tell her "fuck you."

"I shot Brizinski," Josh said. "He didn't make it."

"Did he confess?"

Josh gave a quizzical look. "Confess to what?"

Tish burst out laughing. "Josh is pulling your leg. Brizinski tried to shoot me just as Josh shot him. Josh saved *my* life, while we're on the general topic. We learned some ugly stuff about Brizinski. He raped his wife to get her pregnant and threatened to kill her if she left him."

"And he sort of confessed," Josh added. "His last words were, 'Good luck finding Number Thirteen.' Good work, Joe."

"Now we see why Myra brought you here," Tish concurred. "Once we find the thirteenth body, it should be a wrap."

"But why were you guys even there?"

Tish said, "Boy, you are out of it. We were in the van, remember?"

I couldn't keep track of the most basic things. The fucking van. Brizinski was accurate when he labeled me psycho. The FBI had it right when they fired me. Why did I keep living when I didn't deserve to? What purpose did I serve anyone? Good people, so much better than me, died every day. Blameless children succumbed to cancer. Yet worthless, stupid me went on existing, like a loud car alarm that won't shut off.

"You don't have to worry about Esteban from IA," Josh said, though in my confused state of mind it took me a second or two to remember him. "Some higher up worked it out. In the Bureau, solving a high profile case is like deodorant."

"That's great to know."

"You'll be out of here in time for Myra's birthday party," said Tish.

"Lonnie brought your gift. It's an old book, if you want to read it." Josh handed me a shopping bag from a metal hospital chair. "He included a birthday card for you to sign and said he'll be by to gift wrap it if you'd like."

"He even thought to bring you the computer tablet from the beach house, in case you get bored," Tish said.

Oh, great. Myra's birthday present. And of course the party. "Very kind of Lonnie. Tell him thanks."

Tish said, "They say you can judge a person by how their kids turn out. Myra gets an A-plus as a human being."

That hurt much more than my bullet wound, but I let it pass.

"Thanks so much for stopping by, guys. I need to rest some more." I kept sneaking looks at the morphine drip. I wondered if I could turn it up to max and OD.

"We can take a hint. We know when we're not wanted," said Josh.

"You know he's only joking," Tish added.

I kind of said ha-ha-ha.

"Oh, and Shannon said to tell you she's sorry," said Josh. "You should be getting a much fatter check any day now."

"Through some amazing coincidence, will that fat check coincide with my agreeing not to sue for wrongful termination?"

They both chuckled. "You're really a card," Josh said.

As soon as they left the room, I checked out the morphine drip. Just my luck, I couldn't reach the knobs. Hospitals kept you alive only when you didn't want them to.

Resigned to my fate for the time being, I got the antique book out of the bag. I figured I might as well look at what I was giving Myra for her birthday. Published in 1875, it bore the curious title of *Shadow Language*. It looked to be in mint condition, other than the yellowing of the pages. I opened the book and read:

"This being the true account of the heinous bondage experienced by my twin brother Emmett and me, and how Shadow Language saved our lives."

The Welsh author, Emma Sleet-Badger, made me think of Annabelle Sleet, author of *Supernatural or Psychotic?* But stranger coincidences have happened. The tale told by Emma captured my attention much more:

She and her twin brother Emmett were orphaned at age ten. A considerable inheritance awaited them upon their eighteenth birthdays. However, their legal guardian, a magistrate referred to by the pseudonym of "Clarence Creed," sought to have them both declared insane by locking them up and hoping to drive them mad through this "heinous bondage." Their sizeable estate featured a home with twin spires at each end. Emma was locked in one tower room, her brother Emmett in the other. Though they were fed and given "normal amenities of daily living," they could not leave their rooms. At night, under gaslight, their bodies made silhouettes upon the window shades. Thus, they were able to devise a code of communication with their hands upon the shades, which each twin could see from its respective tower. They came to call this their Shadow Language.

They were rescued just before turning eighteen, which sounded to me like a classic Victorian melodrama come to life. "Mr. Creed," the reader is told, "cowardly disappeared rather than face the justice of Her Majesty's Court." Emmett committed suicide after turning eighteen, but Emma insisted in her book that this occurred because of "an unusually dreary winter." Emma said she remained "content to live my days honoring my brother's memory, with fond memories of the Shadow Language that kept us so verily close to one another that we became but One Heart, even while locked away in our demonic prisons."

The book contained illustrations of the hand configurations of the various letters of the alphabet.

On the computer tablet, I did a few online searches. It would appear that Annabelle and Emma were related, albeit about five times removed. They had descendants in both Britain and the States. (However, I still could not find out what happened to Annabelle.) I also learned that the case of the Sleet-Badger Twins received a fair amount of local attention in its day.

Contrary to Emma's book, no magistrate did anything to them. It appeared that she and her brother chose to stay in seclusion in their respective tower rooms; no one knew why. Emmett did die by his own hand at eighteen, which inspired the writing of the book. Emma died of pneumonia in 1876, a year after the book's release. No one knew for certain if she and her brother ever used Shadow Language, but it became something of a cult-like pursuit among young people of the time, spreading south from Flintshire (where the twins lived) to London among some of the elite as a kind of party game.

I looked again at the photos of the dead speed daters lying with their hands across their chests. I only had the first ten photos on my tab. But I had enough to make sense of the placement of the fingers.

I experienced the peculiar and narcissistic elation of a detective who discovered something major, as if all the murder and mayhem occurred just so I could solve the puzzle.

When Lonnie came to my room a short while later, I thanked him. We talked a little about the possibility of his running for public office. He offered to pick me up the next day when I got discharged from the hospital, and drive me to his mother's birthday party in the hotel reception room.

Then came the hard part. I had to call McKenzie. When she hung up on me, I called back. When she hung up again, I texted her that if she'd at least listen to me, I'd make a hearty donation to the environmental cause of her choice.

"What is it, Carlo?" she said upon answering the phone.

"I wanted to see how you were."

"How do you think I am? I'm lousy. Completely mortified by how I behaved the other day. Did you call to make fun of me?"

"Certainly not. In fact, I wanted to ask if you'd be my date tomorrow at a birthday party."

She didn't say anything, but I could hear her breathing. Then I heard a dial tone.

I called back three more times before she answered the call.

"Why do people like you think people like me have no feelings?"

"Of course you have feelings. Everyone does. I'd like you to come with me tomorrow. There will be nice people. I promise no one will make fun of you."

"You just want me to be. . . like that again. Am I the entertainment?"

"Not at all. And if you're truly uncomfortable, I promise I'll take you right back to your home."

"When did you last feed Trio?" she asked, as if all the same conversation. My presumed negligence toward Trio became, in her mind, part of the larger whole of people making fun of her.

"I'm feeding him as we speak," I said, telling the truth. "Look, I'll double the donation."

After a pause, McKenzie said, "Oh, all right, if it's so important to you. Whose birthday is it?"

"A nice woman named Myra. She has three nice children. I'll tell you all about it tomorrow."

I almost forgot to do one of the most important things: I called Myra and told her that I invited McKenzie to her party, everyone must call me Carlo Rizzo, and no one but me should mention anything about the case or even the FBI. You'd maybe have to know Myra to understand how I could say all this while she still insisted that the party be treated as a surprise.

I studied the book and the photos some more and fell asleep like a baby. My family continued to leave me alone. I had a dream about the Sun People, only for the first time something different happened. I learned that if you touched them, they deflated like popped balloons. As if playing a crude computer game, I deflated them all.

Then the weather turned gray and intense, the waves angry and twisted and full of wrath. I seemed to be in the midst of a hurricane, but I knew no fear. Instead, I never felt more alive. The wind blew fierce and uncensored, and I felt secure and at one with the havoc.

23

I had Lonnie pick me up at the hospital with enough time for us to get McKenzie and still arrive at the party right on the dot, so that I wouldn't have anxiety about being late. Or maybe even arrive a little early. Old habits die hard.

Though I didn't care what I wore to Myra's birthday bash, I knew she'd be offended if I showed up in a T-shirt, shorts, and flip-flops. Some of the clothes I carried to the dumpster the other day were still there; I assumed homeless people had little use for suits and ties. I found a blazer, dress slacks, a wrinkled white shirt, and an uncomfortable pair of wing tip shoes. My arm no longer required a sling, so I wouldn't stand out at the party.

Lonnie arrived on time, as if a sign of respect.

While we buckled ourselves into his rented car, I said, "I read through some of that book, *Shadow Language.* Very interesting. Thanks again."

"I don't like old stuff. It gives me the creeps knowing that someone dead once owned and touched whatever it is."

"It must be fun shopping for gifts for your mother. Or I guess sitting on her furniture."

He laughed. "My mom is like a cat we had once. Any habit it developed guaranteed to be a pain in the ass, but also part of its charm."

I told Lonnie the story of Emma and Emmett Sleet-Badger.

"Just goes to show people have always been weird," Lonnie commented. "I kind of like the idea of communicating across the towers with their hands. I feel that way sometimes, don't you?"

"How do you mean?"

"Gee, I dunno. Just how hard it is to communicate with people. Like everyone is only a shadow talking to another shadow. I can't explain it very well, but I think you know what I mean. It's the kind of thing Mom wouldn't get. She's very concrete. Sometimes . . . "

"Please, say what you were about to say."

He took a deep breath, as if fearing he'd be punished. "She doesn't really know me, know any of us. We get good grades. We do all these things. But she doesn't pay attention to us. Not genuine attention. I'm probably not making any sense."

"Actually, you're making a lot of sense." I almost told him about my own shadowy dead family, but as happened so often I didn't say what I wanted to say. Who knew how Lonnie would react, and anyway the three of them still hadn't been showing up since Brizinksi shot me. I did not wish to tempt Fate. In my obsession with wanting to die for them, I only now realized how much they terrified me whenever they appeared. Though it made me guilty even to think it, I hoped they wouldn't reappear.

The GPS led us to McKenzie's apartment building, where she already waited outside. She wore her brown skirt, the same one she wore at the speed date. I guessed it to be her idea of festive.

I told Lonnie, "Remember, I'm Carlo Rizzo, real estate developer. Oh, and don't mention anything about *Shadow Language*. Trust me, it will all make sense." I got out of the car to greet her.

"McKenzie, how wonderful to see you again."

She looked over at Lonnie in the driver's seat and turned paler than usual. "You didn't tell me someone else would be in the car."

"Lonnie? He's just the son of Myra. You remember, the woman whose birthday it is. I assure you he's harmless."

"Carlo, you told me that you were coming to pick me up. I did not expect to have to ride with someone else."

It took about five minutes of coaxing to get McKenzie in the car. Plus I offered to triple my contribution to her favorite environmental cause, which turned out to be campaign to save a rare species of sea turtle.

"Did you remember to feed Trio?" she asked as she climbed in the back seat.

"Of course." Actually, I'd forgotten but I knew it would in some strange way reassure her if she thought I had.

Lonnie and I tried to make conversation in the car, but McKenzie made only one comment: "I need one of my homeopathic allergy pills."

We entered the hotel reception room that the kids booked for the occasion. They ordered quite a spread of unfamiliar finger foods and engaged the services of a hotel bartender. Laura and Lisa were in fancy dresses that were unrevealing and understated. I wondered if all three kids practiced abstinence before marriage, but decided it rude to ask. Still, they seemed like sex workers beside the uptight McKenzie. Each sister kissed my cheek.

When I introduced them to McKenzie, they extended their hands but McKenzie crossed her arms and lowered her head. She managed to mutter hello.

"You're the first ones here," Lisa said, full of party spirit. "Mom should be arriving soon. We had Shannon tell her it's a special reception for someone else. Like she doesn't already know. It's totally screwy."

"Carlo—oh, and McKenzie," said Lonnie, "just wait until you see my mom open her gifts. She's like Old Faithful. If she really likes the gift, she'll say, 'Oh my God, you're killing me.' If she thinks it's only so-so, she'll say, 'How thoughtful.' And if it's a gift she already has since she has so much old stuff already, she'll say, 'My, isn't that quaint?'"

His sisters laughed in agreement. Lonnie said, "Can I get you folks anything to drink?"

"No, thank you," said McKenzie. "I'll wait until I get home to have some natural water. I do not pollute my body for the sake of capitalism."

I said, "I'm on painkillers. A Coke is about as wild and crazy as I should get."

"A Coke? Really, Carlo. Think of what that does to your intestines and digestive track. You won't have a normal bowel movement for days."

"Do you work, McKenzie?" Laura asked, with an obvious wish to change the subject.

Lonnie walked to the bar area and returned with a plastic glass of Coke on ice.

Lisa said, "By the way, Carlo. I had a strange dream last night. Some unseen voice told me to strangle you. I started doing it, even though I didn't want to. Then I woke up."

"And it's a good thing you did," I said. "I wouldn't be much fun strangled."

Laura disagreed. "I heard somewhere that in dreams, death is a sign of rebirth."

"Or that you ate too much spicy food," Lonnie added. I could see he annoyed his older sister, but she let it pass.

"I can't wait until Jasper comes," Laura said.

"I look forward to meeting Lieutenant Colonel St. Cloud," I said.

McKenzie looked aghast. "Lieutenant Colonel *who*? What kind of party is this, a bunch of fascist government war mongers?"

Lisa looked ready to say something angry on her sister's behalf, but I held up my hand. "McKenzie is a pacifist. She's very sensitive about these things."

McKenzie's face turned red. "I can speak for myself, Carlo."

Fortunately, Shannon arrived with her husband, so I used them as a distraction. "Look, Shannon's here," I said. After introducing me to her husband, Shannon winked, as if to say sorry and thank you. I noticed over the years that many people found it difficult to apologize. I never understood why.

I introduced them to McKenzie, but she didn't say anything. She looked away. In spite of myself, I felt a little guilty manipulating her to come. I knew all too well how she felt not knowing anyone. But my plan had to be executed.

Soon Shannon and her husband nursed vodka martinis. Tish came with a date, as did other agents whom I'd seen at the Bureau. Josh arrived with his wife. McKenzie chatted with them for quite some time, though I didn't know what about.

All the FBI agents knew to call me Carlo and not to discuss the case, which meant I had nothing to say to any of them. As always happened at parties, I stood by myself, hopeless as to what to do next. The rest of the room grew electric with party chatter.

Out of pity, Laura did her best to have a conversation with me, consisting of the man she planned to marry.

She opened the shiny clutch she carried. "Here's a picture of us together."

I looked at it and saw Laura with a young man standing in front of the Pentagon.

"He's adjusted to his prosthetic legs very well," she said. "Honestly, you hardly even notice it."

"That's wonderful. Have you set the date for the marriage?"

Before Laura could answer, Lonnie shouted, "Mom's on her way up. C'mon, everybody, let's move to the back of the room and get ready to yell surprise."

For maybe a minute no one spoke, save for the occasional cough. I heard someone walking on the tiles in the foyer. When the sound stopped, I assumed the person stepped on to the reception hallway carpet.

Caitlyn's voice said, "This is no party, this is hell." But I could not see her. Were they coming back full force? Would they hate me for being alive? I tried my best to ignore the sinking feeling I got in the pit of my gut. It's strange how mercurial the mind can be. One moment you're fine, and the next you. . . well, you wish you were dead.

McKenzie said, "This is no party, this is hell." She wore a vacant expression. No one seemed to notice.

Lonnie turned to direct the group and mouthed the words, "One, two, three . . ."

Just as everyone shouted, "Surprise," a decorative candle on the buffet fell over and ignited the tablecloth. In a matter of seconds, the refreshment table burst into flames, some of which looked like human forms—to me, anyway. Sparks ignited the window curtains.

Myra screamed upon entering the room and ran to her children who, like the rest of us, ran toward the doors. An alarm sounded and a computerized voice instructed us to leave the room.

"Oh, fuck you," I heard someone say. Some people coughed from the smoke. McKenzie stared at the fire. Lonnie grabbed her arm, but she kept looking backward at the flames.

Myra had fallen onto the floor. As I helped her up, she said, "Damn it, this is my birthday party."

From out of nowhere, powerful water sprinklers turned on. By the time I led Myra out of the room, we were soaked. The smoke that irritated her eyes made it look as if she'd been crying.

The fire didn't spread beyond the one reception room, but the party appeared to be over before it started. Guests left in a hurry; some talked about going out to dinner. I couldn't help wondering if many people saw the fire as a convenient excuse not to celebrate Myra's birthday.

In the busyness of firefighters and other people coming and going in the hotel lobby, I turned to Myra and said, "Let's move the party to the beach house. Just your closest friends."

Her face glowed. "That sounds lovely. But I need to go to my room and change." I thought she looked better in wet hair and clothing, not as stiff as her normal appearance.

"Carlo, I should go home," McKenzie said. "I don't know these people. The smoke upset the magnesium balance of my body. I can feel it."

"I'm sorry to hear that," I said. "Please stay with us. The ocean air will make you feel better. It will just be a few of us."

She frowned, deep in thought. "All right, but only for a short while. The sea is rich in magnesium, so that may help. Not that I ever go into the water. UV rays are deadly. But I can do deep breathing exercises with the air."

Laura told me she got a text that her boyfriend's plane had been delayed, and he wouldn't be able to make it. "I'm so sorry. I really wanted you to meet him."

I smiled for her sweetness. She sounded disappointed on general principle but needed to project her feelings to someone. I thought it touching that she chose me.

"I'm sure I can meet him another time."

She cried a little. "I just love him so much."

I found myself giving her a hug. Except for lying in bed with Swann, I couldn't remember the last time I hugged someone. It felt sort of okay.

Myra and her kids, Shannon and her husband, Josh and his wife, and Tish and her date, were rounded up to join McKenzie and me at the beach house. Despite the pandemonium, everyone retrieved their birthday gifts to bring along, though a few had gotten wet.

In a short while, we all gathered in the beach house living room. I changed out of my wet clothes and back into my casual wear. We ordered some pizzas and while we ate and drank beer, I withstood an uncomfortable interlude of Myra reflecting on her birthday and raving about how magnificent her children were. McKenzie criticized us for ordering pizza and drinking beer, but no one commented on her remarks.

"Now it's time to open my gifts," Myra said. I had a passing thought that in her view this had to be the happiest statement possible for one to utter.

Lonnie looked over at me, having predicted how Myra would react to each gift. She first opened her present from Lisa—an elaborate vintage top of a staircase newel.

Myra hugged her daughter and kissed her check. "Oh Lisa, you're killing me." Exactly as Lonnie prophesied.

The middle-aged birthday girl next picked up a tiny box that had gotten wet. "The ink ran. I can't read who it's from."

Laura said, "It's from Jasper and me."

Upon seeing the antique cameo, Myra said, "I'm just being killed with love and kindness today." Laura helped her mother clasp it around her neck. "Oh, Mom," she said, hugging her mother.

Myra found Tish's gift of a second edition obscure Victorian novel to be thoughtful, as she did the gas lamp from Shannon and her husband.

Myra said, "I just realized all the women's gifts were opened first. I guess I'm just a natural Victorian." Everyone felt compelled to chortle.

The only remaining gifts were, Josh's picture of some kind, Lonnie's large box and my small book. All three gifts sported the same wrapping paper. I guessed that Lonnie wrapped Josh's gift, too.

She opened the gift from Josh and his wife, an elaborate "Home Sweet Home" tapestry that did no better than being deemed quaint. Lonnie mouthed to me that his mother already had a million of them.

"Do Joe's next," Lonnie said. "It's the small one."

I would've preferred she opened Lonnie's first but didn't say so. My plan could still work out fine.

"*Shadow Language*," Myra said upon unwrapping the present. "I've never heard of this book." She started thumbing through it. "Carlo, I might as well drop dead right here and now. It looks fascinating." I winced as she kissed me almost on the mouth, but I hoped it didn't show.

I said, "Yes, Myra, it is a fascinating story." I once again shared the tale of Emma and Emmett Sleet-Badger. However, I made a point of not mentioning Annabelle Sleet's *Supernatural or Psychotic?,* so as not to compromise my credibility.

"They sound psychotic," Josh's wife said. "How sad."

Josh himself added, "It's a BP story. Before Prozac."

Shannon's husband laughed, but several women found Josh's remark insensitive.

I looked at McKenzie, who'd been sitting with her arms crossed in a corner of the room. "You know, McKenzie, the Sleet-Badger clan has relatives in the states. In fact—"

Myra said, "Sleet. That Annabelle Sleet person who wrote that nutty book."

"Uh, yes, she is related," I continued. "It would seem that so is the wealthy Schultz family. Like many such families, they probably take good care of family heirlooms."

McKenzie grew cross. "Why do you keep looking at me, Carlo? And what about my family?" Estrangement did not prevent her snooty family pride from appearing as needed.

"The *Shadow Language* alphabet," I replied. "The positions of the victims' fingers one by one spelled out, 'I am so lonesome.' We're still missing the last 'e' of the thirteenth victim, but we have the general idea."

Myra flustered and said, "I knew all along the placement of the fingers mattered. I only acted stubborn to. . . to make you work harder on finding the answer. Good work, Joe. And let's all remember that if I hadn't brought him into the case, we wouldn't know this."

But everyone ignored her.

McKenzie put her hands over her ears. "I don't know what you're talking about."

Josh said, "But Brizinski—"

"You told me he said good luck finding the last victim. He could've been mistaken or confused. He never said he murdered them. He was a bastard, but not a murderer. Willow was. She had the Roofies hidden in her shawl. I guess her purse was too obvious. But there was a second killer." I turned to McKenzie. "I hope you're not too disappointed I'm still alive."

"What are you talking about? Why is everyone looking at me?"

Shannon read McKenzie her rights and helped her remain standing as her knees buckled. She turned to me, narrowing her eyes behind her tortoise shell glasses. "A boy and a girl on swings," she said. "All bloody and rotting.

They're saying, 'You said we broke your heart. You said you don't even know us.' Now they're laughing."

Everyone looked at me, but I didn't know what to say. I could not see or hear my family, so I didn't know if McKenzie saw them at that very moment, or if she recalled them from the other day to scare me.

I said, "I have no idea what she means."

"Death consists of many phases," McKenzie added, as if explaining how to fix a paper jam in a photocopy machine. "My God, I can't believe I socialized with a bunch of cops. Is Carlo even your real name?"

I responded without answering her question. "I feel sad for you, McKenzie. You have special gifts. You could have put them to good use." I had many questions for her, but they could wait.

She cleared her throat as she straightened her glasses. "The air is polluted. The electrons are out of control. They're doing something to my brain. Nothing's been proven about what you call my special gifts. Life has no special gifts."

"Nice meeting you," I said. A serial killer deserved cruelty.

"I wouldn't exactly say we met," McKenzie replied.

Shannon took out a pair of plastic cuffs but decided not to use them as she put her arm around McKenzie's shoulder and led her out the door and into her car. Shannon's husband went with them.

"Well, thanks for solving the case again, Joe," Tish said. "I guess having been molested by her uncle. . . and if mental illness runs in her family. . ."

"And she told us the truth in her secret code," said Josh. "Have you ever seen anyone so lonely?"

I said, "Brizinski died over nothing."

"I beg to differ," said Josh. "His wife actually thanked us. She tried to leave him but he found her. He tried to kill you and Tish. He could've been charged with murder for killing Willow and her husband."

"Yeah, I guess so." But I still felt bad. It occurred to me
I didn't even know his first name but decided not to ask. It
seemed a dumb thing to do.

For a few minutes, no one spoke.

Finally Lonnie said, "C'mon, Mom. Open my gift."

"You're right, dear. It is still my birthday, after all." But
Myra's *joie de vivre* struck me as more forced than usual as she
walked over to the large box. I guessed it to be about three
feet in height, width, and length. As Myra took her time
unwrapping the box, I saw that Laura looked upset.

I took out my phone and got online to do a search for
Lieutenant Colonel Jasper St. Cloud, to find a photo or
something to cheer her. I knew something was odd when the
resulting links concerned an officer who served in Iraq and
died from complications following the amputation of his legs.

I looked at Laura again. She told me she missed Jasper
but that could have at least two meanings . . .

Myra opened the box. Everyone gathered around to
watch as one layer of tissue paper led to another and another.
At the bottom of the box was her gift from Lonnie.

It was a second copy of *Shadow Language*.

Lonnie burst out laughing and put his hand on my
shoulder. "I thought it would be fun if we gave the same gift.
Mom can always auction off the extra copy on eBay. I got
them both a few weeks ago. I hate sitting on surprises."

Laura and Lisa looked at their brother in something like
a state of shock. Then they looked at me. I glanced at the
information on Jasper St. Cloud on my cell phone. . .

I could tell Myra experienced a deep wound to her soul,
though she tried not to show it. Imperfection had reared its
ugly face upon her birthday gifts. "Gee, Lonnie, I guess
you're right, though you know I don't like to sell—"

"That dream you told me about, Lisa," I interrupted.
"About Katy. About dying. How smart to make it not quite
Caitlyn. That would've been too obvious. But the ax—you
remembered to mention the ax. Or this other dream about
strangling me. Or excuse me, not strangling me. Just a little

extra seasoning, I suppose. Your mom all but called me psychotic. Why not help my craziness along, to prevent me from figuring anything out? Or even if I did, who'd believe a lunatic? Were you hoping I'd kill myself?"

Myra slapped my face. "How dare you talk to my daughter like that."

I ignored her and stepped toward her kids. I could feel my nerves tremble with an inner fire as the words came to me faster than I could say them.

"Lisa, your mom considers me a good detective—no, a great one. Your mom exaggerates. But a great detective, even a good one, could figure things out. Your brother and sister put you up to it. They saw I had a book about. . . about the supernatural, okay? So maybe I had some crazy idea about communing with my dead family. Maybe it would drive me over the edge.

And Laura, did you resent men who were still alive when Jasper gave his life for his country? Did you think that if you said he was still alive, no one would connect the dots? But why these men? Lonnie, when you gave your mom a second copy of the book, were you trying to see how far you could push it without getting caught? Do you think you're smarter than everyone? Is that all it's about? The perfect crime that makes the FBI look like dumb shits. But you're no genius, either. You just said you got *Shadow Language* a few weeks ago. The other night you told me you bought it that day."

Lonnie smiled, but I could see him getting shaky. "I bought the first copy a couple of weeks ago, and then went back for the second."

"So you didn't just arrive here a few days ago? You've been here a few weeks at least. Long enough to be here for the first killing?"

"Hell no. The killings already started. I mean. . . the other day. . . "

"You say they already started? So Willow was the murderer. But then along came a copycat. Or should I say three copycats? Did you kill more of the men than Willow did?"

Laura interjected, "Look, we had our reasons. You should be thanking us. The men we killed weren't just any men. They belonged to a secret group—"

"Shut up," Lisa shouted.

"They were terrorists," Laura continued, her voice gaining momentum. "All seven of them that we killed. My father died for our country. My fiancé did. How could those men betray their country? What right had they to live?"

"I told you, shut up," Lisa repeated.

I said, "So you figured you could just copy the MO of the original killer, and no one would notice. You know a lot about DNA and crimes scenes from your mother. In fact, she trained you all too well without realizing it. When Willow and I walked on the beach, she said, 'You don't even know the people you affect the most. Total strangers want to be just like you.' It must have been the last thing she expected—to have her mind set on killing a man who someone else ended up murdering.

"In her unbalanced way, she felt sorry for the three of you. Not that she knew who you were. The only missing piece is how she got away with murder if her husband had her shadowed."

Myra said, "Is this a joke? I appreciate getting my leg pulled as much as the next person, but kids—and you, too, Joe. Please, this isn't funny." We could see her heart breaking right before our eyes. Damn it, I felt sorry for her. She got her comeuppance for a lifetime career as a control freak, and a primitive part of my nature told me to celebrate. Yet all I felt was sad.

"They belonged to an ultra-left-wing party," Lonnie hissed, his face a deep crimson. "That's all we needed to know. These kinds of people are always terrorists. They want to destroy America. We saw a file about it snooping around the FBI last semester break. Mom's hands were tied, so we left school to come here and take care of them. We're patriots. And we're smarter than all of you. And we're better people. Our mom raised us the right way."

Myra put her hands to her face in horror. Tish tried to touch her, but Myra flinched.

Josh said to his wife, "Please, wait in the car, honey."

"No way," she replied. "I have to hear this."

Myra started crying hard, but she managed to say, "I had a file on one man. And we didn't even know for certain about the terrorism, so I wasn't supposed to mention it."

Laura said, "We didn't want to get the Bureau in trouble. We saw that he went to a speed-dating service, and I hacked into its files."

"We saw the first victims, and figured the long hair would continue to make a good MO," Lonnie said. "Keep everyone thrown off. We don't know what Willow had against the guys she did in. Maybe they were subversives, too. No good hippie left-wing anti-Americans. Dad taught us to be mindful of such people."

He reached into his pocket and swallowed a few Xanax. "No one noticed the fingers until you did, Joe. I have more respect for you than ever. And I sincerely mean that."

"We did it for Dad and for Jasper." Laura stood up, hand over her heart, and started reciting the Pledge of Allegiance.

Lisa said, "Damn it, will you two just shut up?"

Lonnie grinned. "So we fooled you all. Especially you, Mom. Pretty funny, huh?"

"I knew about it, but I didn't kill anybody," said Lisa. "Honest."

Laura finished with her pledge. "But you agreed to find out the code to the beach house to drug the ice cream. Don't try to play Little Miss Innocent."

They sounded like they disagreed about an incident at a family picnic when they were little kids.

"But I still didn't kill anyone."

"Would you stop saying that?" Lonnie inquired. "It's really getting annoying. Jeez, the bratty youngest kid. Always so spoiled. Thinks she can get away with anything."

Laura added, "It used to be such a pain in the ass when you'd go running to Mom to tattle on us."

Without her fake perkiness, Myra was as listless as a blank sheet of paper. "You sent the e-mails, too, I suppose?" she asked, to no one specific. "You called your own mother a—a cunt."

I found it remarkable that this would be the one heinous act she commented on, but I reminded myself not to be too harsh a judge.

Myra collapsed on the floor. She seemed catatonic. We called for an ambulance and for a squad car. None of the kids put up any resistance to being arrested.

As they lifted Myra into the ambulance, I asked her if I could do anything to help.

She lifted her head and looked at me without blinking. "Why would I need you? My children know they can come to me with anything."

## 24

It took the FBI months to sort things out. A thirteenth victim never turned up. Laura, Lisa and Lonnie insisted they knew of no other victims, so either they lied, Brizinski couldn't add, or Willow killed someone whose body never was found. But that a top homicide agent such as Myra never reported the mental illness that ran in her family, that people committed suicide or got committed and that no one noted this on a background check, did not look good.

The case got buried in a hurry, and all three kids agreed to lifetime commitments in separate mental facilities. In theory they were eligible for parole, but I imagined such a day would never come. I tried but failed to find out if their victims were terrorists or even just left-wing—or if the whole thing was a delusion. Myra took her second and final retirement from the Bureau. Her last official act was to declare that she stole Willow's purse at the crime scene, just to throw things off. She claimed to already know her kids were in trouble, and so like any good mother, she'd do anything to protect them.

I of course did not believe her story. I think the purse simply got lost.

I have no idea if Myra visited her children, and if so, how often. Nor do I have any idea if she ever engaged in any self-reflection on what her children did or why. I did, however, get a postcard, telling me that she loved "gorgeous" Jamaica and that "life has a way of working itself out." She drew a little smiling face next to her name.

I forced myself to send a postcard back expressing pleasure in hearing she. . . I started to write "healed," but thought she'd get defensive at the suggestion that she had any problems whatsoever. Instead I wrote I was pleased she loved Jamaica.

I never found out for certain how Willow knew about Shadow Language, though I did find out she had Welsh ancestry, and through the internet I learned that the small Shadow Language cult still existed. I'll also never know what word she planned to use, since her killings ended with the fifth victim: *I am so—*. Lonnie and Laura made it the word, "lonesome," but maybe Willow thought she was so something else.

McKenzie got released from custody the same day they brought her in. The incident left her traumatized, but before Josh left the Bureau, he told me he ran into her and she told him her doctor put her on anti-anxiety drugs. According to Josh, she acted much more like a normal person. Maybe it all happened for the better. I have no idea if the meds affected her apparent supernatural ability, but she never wanted to use it, anyway. I e-mailed her an apology. She never replied.

Josh also told me that the detective that Chris McBride hired to follow his wife admitted to having an affair with Willow, and helped cover her tracks. He did it because they were supposed to have fallen in love. When he realized she used him, he told Chris she was screwing around. The detective struck some hushed up plea bargain for obstruction of justice and evidence tampering.

I later heard that Shannon, Tish, and Josh all took early retirements. The McBride cover-up came back to bite them in the ass after all.

I didn't know for certain if at least some of my blackouts were a product of my bizarre state of mind. For whatever it meant, they stopped happening once I moved out of the beach house. I remembered that the first time we had ice cream in bed, Swann didn't eat any herself, which explained why she passed out only the second time.

Out of curiosity, I asked an agent who still worked for the Bureau to look at the file on Swann's husband. A week or so later, he called to tell me that all evidence pointed to the death having been an accident. I thought so, too, but I wanted to hear it from an objective outsider.

I stopped dreaming about the Sun People. I never found out what happened to Annabelle Sleet.

My family did not revisit me after that brief moment with Caitlyn's voice at Myra's party. I found myself thinking of a prisoner on death row who just found out the governor approved a stay of execution. I agreed to work on the case in order to die peacefully in my sleep. I even experienced genuine frustration when Willow failed to do as she intended.

Yet I couldn't kill myself, and maybe that told me something. Even when I wanted to die I still wanted to live. Maybe life, even at its worst, is worth living. At times the percentages were 51 to 49, but even that was enough to make me hold on as long as possible.

I even had some nutty moments with Swann that I enjoyed a little. She reminded me that life had some good things going for it. I knew I'd never see her again, but I hoped she knew somehow that I appreciated meeting her.


When I returned to my cabin, it was hard to believe I'd only been gone such a short time. I shaved my head. I wanted to get rid of all that dyed hair. I got a mutt from the nearest dog pound, and named him Ralph Jr. In exchange for a donation to an animal shelter, I arranged for Trio's webmaster to "adopt" him. As much as I hated admitting it, I missed him a little. That little dance he did—he had such a delicate existence.

A few days after returning home, something happened.

I thought about my family and started laughing.

I remembered some stupid argument the kids had at the dinner table over who had greater strength, Spiderman or the Incredible Hulk? I saw the four of us sitting around the table like a normal family, passing the mashed potatoes and green beans, and—well, yes, maybe being happy. Then I thought about Caitlyn, and when we first started dating. I don't remember the movie we saw, but as we took our seats and settled in, she smiled at me and said that she turned down a date with someone else because she'd rather be with me.

I don't know why remembering happy things should've made me cry, but it did. I cried for my wife, son, and daughter for two solid weeks. Or to be more accurate, I cried for two weeks when not shooting targets and breaking things to vent my rage. At the end of the two weeks, I made burial mounds for each of them next to Ralph, even though there were no bodies or trinkets to bury.

I swear I saw the three of them linger over the mounds, whole again, the way they'd been for all but the final minutes of their lives. "Hi, Dad," my kids said, while Caitlyn beamed.

"Go on now," I said. "Scoot. Skedaddle."

Call it coincidence, call it psychological, or call it mystical. But the horrific visitations from my family didn't come back.

In the spring, I grew colorful flowers on the mounds.

But I never could bring myself to celebrate my birthday again.

I deleted my e-photo album of happy families. I wished the people well, but whatever I acquired from them I no longer needed. As for wanting to die in my sleep or hoping that the world would end, I'd like to say I had some profound moment of clarity after which I never felt this way again. But that's not how it happened.

Instead, I found happiness in small things, like the day in the park when I saw a blizzard looming over the horizon. Loss was a part of each day, but something magical happened in flickering moments: the crackle of a log in the fireplace or the wingspan of an owl silhouetted against the moon. Sometimes I drove into town for supplies, as opposed to texting for them. I said hello to local people or commented on the weather and the football scores, and I didn't mind it much. Sometimes it even made me feel better.

For reasons I never understood, people I didn't like always were drawn to me. I think I figured out why. They were inviting me to be part of life with all its flaws, as if asking me to taste an unfamiliar food or listen to a new kind of music. To let the imperfection of humanity touch my life.

As a cop, as a husband, and as a father—or even as a son—
the death tolls were high, and I wished with all my might that
the deaths could be taken back. But surviving everything
somehow cleansed my life. I felt clean.

As for ghosts, or whatever you'd call them, I realized it
didn't matter if they were real or not. McKenzie's strange
actions lent credence to the notion they existed, and
sometimes I let myself believe that Caitlyn started the hotel
fire. But what matters most is sensing the spirit in things, no
matter how small. It's in whispers or the blink of an eye, so
fleeting and yet that's what makes it special. Looking back, I
sensed something spirit-like in Caitlyn slipping off her
negligee in the dark before we made love to conceive our
kids. Anytime something lives and dissolves at the same time,
there is spirit. Maybe you've experienced these momentary
glimpses into otherness, too. I think that Ralph Jr. did in the
cabin at night, barking at nothing in the fireplace.

Shannon told me that solving murders took talent. I
knew I possessed this talent, but unless something changed, I
doubted that I'd ever use it again. I felt fortunate to not have
to work anymore because I never did figure out how to be a
good person and have a career at the same time. Maybe
careers outside of criminology placed less of a burden upon
the soul, but I'd never know because I never looked for
another job.

A few months after settling in, Ralph Jr. and I sat before
the fireplace on a crystalline winter evening. Someone
knocked at the door. I thought that perhaps someone's car
stalled in the snow.

I opened the door and saw Swann Baumgarten in the
flesh. I stood there with my mouth hanging open.

She walked inside without being asked. Her first words
were, "Damn it, I'm going to have to call you Joe without
thinking of my ferret."

"Swann, how did you get here?"

She took off her colorful winter coat and muffler and set
them on a workbench. Her hair still sported different colors,

but it had grown out some and the spikes were gone. She sat next to Ralph Jr. in front of the fire, scratching him behind the ears. "Swann's the name. Pleased to meet you." She shook his paw. He wagged his tail.

"Well?" I said.

"Well what?"

"How did you get here?"

She thought about it. "Let's see. Taxi, plane, bus, and taxi."

"And how did you find out my real name? Or where I lived?"

"This woman named Shannon. A real cool lady. She came to my store and told me all about you. She said I should see you and that she wanted to be a good person again, whatever the hell that is. She said if I told anyone what she did, she'd deny it and have me tailed for the rest of my life."

"I'd be careful. Shannon is a woman of her word. But why did you come?"

Swann looked at me with disbelief. "To borrow a cup of sugar. Why the fuck do you think I came?"

I sat down next to her. "I'm old enough to be your father."

"Barely."

"You like clubbing, I like solitude. You like the city, I like the country. You like that hard rock and I like. . . whatever you'd call it. Pretty songs. Oldies."

"Well, I can top that," Swann said. "I'm bipolar, and I'm not sure I should have children. And if we stay here, you'll have to add on to the cabin so that I can start my Internet clothing line. What a hassle."

"You're a heart-bleeding liberal."

"You're a tight-ass conservative."

"There's no reason at all we should get together."

"Not a reason in the world," Swann agreed.

"We met on a speed date, for God's sake. How tacky is that?"

I sat down before the fire; she put her head on my shoulder. "Surely we aren't stupid enough to give it a go," she said. "What would we do when we're both depressed at the same time?"

"There's no place in the world for my love. No one would know what to do with it."

Later that night, we made love. I have to say that one thing about celibacy is that it really feels good when you have sex again. As we lay in bed afterward, I told Swann about the case, leaving out all the supernatural stuff. There'd be time for that later.

I don't know if it happened, but I could swear I saw my family whole and happy, holding up a banner that read: *Welcome home.* But then again, I could've been imagining things. I guess I have a vivid imagination.

In the morning, I woke feeling well rested. I leaned on my elbow and watched Swann as she slept. Ralph Jr. whimpered and plopped on the bed, jealous of his rival for my affection. I laughed as Ralph started licking Swann awake, so she'd get out of bed and he could lie next to me.

Swann must've been wiped out from jet lag because she continued sleeping. I couldn't wait to tease her about it. I brushed my hand along her cheek.

She felt cold.

I rolled her onto her back. She didn't stir. I slapped her face and got no response. I saw that her lips were discolored.

Frantic, I gave her CPR. Ralph Jr. kept licking her, and I shooed him off the bed. I breathed and breathed into her mouth, I kept compressing her chest to stimulate a heartbeat. But her skin was ice cold.

I looked at the floor on her side of the bed. I saw an empty pill bottle and a note:

Joe,

I am sorry for doing this to you, but I had to, and it had to be away from my mom, my life, everything familiar. Except you. You brought me such comfort, though I don't understand why. I'm sure it looks very selfish of me to lay this on you, but I have trouble thinking about anyone's needs but my own. Maybe it's the bipolar. I can't keep on. I work so hard at hiding my pain. I wish I could be happy and normal like you, but it is best for me and for everyone else that I do this. Since you're a cop, I'm sure you'll deal with it and know what to do. Also, let them know my husband made fun of me so I pushed him down the stairs. I felt awful ever since. So you see you are better off without me. Please be gentle when you tell my mom everything.

If it matters, I did like you.

S.

Ralph Jr. walked over to me and started licking my legs. I petted him with one hand while I called 911 with the other. Caitlyn and the kids formed a circle around me, bloodied but with their bodies intact. They each had their arms crossed, and they gazed at me with mean smiles. Caitlyn said, "You thought you could just forget us, didn't you?"

Behind them, in a blurry distance, the giant Sun People danced and laughed.

# ABOUT THE AUTHOR

JP Bloch has a PhD in Sociology but hopes people won't hold it against him. He lives in Connecticut, where he is an indentured servant to his dog. JP writes on his king-size bed with the fan on. His hobbies include eating cashews while watching TV and overdosing on film noir favorites.

JP has published novels and nonfiction, including *Identity Thief*, a #1 Amazon bestseller, and has appeared on TV and radio numerous times. On his own since age 15, he has many sordid tales of survival in the Bay Area and other parallel universes.

His turn-offs include Brussels sprouts, bigotry, and people who think life is simple. He enjoys people who have gained wisdom from hardship and ask questions more than they assume answers. Tumultuous skies are preferred over sunny ones.

Author info:
Email: jpblochauthor@gmail.com

Social Misfit Times Blog:
http://jpblochauthor@blogspot.com/

Facebook: facebook.com/jonpbloch
Facebook fan page: facebook.com/jpbfan
Twitter: @JPBlochauthor

Other Recent Books:
Identity Thief

order at www.pegasusbooks.net

www.ingramcontent.com/pod-product-compliance
Lightning Source LLC
Chambersburg PA
CBHW050427260626
47156CB00003B/1183